To Ro!

My ∑
frie...

Sentio

JC Howell

Sentio, Published February, 2017

Editorial and proofreading services: Kathleen Tracy, Karen Grennan

Interior layout and cover design: Howard Johnson

Cover artwork: Oil on canvas, created by Randi Jane Davis,

www.randijanedavis.com

 **SDP Publishing**

Published by SDP Publishing, an imprint of SDP Publishing Solutions, LLC.

ISBN-13 (print): 978-0-9981277-9-8

ISBN-13 (ebook): 978-0-9984240-0-2

Library of Congress Control Number: 2016962201

Printed in the United States of America

To Michael and Jack for their love,
for believing in me, and to my readers
who direct their attention to channel
goodness into the world.

This book would not have been possible without the encouragement and support of Jacqueline Flynn, Rachel Bottoms, Lisa Akoury-Ross, and Kathleen Tracy. Jacqueline and Rachel provided invaluable support early on. Lisa embraced the story and brought in Kathleen, a distinguished writer who elevated this manuscript with her incisive observations, suggestions, and edits. And last, a special thank you to Randi Jane Davis and Howard Johnson for giving this story majesty through the storyline cover artwork and elegant paging.

After studying the works of the greatest men and women thinkers of western civilization, I found a thread about the wisdom of love, the way to the truth, and the way to greater freedom for all. It is my pleasure to present, **Sentio.**

Prologue

Helen approached the university grounds, somewhat annoyed that Poulou had demanded her presence for a surprise announcement. She looked across the street at the historic, three-story building and glanced at the words on the doorway window: *Ecole Normale Supérieure.*

ENS, she thought while crossing the cobblestone walkway; *Poulou's new hangout, where he is studying existentialism.* He had requested their meeting at his favorite spot in the park, on the other side of the campus.

Wearing a grey wool dress, blue scarf, and dark sunglasses, Helen pushed through the wrought iron entrance gate on the sunny afternoon, the first Friday of autumn in 1949 Paris. She strode in her pumps down a double-wide, brick sidewalk between the classroom buildings, continued through the courtyard of trees where students had gathered at tables for lunch, and hurried past the philosophy building to avoid running into Poulou's existential comrades.

A dark-haired man in a suit approached her. "Helena Moyen? What are you doing here?"

She stopped, and he moved close, peering into her eyes. It was Maurice Merleau-Ponty. Helen smiled, took off her sunglasses. "Hello Maurice."

They kissed cheeks. Maurice had been a student of Husserl's phenomenology, and she had worked with him years ago.

"What are you doing at ENS?" he asked.

"I'm living in Paris now and am on my way to meet a friend in the park."

"Have you heard from Martin Heidegger?"

"No," she said, and lowered her eyes toward the sidewalk.

"That was too bad what happened to him."

"Yes, it was."

"What are you doing in Paris?"

"I'm working on a book and special project to free humankind."

Maurice smiled. "If anyone can, I hope it is you." He handed her a card with his number. "Call me and we'll have lunch. I would love to talk."

"Thank you." Helen took his card and waved good-bye, quickening her steps down the sidewalk.

Maurice and Martin had gotten closer than any of the others, almost discovering the truth about what we are, as beings in the world. Martin lived in an asylum in Germany now, and Maurice appeared to have lost his way at ENS. Slowing her pace, Helen put on her sunglasses and step-by-step slipped into a trance recalling her journey to the truth.

Years ago at Freiburg, she'd been a professor of philosophy and had worked with Husserl, the founder of the school of phenomenology, and his protégé Heidegger. A couple of years before WWII, she'd studied Heidegger's work and believed as he had that Cogito, language-thinking consciousness, obstructed our ability to perceive the truth and freedom, and like a perceptual veil, Cogito had separated us from who we are, obscuring what it means to be and to experience the world as the pre-Socratic beings that we are.

She remembered before the war began, when she tried to expose the Nazi veil, when she fell into the abyss of despair, and when she underwent experimental shock treatment. After the war ended, her despair lifted, and she found the way forward to greater freedom for all while living in the Black Forest of Germany. Alone in nature, she experienced Sentio, her proper name for true sensory consciousness, which projected immediate sensory data into her perception. Her consciousness of nature returned to what she had imagined Eden looked like.

Embracing her new window of perception, she reflected on Husserl's phenomenology—Intentio, attention, and selective attention—and discovered why she had not been able to experience the world through Sentio previously: her Intentio had been trapped, addicted to language-thinking consciousness. Then she found the way back to her pre-Socratic being state by using her new paradigm for being in the world: Intentio, Sentio, and Cogito. And she created a new philosophy of freedom, intentialism, after she experienced the compass—

A bell rang, rousing her. She stepped quickly to her left to avoid students rushing from the classroom building. Adrenaline rushed through her veins, delivering a sense of exhilaration, the lift of a student when school let out. She hastened toward the park, and when Helen's heart slowed, her thoughts returned to her compass experience, the language-free vision for freedom.

She remembered it was 1946 in the forest, just after sunset on the first day of spring, when she experienced the Compass of Freedom, which gave her the vision to move to Paris, build an international orphanage, and free humankind from language-thinking consciousness. She had visited that memory many times over the last three years. She hoped to deliver the compass experience to the world on a grand stage someday.

Helen slowed, looked over the top of her glasses toward the heavens in gratitude for her journey, and then lowered her eyes as a garrulous couple approached: a short fellow wearing a beret and a tall woman wearing slacks and a blouse. Sartre and Simone, the famous existential couple she had met in a café the previous spring, walked toward her. She ducked behind a building, not wanting to argue with them about freedom. Once they passed, she hastened across the lawn toward the cluster of trees where Poulou was supposed to be waiting for her.

She stopped and looked for her lifelong friend. She and Poulou, both orphans, had moved from Germany to Paris almost three years earlier and had adopted each other. Last summer on Bastille Day, lying on a blanket on the rooftop of their apartment, tickling each other in laughter, and gazing far above the Eiffel Tower, they had pledged to lead the world to freedom together.

"Helen! Helen!" a voice called out.

She turned, and there was Poulou, an athletic, energetic man, sitting on a grassy knoll under the canopy of a large tree with heart-shaped leaves. His girlfriend Hana lay beside him on a blanket near a picnic basket.

"Come join us. We are having a picnic," he said in a cheerful tone, raising a bottle of wine into the air.

"Hello, Hana," Helen said as she approached, giving a cordial smile.

"Hi, Helena," Hana replied, and giggled as Poulou reached over and tickled her ribs.

"Poulou, I came because you told me you had a wonderful surprise."

"Yes, I do. Please have a seat over here on the blanket beside me."

"I'm fine," she said, taking off her sunglasses. Helen could see he had been drinking, was perhaps drunk. His blue eyes were red. An empty wine bottle lay on the ground beside him, and the one in his hand appeared almost empty.

"Let me pour you a glass of wine," he said, and looked toward the basket. "Hana, do you have a glass for Helen?"

"I'm fine," Helen repeated. "Tell me the surprise. I want to go back to the apartment. I do not like being here on the ENS campus."

"Oh, Helen, you should be teaching here. Hana, did I

ever tell you that Helen made the highest score ever recorded on the admissions test to ENS?"

Hana shook her head no and wrinkled her nose. Helen had applied to the school in 1924 but declined admission and attended Freiburg University instead.

"Poulou, you've had too much to drink; I'm leaving." She turned and walked.

"Wait! You haven't heard my surprise."

Helen stopped and turned around in curiosity. "Okay, what is it?"

"I've started a women's garment business."

"For heaven's sake, that's your surprise?" Helen shook her head.

"Yes, but wait. You know how busy I've been for the last two years collecting American nylon parachutes left over from the war? Well, earlier today I made a trade with a Japanese fellow for several thousand silk parachutes. Soon I will have a warehouse full, thousands of yards of silk and nylon."

"So what can you make with the material?"

"Hold on a minute." Poulou took a swig of wine, corked the bottle, and then asked, "Do you remember during the war when there was a shortage of corsets?"

Helen nodded. "Yes, because of the shortage of metal."

"Well, women stopped wearing them, and that has increased the demand for brassieres."

"Brassieres?"

"Yes, nursing brassieres and comfortable bras. Since the war, babies are being born right and left, and women need nursing bras—*Poulou's Brassieres.*" He paused then asked, "What do you think of our company's name?" He shot a smile at Hana, saying, "Hana is going to be our model."

"For goodness sakes, I will see you later," Helen said. "Goodbye, Hana."

"Wait, Helen. I'm going to fund your orphanage," he said, and laughed as Hana tickled him.

Helen watched him tickle Hana in retaliation. She loved Poulou like a brother, and they had been through so much together, but this idea was ridiculous.

"Tell me again why you want to name the orphanage Essence?" Poulou asked in a jovial tone as he released Hana.

Helen put on her sunglasses. "Aristotle used the term *essence* to refer to the potential of what something can become, what it is meant to become. But who gets to say what humans are meant to become now? Existentialists?" She shook her head no. "Even though the existentialists decided it should be up to the individual to determine what one is meant to become, they turned around and condemned humankind to language-thinking existence and false freedom."

Poulou raised the corners of his mouth into a smile, as if to agree with her. Helen smiled back knowing her paradigm for being and the compass could provide the orphans of the world with the opportunity to lead true essence lives. Lives dedicated to finding greater freedom for all while using Cogito as a plowshare instead of as a weapon for power.

"What about meaning and purpose?" Poulou asked.

"When the will for meaning is extrapolated to infinity, it becomes the will for the ultimate freedom, the freedom from the misery of need and time. It becomes the will to experience the ecstasy of infinity." Helen looked over the top of her sunglasses at Poulou, grinned, and walked away.

"We'll celebrate tonight," he cried.

CHAPTER

1

"**Our orphanage Essence will** become the birthplace for a revolution of consciousness. A revolution needed to restore the vision for freedom and love, for humankind," said Helen Moyen in her final remarks at the tea party.

The sisters cheered and put their hands together in loud applause. Helen shared embraces with her fifteen sisters and kitchen staff before they departed to their villas. The tea party, a get-together to discuss the new school and to welcome her newest Sisters of Freedom, had been a wonderful success.

After giving Josephine and Mary Elizabeth hugs, Helen dismissed them and finished cleaning the kitchen by herself. She stood all alone at the sink thinking about the lovely young women—her newest recruits—and the desire for love and freedom visible in their eyes. Several moments later she found herself staring out the villa window at the horizon where snowcapped mountains reached through wispy clouds toward the heavens far above terrestrial existence.

It was a wintry Sunday afternoon on her mountaintop in Andorra and just five days before the christening ceremony for her newly constructed international orphanage, the embodiment of her longing to lead humankind to freedom through Sentio.

Turning her eyes toward the campus, she smiled,

1

admiring the cedar and stone structures, the school building and dormitory, nestled among pine trees. She had followed her vision of freedom and built a Garden of Eden for the forlorn beings of the world.

Soon she would introduce the orphans to her new philosophy of freedom, so they could experience their sense of being through the consciousness of nature. She would introduce them to her paradigm: Intentio (attention and selective attention), Sentio (sensory consciousness), and Cogito (language-thinking consciousness). Using her paradigm and nature, she would free their Intentio from its institutional enslavement to language-thinking consciousness. The orphans would experience a new vision of freedom and love and would have the potential to live true essence lives guided by the Compass of Freedom.

She could still hear the cheers and thunderous applause from the sisters echoing in her head as she picked up a dishtowel and dried one of four shining, porcelain, oriental teapots, gifts from Poulou, who indeed had arranged the financing for the orphanage. While drying the second pot, she lowered her gaze from the horizon and enjoyed a bird's-eye view of Pierre, France, where Tudor buildings, cobblestone roads, and gas streetlights decorated the sleepy valley town, bounded by pine trees on the east and by white water rapids on the west. She could see a young couple strolling down a side street, a motor vehicle creeping down the main street, and the grocer preparing to make a delivery on his moped.

Helen finished drying the last pot and wondered why she had not heard from Poulou in more than two weeks. She had concerns about their financing and hoped he would attend the christening on Friday. He had not seen the campus since the ground breaking nine months earlier and had not met her sisters. She stored one pot in the cabinet, left the other three on the counter, needing to return them to the other villas. She folded the towel over the sink and looked again toward the majestic horizon—

She heard a familiar rap coming from the front door.

Could it be? She smoothed the front of her habit and hurried to the door.

2

Helen jumped with excitement the moment she laid eyes on her visitor.

"Poulou! Oh, Poulou, I knew you would come."

She threw her arms around her brother, leaping into his arms, and kissed him on one cheek then the other as he twirled her in the air. When he eased her down, Helen stepped back holding his hands and took him in from head to toe. He was a dashing gentleman with a charming smile.

"You look wonderful," Poulou gushed. "The habit becomes you."

"Thank you," she said, squeezing his hands in gratitude and pulled him inside.

They stood on the marble floor in the foyer holding hands and basking in each other's auras.

"I've missed you," Helen said.

"I've missed you," he replied in a warm, soft tone. "This is such a magnificent place."

"I want you to meet my sisters," she said and then called back into the villa, "Sisters, come here!" She released his hands and moved to shut the door.

"I would love to meet them," he said, gazing toward the sitting room. "I parked my Dauphine on your terrace. I hope that is okay."

"Of course." She closed the door and yelled once more

for her sisters. "They must be upstairs, freshening up after our meeting. Take off your overcoat; I want to show you around."

"That would be wonderful," he said, rotating toward the coat rack. He hung up his overcoat, removed an envelope from the side pocket, and placed it in the inside pocket of his dress coat, saying, "What a view! The town of Pierre looks so beautiful from up here."

"Yes, gorgeous. I was admiring the vista earlier from the kitchen."

His mood changed as he turned back toward her. Helen knew that something was up. His face flattened and grew pale as he spoke in a soft tone.

"I can't attend your big day. I have an important meeting in Paris on Friday."

"What?" she asked in disbelief.

"I can't be here for the christening," he repeated.

After shaking her head in disappointment, she wanted to ask why he had not rescheduled the meeting. Instead, she turned toward the mahogany staircase, and gazed at the beautiful vaulted pine ceiling, focusing her attention on the pleasing sensory of her new home, and remembered that without Poulou's support there would be no orphanage named Essence. She gazed into his apologetic eyes.

"I wish that you could be here for the christening, but I understand you have your businesses, meetings, and such. I wish . . . never mind."

She stepped toward the sitting room, and he pulled at her arm. "I will make it up to you, just wait." He grinned like a schoolboy.

Helen stared in silence, transfixed by his hope-filled grin, which had brought her out of despair so many times after the war. Now 1958, it had been almost ten years since they had adopted each other and lived together in Paris like brother and sister. Over the past year, they had lived apart.

While she built Essence and founded the Sisters of Freedom, Poulou had expanded his woman's undergarment company in Hong Kong.

He continued grinning, and she could not prevent the corners of her mouth from lifting into a smile, thinking about their good times together in Paris. And she knew him too well for him to come such a long way to disappoint. Something else was up, so she played along.

She took him by the hand. "You owe me nothing."

"But I want to owe you something." His grin became a mischievous smile.

She slapped him softly on the derriere. "There! That is your punishment for missing the christening."

He returned a soft pat to her fanny. She tickled his ribs then pulled his hand and led him on a tour of the villa.

"I had all of the rooms painted from Monet's impressionistic color palette. Look at the beautiful shades of green in our study . . . and my bedroom," she said with excitement, and proudly pointed to the large crown moldings.

"Yes, beautiful work. I see Monet's pastels," he said.

They meandered through the hallway toward the back porch then turned toward the large opening.

"Whoa—your kitchen is canary yellow. How beautiful," he offered.

Warmed by his compliments, she showed off the cedar closets, the pantry, and the kitchen cabinets. They ended up in the sitting room on the sofa with tea and biscuits. Their spoons jingled against their teacups as they searched for more to say. Helen called to her sisters again and heard a commotion.

"Ah, the scent of pine . . . your villa smells wonderful. I noticed you used cedar shingles, and I love the shade of green—excellent choice for the exterior."

"Thank you," Helen said, and took a sip.

"Those guys we found in Catalan can really swing a hammer," he said, adding more sugar to his tea. "And they can stack stone; the dormitory and the chapel are gorgeous. The entire campus looks marvelous." He lifted his cup for a drink.

"Yes, they were impressive builders, but they loved to argue," she told him.

"Oh, of course. Good builders are like artists. Everything has to be perfect. They become their creations in a way. I think Marx was right about that."

Helen put down her cup and looked him in the eyes. She wanted to remind him about how workers can become alienated. She knew he had employed cheap laborers in Hong Kong for his woman's undergarment business. She wanted to encourage him to let his workers share in the ownership of their products.

"Man incorporates his sense of being into what he builds. His attention visits in his consciousness every corner, crevice, eave, and overhang in the process of building. I can see Marx's point about workers becoming alienated when they are separated from the products of their labors, their sense of being," Helen said and maintained eye contact. "The Catalan builders will always be a part of Essence. How about your workers?"

"Enough of Marx," said Poulou with a wave of his hand. "Nobody wants to experience his or her sense of being in someone else's underpants. Let me look at you."

"Oh, Poulou, you understand what I meant."

He smiled and nodded. "Take off your veil. I want to see your beautiful curly, brown hair."

"You know my hair has turned gray," said Helen with a rush of blood to her face.

She did not want to reveal that her hair had returned to the color of her youth. Since the construction of Essence, Helen's mind had become more sensitive and her body younger. She did not want to create a fuss, and her black and white habit concealed her rejuvenated appearance.

"Yes, but a little gray will become you," he said. "Your eyes still reflect the most beautiful shade of brown, and your face," his eyes narrowed as he scrutinized her smooth skin, "has not a single wrinkle. You have indulged in the fountain of youth," he said, his voice reflecting surprise. "You look like a twenty-year-old woman."

"You always say that," she grinned. "You said that last year, before we started building. I experience life through Sentio, my fountain of youth. Cogito, language thinking, creates the worry lines of old age."

"Of course . . . how could I forget Sentio. What about me, how do I look?" he asked. He pulled his beret tight over his head, raised his shoulders up towards his ears, and puckered his lips. "I have lost most of my hair," he said and lifted his beret as evidence.

"Yes, but your mustache and chin hair with your baby blue eyes make me want to cuddle you," she said, cupping his chin with affection. "You are a handsome man with strong shoulders, and your short stature makes you more interesting."

A desire kindled within her after admiring how his red-brown sideburns curled in front of his cute ears.

"Thank you," he said, and wrapped his arms around her shoulders in a sensual embrace that ignited a warm tingling sensation within her.

She could feel that he wanted more; she did too but not here, not now. Her sexual arousal buttons had returned to the sensitivity of her youth. She had related to Poulou as a brother for most of her life, but now she saw him differently. She experienced a strong desire for him but would not dare admit it; he might overreact. When she heard the sound of feet pedaling through the hall and down the stairs, Helen pulled back from their embrace.

3

One by one Josephine Joseph, Jahn Phillips, and Mary Elizabeth Braun careened into the sitting room. Their faces blushed red when they saw Poulou. Helen sensed their surprise at seeing a man in the villa.

She stood, pointing to her head. "Your veils?" she admonished. She had taught them never to let a man see them without their veils. The sisters turned toward the stairs in unison.

"I know they aren't real nuns," he whispered.

"Come back," Helen said. "I forgot. He knows."

Another simultaneous quick turn from the three sisters and Helen saw Poulou hold back a laugh. He removed his beret and got comfortable on the sofa. His arms stretched over the top of the cushions, and his belly listed to the right.

"Sit up. You are slouching," Helen softly reprimanded.

She looked at her sisters and gave informal introductions. Poulou stood and smiled big. His cheeks filled with color as he touched each woman's hand giving a cordial greeting. As quickly as he sat down, he stood again and offered the sofa to the sisters. They remained standing as Sister Phillips spoke.

"It is so nice to meet you, Loulou. So you are the man behind Helen," she said with a husky tone to her voice. She sounded as if she had been drinking.

Helen corrected her, "*Poulou*, Sister."

"Hello," said Josephine.

He smiled and looked toward Mary Elizabeth, who said nothing, her face guarded by a cautious smile.

"Poulou, sit there," said Helen, "in that nice chair." She pointed with her gloved hand to a large, cushioned chair in the corner.

He moved toward the chair, but his attention remained on the three sisters until Helen raised her gloved hand again. "Please, sit down, Sisters, or Helen will give you the glove," he joked. "No one is in front of her. Save God, maybe. You might say that we are all behind Helen."

Mary Elizabeth ended her silence as she took her seat. "Poulou Marcel, I read your book *Me and Nothingness*. It is so nice to meet you."

Helen watched him swell with pride. Only a handful of people had bought his philosophy book about the nothing man behind consciousness.

"It was just a compilation of some late night thoughts. It was really nothing," he said with a big smile at Mary Elizabeth.

The three sisters sat together on the sofa with their backs straight and their hands folded in their laps. Meanwhile, Poulou relaxed into his chair and crossed his outstretched legs. Helen sat facing the group at her stationery desk. The group formed a tight circle that grew warmer by the moment. They shared pleasantries about the weather and talked about Poulou's nine-hour drive from Paris to Essence.

"I found a nice two-lane highway for most of the trip then a single road through the mountains," he shared. "I stopped twice, once for lunch and once for mountain goats. Snow covered the road, but it was drivable with my new Dauphine. Maybe we can go for a ride later; it's a wonderful machine."

"That would be nice," said Helen.

"You must be tired from your journey. Are you hungry?" asked Josephine.

"Oh no, I am overfed as it is," he joked and patted his belly.

The pleasantries subsided as Poulou leaned forward with intent. With his change in demeanor, Helen and the sisters leaned in as well. Then he announced the reason for his visit.

"**An anonymous family has** donated a large sum of money," Poulou explained. "I redirected the donation by proxy through my mission fund to your outfit, the Sisters of Freedom. A family from Alsace-Lorraine created the endowment to support compassionate organizations. I know that they will be proud to know your group will benefit. I am sure of it."

Helen stood and reached toward her brother, almost falling over her desk in the process. She grabbed him by the neck and kissed him on the cheek. The sisters leaped to their feet, jubilant about the news. Mary Elizabeth hugged Josephine and then Jahn Phillips. The hugging went on until Poulou tried to hug Helen a third time.

"That's enough. Where is the brandy? We must celebrate!" said Helen.

Poulou smiled at her as if to communicate that he had made up for the earlier disappointment. She acknowledged him with a warm grin, shaking her head.

"How about a prayer—I mean praise," suggested Josephine.

"Yes, of course," agreed Poulou, lowering his baritone voice. "I thank you. Helen thanks you. We all thank you. Amen."

The sisters looked puzzled at his short and informal praise.

Helen waved the raised index finger of her gloved hand. "You know what I think, Sisters." She opposed prayer and praise unless in private.

"Oh, a little public praise will not hurt God," Poulou said and handed Helen a glass.

Sister Phillips lifted her large brandy flask and filled their glasses. "One, two, three, four . . . over the lips . . . look out stomach . . . here she comes," Sister Phillips sang and then guzzled her shot.

Poulou sniffed, threw the liquid to the back of his throat, and swallowed, producing a frown. "Wow, I can't believe that you women like this stuff," he joked. "Give me a shot of Russian vodka. I won't complain."

"The tavern owner in Pierre gave us the brandy as a gift," said Helen.

"It has a bite, but now it feels rather smooth. I can see why you like it. What a nice gift. I might like to take some back to Paris."

"The grocer in Pierre can get you a case real cheap," said Sister Phillips.

"Tell us about the money," Helen encouraged as everyone found their seats. She was filled with gratitude and wanted to hear more.

"Helen, you always get to the point," Poulou noted with affection. He pulled the envelope from his jacket and handed it to her. "This is your account. The endowment's interest will be enough to cover your expenses for the Essence orphanage for the year—maybe more depending upon your future expenses and the interest rates. The money will give you breathing room to train your orphans."

There was also enough left over to support the Sisters of Freedom's motherhouse, which was located an hour away in Vichy, Andorra.

"Thank you," Helen said, her voice filled with genuine appreciation after glancing at the deposit slip and placing it in her desk drawer. She felt instantly lighter; the air smelled a bit sweeter, and her smile was effortless. "This is the best possible news."

Poulou stood and looked around. "I need to excuse myself to your privy or indoor plumbing. Where might that be?" Before Helen could answer, he asked with more urgency, "Where is it? My damn prostate!" he grumbled.

"On the other side of the pantry," Helen said, pointing toward the kitchen.

She turned toward the sofa and directed her attention toward Mary Elizabeth. She wanted to expound about their Freedom Order for the benefit of Mary Elizabeth, the newest Sister. The brandy had loosened her tongue. She felt warm and jovial making eye contact with her sisters.

"What does Poulou do?" asked Mary Elizabeth.

"He is our broker and my adopted brother. After establishing our incorporation in Andorra, he arranged the financing for the Sisters of Freedom to build Essence," Helen said, looking toward his whistled sounds coming from the bathroom. "He helped us qualify for tax-free donations by taking advantage of Title IX of the Napoleonic Code, which also encourages reformed French women to move to Andorra."

Mary Elizabeth gave a nod of understanding as did Josephine.

"I was wondering, when I joined the Freedom order, did I make a vow of celibacy? asked Sister Phillips. Her face had twisted into a question mark, and Helen could see that she was tipsy. Sister Phillips became more forgetful when she was drinking. The Nazis had experimented on her while she was imprisoned by them, inducing a memory disorder by depriving her of thiamine.

"No. We are not institutional nuns, but we are authentic human beings. Compassionate women in search of greater freedom," Helen said and looked at Mary Elizabeth. "We are not all French either. Some of us are from Catalan and

Germany. I remind you that we keep our institutional nun status private. No one else needs to know our business, especially our neighbors in Pierre." Helen smiled, lifting her glass for a refill, and Sister Phillips rose up and topped it with brandy. "Let me also remind everyone that each Sister has had their own personal fall and is now under the corporate parasol of the Sisters of Freedom. We have all lived as holier-than-thou institutionalized people in our past, but now we are true essence women."

"Hear, hear," said Sister Phillips, taking her seat on the sofa. "I am the worst offender. I worked as a tax collector during the war, and I helped put my own mother in jail. Before I became a Sister, I thought that I was a man . . . not really, but sort of." She slapped the top of her thigh.

After the war Sister Phillips was branded in a public display as a German sympathizer. They cut off all of her hair, and Helen believed that she drank to suppress those painful memories and shame. Helen watched Josephine arch her brow and noticed that Sister Phillips' face had elongated after her disclosure.

"Yes, you did, but now your mother is free, as are you," Helen said, gaining Sister Phillips' attention. "A woman is not born a woman. She becomes an institutionalized woman by the forces imposed on her by the male-dominant culture and the yin and yang misogynists."

Helen produced a fake smile for her sisters and connected with Mary Elizabeth's smiling eyes. "We take the woman back to her consciousness of nature and help her redirect her attention to live a true essence life. We have no ties with institutionalized religion and have made no vows to anyone. We are free. We are a simple order of reborn, compassionate human beings. Aren't we?"

She looked toward Sister Phillips who nodded. Josephine also gave a nod then Helen caught Poulou's eyes as he returned from the lavatory.

"Aren't we what?" he asked, jumping into his seat. "Yes, of course, whatever you say, Helen." He kicked up his feet then crisscrossed his legs.

The sisters let out restrained laughs at his jovial behavior. Their faces were lifted. They looked younger, and their eyes reflected new curiosity and amazement. Helen realized that she was opening up to them for the first time.

"Poulou gave me the spark for the idea of creating our Freedom Order," Helen explained. "He told me that if I put a habit on my head, then I could sell anything to anyone."

"Yes, I did," he said. "And I told you to take off that glove, and you did not listen, Helen Strange-Glove. I read your letter about the orphans' nickname for you."

"I wear the glove as my reminder that I was addicted to Cogito. But since it seems to scare the children, after the christening I will no longer wear it."

"Thank God," he said. "I was worried about the effect on your neighbors in Pierre. It seems a funny way to remember your past."

Helen turned her eyes from him and continued addressing her sisters. "My brother has served as the business brain and scrounger for our budding order. Our orphanage will be the first of its kind to provide children the opportunity to lead true essence lives."

Poulou added, "It is an ingenious plan to export Helen's brand of true essence to change the institutionalized world."

The sisters smiled at him. He downed another shot of brandy, and his cheeks turned rosy. He removed his jacket and sank deeper into his chair. After thanking Sister Phillips for the brandy, he focused on the face of Mary Elizabeth. His eyes pawed at hers and lingered for an uncomfortable length of time, and Helen took notice. Mary Elizabeth had beautiful eyes and long blonde hair with a confident smile that had clearly triggered Poulou's sexual arousal.

She had seen her brother like this before. It reminded

her of his French kisses in taxis and gropes in cafés. He had tried to have his way with her on many occasions in their youth. She understood his hominem, the man. She sensed Mary Elizabeth's uneasiness and spoke up to regain Poulou's attention.

"How is that French feminist girl you wrote to me about, the pretty blue-eyed tot? I mean tart?"

"Oh, she was just fun for my sensibility," he replied. "She was young and beautiful, nothing serious or essential."

Helen was going to ask about his business trip to the French Riviera, but she dared not.

Josephine looked up and asked her, "How did you and Poulou meet?"

Helen's lips spread against her teeth as a knot formed in her throat. Her insides squeezed together and her mind filled with unpleasant memories, but despite her misgivings she wanted her sisters to hear their story.

"I will let Poulou explain," Helen said. "He is a brilliant writer. He tells wonderful stories."

"You're so modest," he answered. "Are you sure you want me to tell our story?"

She nodded as her insides grew tighter still.

"**When I met Helen** . . . oh boy, let me think for a moment. How should I start?"

While Poulou pondered, Sister Phillips brought more brandy and shared with Josephine.

"How about some more for me and Mary Elizabeth?" Poulou asked.

She poured another shot for him and turned toward Mary Elizabeth.

"No, thank you, Sister Phillips," said Mary Elizabeth.

Poulou downed his shot and gave a little roar. "Okay, I'm ready," he said, flashed a smile at Helen, and then turned toward the sisters. "We were both born in 1905. Helena Moyen was born as a victim of a crime near Freiburg, Germany, and I was born to farmers in Alsace-Lorraine. Helen became an official orphan at the age of six after her mother died. The Sisters of Charity picked her up off the streets and raised her." Poulou shook his head. "Charity is such a messy thing—"

"Go on, please," Helen interrupted, not wanting to discuss how most charity is not given freely for true freedom.

"Of course . . . my devout Catholic family raised me accordingly. I spent part of my youth in a boarding school at the *Realgymnasium* in Vienna until I flunked out. I got home-sick," he said, and stopped to look at Helen. "I met Helen at church of all places while visiting Freiburg on holiday."

Helen grinned at her sisters who listened with rapt attention. They uncrossed their legs and arms in succession and relaxed against the back of the sofa.

"I met Helen when she was a teen or maybe twelve. I can't remember. Oh, yes, we were both thirteen. She was the most beautiful girl I had ever seen, and she smiled at me on her way back from Communion. She had the prettiest brown eyes and long curly, brown hair. She fascinated me in her light green dress—or was it yellow? She walked graciously like a princess, and my eyes were drawn to her curves and feminine things that jiggled, well beyond her years."

Helen saw her sisters' blush and watched Poulou pause to enjoy their response.

"We had our first kiss together. Do you remember, Helen?"

She smiled then glanced toward her sisters, "Of course, our first kiss together. We were having a picnic by the Rhine, and you had given me two glasses of wine. I will never forget. I have revisited that moment many times when I feel despair. Poulou acted so debonair at thirteen, and I was just a young innocent girl." She turned toward Poulou with a grin and went on. "I remember your lips landed a little low then you repositioned them and pressed against mine, and the gates of sensual pleasure opened wide. The moment of bliss was divine. I opened my eyes, and yours remained closed. Out of the corner of my eye, I watched the blue-green river pull two young men in a rowboat."

"Yes, my eyes were closed, and I enjoyed every minute," he said, and stared into Helen's eyes.

"The sky looked so blue and the grass so green. It is a memory to which I often retreat," said Helen.

Poulou turned his smiling eyes toward the sisters and picked up the story. "Yes, it took two glasses to break through the institutionalized Helena. I resuscitated her, but it led to my own demise. She began to like other boys. The next thing I knew, Helen had earned a scholarship and entered the University at Freiburg. That is where it all began. She fell under the influence of Husserl and his phenomenology. Husserl placed brackets around the physical world; the idea that everything is perception and very little is real appealed to Helen. She became a great holier-than-thou philosopher.

"When she challenged the ideas of Sigmund Freud and his three-component psyche, Helen received criticism from some of Freud's students, and things got ugly after that. Helen lost sight of freedom as she became addicted to language-based arguing."

Helen nodded in agreement, and her demeanor changed as she looked toward her sisters. She felt sad as she confessed, "Yes, I thought that I had everything figured out. I was so naïve, and I despised Freud."

She wanted her sisters to hear her contrite statement even though she knew she was right and Freud was wrong. Her arguing had taken away her vision of freedom. The dialectic had almost cost Helen her life.

Poulou hesitated until Helen urged him on with her eyes. "Helen fell in love with Husserl's assistant—head over heels in love with him. I remember that spring before the Second Great War." He turned to Helen. "You were going to be married. I remember trying to tell you that he was a brute, but you would not listen."

"I was young," Helen scoffed. "I was listening to my institutional thinking and my conditioned feelings driven by hormones, which you had a hand in, I might add."

"Yes, but my hand was always pulling for your attention. The beautiful woman that you were and are."

"I know, my brother. You have always been there for me."

"Well, then there was the war," Poulou continued. "Helen came down with alopecia and began losing her hair. Her brute lover sided with the enemy. It was a terrible time for Helen and me. My family disintegrated in an explosion, and I crashed into a pit of despair. Helen and I ended up at Munchausen's Institute in the Black Forest region. Do I need to say more?"

He stopped and looked at Helen, and she gave him a nod. "Please go on; each of us has had to rise after a fall into the abyss of despair," she said. "I want my sisters to understand my story—our story, the Sisters of Freedom."

Her heart pounded and left hand trembled. Sister Phillips poured her another shot of brandy while Josephine stepped into the kitchen and returned with biscuits. Poulou took a bite and chewed. After everyone was seated, he washed the biscuit down and continued.

"Helen had fallen down and needed help. She had met the love of her life and then lost her hair and her love at the same time. She was taken to the Munchausen's Institute where we were reunited in the dark. Only she did not know I was there, at first. I followed her recovery as if my own depended on her getting better."

Poulou's eyes filled with tears, "I remember as if it were yesterday." He paused. Helen moved her chair next to him and took his hand. "I'm okay," he said as he wiped his tears on his sleeve. Helen gave a gentle pat to his shoulder.

"Munchausen's had a dark hollow feel with walls of large stones. A depressing place," he said. "The treatment facility looked as if it were restored from medieval times." Helen nodded in agreement as he continued. "I was in a room with three other men, and we shared two windows. Thank God, my bed rested adjacent to the largest window. By looking out into the thriving forest, I could escape my despair, and I did. I got better.

"One night I saw a man and a couple dressed for a night in the city standing outside of my window, and they appeared lost. I snuck out to help. A French underground operative had assisted a Jewish professor and his wife in flight from

Freiburg. I helped them find their way to the river, and that is how I became a spotter for the underground. I helped others find the river, and for my assistance, they brought me gifts.

"After that, I became friends with several of the nurses when they found out I was a scrounger. I used the cigarettes, chocolate, and nylons to bargain, so they allowed me to watch some of Helen's therapy." He released a sigh and shook his head in sadness. "They performed experimental therapy on her . . . they electrified her at night." He choked. "I watched Dr. Menglev hold the paddles to her temples and deliver the shock, causing Helen to convulse while she was tied down. The experience was shocking . . . I remember crying while I watched." He looked toward the sisters as his eyes filled with new tears and mumbled, "There was nothing that I could do . . . I . . . "

He choked up when he tried to continue. The mood in the room had changed. Poulou leaned over and hugged Helen. Josephine's eyes filled with tears, and Sister Phillips began to sob. Mary Elizabeth looked down at the rug. A few moments of silence passed, and Poulou pulled Helen onto his lap and began caressing her shoulders.

Helen reminded him of her nickname at the asylum and produced a chuckle to lighten the mood. She shared some of her brandy and reminisced with him about Sparrow, her feisty roommate at the Munch. His face broke into a grin.

"The Sparrow, she was something," he said, his mood improving. Poulou regained his composure, and Helen shared a kiss with him before retreating to her chair. "During most of her therapy, Helen lay naked in a room with mattresses for walls. The nurses protected her by taking away her clothes, so she would not take her own life with a slip around the neck or a suffocating dress. Helen, the visionary, stared at the ceiling in her padded room. Lost in existence, she had no essence to call her own. She had fallen down into the godless path of the institutionalized world.

"Oh, she still tried to hurt herself. She had visible scratches all over, and at least once she attempted self-strangulation. One morning she wrapped her legs over her head and twisted her arm around her neck like a pretzel in an attempt to choke herself. I believe she would have taken her own life if not for the straightjacket that was pulled tight around her body at night. After the pretzel, I made sure— every night."

Helen gave him a sweet look of affection. Poulou smiled with tears in his eyes and continued.

"She was nicknamed the *bald beaver* for her attempts at chewing through the jacket that saved her life. Imagine that." Poulou leaned forward and looked around, gathering everyone's attention. "Then something wonderful happened. A young nurse with blonde hair and green eyes, I had never seen her before, came to our room and exclaimed: *The Americans have landed at Normandy!* We jumped and screamed for joy at the news, but I could not get word to Helen. Yet somehow she knew.

"Later that night, they played the song on the free radio about the rainbow, and Helen smiled at me as she listened. Strapped supine on the stretcher, awaiting her shock therapy for the night, she produced the most angelic smile, and I knew that she knew the Americans would set us free. That is how I remember when she began her recovery, the night they played the rainbow song. They played the song on the streets when we got back to liberated France, and the tune liberated our spirits.

"But I am getting ahead of myself. When Helen was released from the asylum, she discovered an alternative consciousness. Her journey through shock treatment, I believe, freed her to experience Sentio. From there she made a journey to nature much like Thoreau on Walden, and her journey was into the deep Black Forest. Her hair grew back, and she rejuvenated. She began experiencing things without words or language. She realized that she was connected to everything through Sentio, without the need for words; she had discovered nature's language."

Helen spoke up, "I lived in a one-room cabin near a creek. I befriended an otter who brought me fish to eat. I befriended a mother raccoon, a doe, and three fawns. They helped me, and I helped them. I gathered canned food and grain from a nearby deserted farm and fed the animals during the cold winter. An owl and a wounded hawk lived inside my cabin with me. I shared with them, and they cared for me. Animals have Sentios too."

Helen sat back in her chair and relaxed. Her sisters' eyes widened, and Poulou looked around with a big grin.

"Yes, well, she did look like Doctor Doolittle—or Mrs. Doolittle. I brought her care packages once a month until she requested my absence. Then I watched from a distance, giving her space and time. One day on my planned visit, she came to the edge of the forest to meet me. She had experienced the famous Compass of Freedom the day before, and she wanted to rejoin humankind, so I brought her back to Paris."

"Because I wanted to go to Paris," she said. "My compass pointed me there."

"Of course it did, and you helped me recover from the loss of my family. I was able to focus on my sensory consciousness, where I directed my attention, and I began to heal," he said. "We lived together in Paris like brother and sister after the war. It took us a couple of years to reinvent ourselves—"

"Poulou," Helen interrupted. "Don't forget about the man in the café. He is part of the reason that we are here today."

"How could I forget the exie?"

After a glance toward the sofa, he said, "The sisters need a rest, Beaver. They look saturated."

Helen blushed, "Of course, they need to recover." She

turned to her sisters. "I'm sorry. I'm sure you're overloaded. Sisters, focus on your immediate sensory, the beautiful colors and furnishings in this room. Direct your attention to the greens, the wood floor, and the lovely fir trees outside the French window. Surrender your Cogito, and experience what I have found."

Helen searched the room for more pleasing sensory, and said, "Let your attention flow through your Sentio and renew your sense of being. I promise that in a few minutes you will feel rejuvenated."

The sisters listened with no words among them and stood to stretch. The best was yet to come.

6

The sisters moved about and remained silent after they stretched.

Sister Josephine spoke up. "Helen, you look too young to have been born in 1905."

Mary Elizabeth and Jahn Phillips quickly agreed.

"Thank you," Helen replied. "Sentio is my secret."

She did not want to explain her rejuvenation, not now. Poulou gave her a look, and she knew that he knew. She gave him a look to communicate she would explain later. Sister Phillips refreshed everyone's brandy, and they returned to their seats. Helen sat down at her desk and looked toward her sisters waiting for them to settle.

"Go ahead," she said to Poulou.

He continued the story. "I will never forget that fateful day. It was spring in Paris, 1949. Helen had joined me at our favorite café."

"No," Helen jumped in. "We walked in together at my request. I was guided there by a strong attention wave, an Intentio directing me to focus on a man surrounded by students. I remember him and his students blowing smoke and pouring liquor into their coffee. He repulsed me, yet I wanted to hear what he had to say. At my urging, you led us to a table right next to him."

"Yes, I remember now," Poulou concurred in a soft

tone. "The large windows, awnings, the mahogany tables, the brick pavers, the large globe lights, the tile ceiling, and the mirror behind the counter created pleasing sensory for a café back then."

Helen turned to her sisters. "I told you he has a writer's eye. As we walked into the café, the arrogant man was puffing on a cigarette held between two outstretched fingers. He thought he was so handsome and intelligent. Oh, he acted so superior. He was leading a small discussion group; they were talking about existentialism. I knew the philosophy from my work in Freiburg, but I was not prepared for what would happen next. The experience that followed would change my life forever."

Poulou nodded as if to concur with Helen and repeated the existentialist's words: *Existence precedes essence; all the existentialists agree. Cogito consciousness is the starting point from which man creates his essence. If man creates essence under institutional influence, then he has created human essence. True essence is created by an authentic individual who lives a life of free choice and makes decisions free from institutional influence but in consideration of others.* I remember Helen started whispering the word *Eden* to herself. What were you thinking at that moment?"

"I was thinking of my experiences in the Black Forest; I was thinking of the beginning of it all in Eden. Sentio was the first authentic consciousness. Humans experienced the consciousness of sensory first, before language." She looked at Poulou and asked, "Remember what I said next?"

"Yes, you said: *Sentio consciousness holds the Compass of Freedom to direct man to live a true essence life for greater freedom for all.*" Poulou turned to the sisters. "The arrogant existentialist overheard Helen speaking and looked at her with disgust. He spoke directly to her: *You are just a woman, and from the looks of your dress, an oppressed one at that. What do you know about Sentio or philosophy? Aristotle discovered our five senses and William James divided the sense experience of feelings into physiological and psychological emotions, reflective consciousness. What may I ask can you add to Aristotle or James? There is no such true essence that you speak of. There are no compasses for man."*

Helen experienced Poulou's words as if she were back in the café listening to the existentialist; her feelings of contempt returned as if it were yesterday. She met each of her Sister's gazes with her eyes aflame. The sisters sat up in unity, and Sister Phillips looked angry enough to hit someone.

"You have a great memory, Poulou. I wanted to slap the fellow for his rude manners, but I held my anger as he went on. I had no words adequate to describe Sentio or the compass experience back then."

Poulou gazed at Helen. "The existentialist announced: *There are no objective values, no compasses. The authentic individual is free from institutionalization and is capable of free-will decisions that will lead to a true essence life. From this point each man will create his own values.* Then one of his students asked: *What about passions?"*

Helen looked at Mary Elizabeth and said, "I remember his reply: *Man creates his own passions. No one is swept away by sex, alcohol, money, or the passion for power, at least not until the passion is created by the institutionalized man or the true essence man who makes decisions that take him near the abyss. All passions are self-created and will take away one's freedom; jealousy is at the top of the list.*

"I remember thinking that passions imprison our attention, our Intentio, and now I realize that language-thinking consciousness was the elephant in the room on that fateful day."

The sisters sat up straight, enthralled.

"Then I asked him: *What about God? You seem to know everything,"* Helen said, staring at Poulou. "You apologized for me. You told him that I was a former patient in Munchausen's facility: *Please forgive her, she has no filter,* you said. I was so upset!" Helen threw up her hands and glared at Poulou.

"I do not remember saying that," he said with a hint of shame.

"Yes, then the existentialist said that his friend was treated at Munchausen's, and he understood. I spilled my coffee trying to stand. I was so furious at him. You convinced me that you were trying to ease the tension while you left out that you too had been at the facility."

With apologetic eyes Poulou added, "Yes, and you said that you wanted to go home. You had closed your eyes. I asked you to open them, when he kept speaking to you, saying: *The deliverer for our sins has come and gone almost 2000 years ago. After the word became flesh, the flesh was pounded into confusing words. For years the Sermon on the Mount directed us, always pointing toward love for your enemy, but now the word has been prostituted for convenience and points in the direction that serves the coffers of the institutionalized man—the enemy has destroyed the meaning of the word. The God that we knew is dead, and man has killed him.*"

Helen's back straightened as Poulou recounted her response. "Helen said: *No God!? You are a fool!* Then she opened her eyes, and the existentialist said: *I did not say, no God. I said that the old God is dead.*"

Poulou leaned close to Helen's ear and lowered his voice. "You whispered to me: *Who is this impertinent bastard? I am leaving.*" Poulou's voice returned to normal. "Rather than agreeing to leave with you, I ignored you as the existentialist continued. Then you knocked off my beret and spat toward him. He watched you and kept speaking. Do you remember?"

Helen replied with conviction, "Yes, how could I ever forget! *Man should act in accordance with and in consideration of how his decisions and actions might affect others. We are orphans, condemned to freedom having been abandoned as it were in a life raft in the middle of this ongoing disaster called life. The woman who gives up her freedom for an institutional life is jumping on the merry-go-round of history. Her life is nothingness. So, enjoy your freedom without condemnation, and always be respectful of another human being's freedom.*" Helen sighed then added, "I got up and politely stomped out. I knew that the existentialist was wrong yet also right in many ways, but I was too upset to respond. I was determined after that day to restore true essence with the compass that points to greater freedom for all humans."

Poulou placed his beret back on his head. It was getting late.

Helen turned to him, "Please stay with us for a few days. I would love that more than anything. We need to join the children for dinner in a few minutes. Rest and have another brandy, and we will be back in one hour."

Sister Phillips filled his glass, tucked the flask in her pocket, and turned toward Helen who pointed to her head to remind her. "I need to get my veil," Sister Phillips said.

Poulou smiled, "Go get yourselves ready for dinner, and do what you need for the orphans. I will stay for a couple of days."

"We'll be back," Helen said and put on her coat.

She caught Poulou glancing at Mary Elizabeth out of the corner of her eye as Sister Phillips came down the steps in her veil. Helen followed Sister Phillips out the door and into the cold, heading to attend dinner with the children.

7

When Mary Elizabeth rose from her seat, Poulou challenged her. "I suppose I can let my Intentio enjoy my Sentio tracks while Helen is gone," he said.

"What do you mean?" asked Mary Elizabeth as she returned to the edge of the sofa.

"You are a grown woman. Helen redirected my attention from you earlier. You know that a male's Sentio infrastructure, which gives rise to Intentio and delivers sense data to the perception window, has arousal buttons everywhere with memory tracks that light up at any form resembling a pleasing part of a female: her hair, scent, voice, face, bosom, bottom, leg, or even her ankle. If the stimulus reaches threshold and the conditions are right, then Intentio rises for the occasion and embarks on a mission for pleasure."

Mary Elizabeth pulled her skirt over her ankles. Josephine covered her mouth with her hands, but could not hide the rush of blood to her face. Poulou looked straight at Josephine as she lowered her hands, crossed her arms, and then turned toward the large window behind Helen's desk.

Mary Elizabeth spoke. "Yes, the male id goes crazy in his cage. Thank goodness Cogito has kept the male id and his subconsciousness where he belongs. I am disgusted at the thought of men being driven by their instincts when I am trying to be cordial."

Poulou thought for a moment and felt a surge of emotion. "I am not talking about the id and instincts. That is hogwash. All consciousness is consciousness. There is no sub-consciousness and no id plotting an overthrow of the ego. There is no ego. Freud's sub-consciousness is not science. It's not falsifiable, which means it can't be proven wrong, so it is no good to us. But Helen's model for consciousness will be tested someday and proven correct."

Sister Josephine looked concerned. "Calm down," she said.

"I am calm. The id is idiotic nonsense. You can't argue against something when your conscious argument is considered symbolic of something else. Freud is probably still laughing at us."

"I'm sorry if I upset you," said Mary Elizabeth.

"I'm not upset. Flush! Did you hear that?" asked Poulou in a loud voice. "The psyche and the sub-consciousness are kaput. Finished!" In a softer tone he added, "Throw the psychopathological jargon in the rubbish bin. Freud's human psyche model with the id, ego, and superego adds nothing but poppycock to the true experience of the sense of being and consciousness. Freud's psyche is only useful for writers, who tell entertaining stories."

He sighed and calmed and then gazed at Josephine's round face and blue eyes before continuing. "I'm sure you've heard Helen speak of her construct to describe the human sense of being. Her model provides a far better way to understand the enterprise of living and the experience of the concrete, the sense of being."

Josephine's forehead wrinkled with worry. "I do not really understand Cogito and Sentio. Helen's ideas seem so abstract."

"Let me try my hand at explaining it," he said.

Josephine arched her brow, and asked, "Are you a philosopher?"

"I studied existentialism in Paris, but please do not remind Helen."

"Oh, I would not dare," Josephine promised.

Mary Elizabeth grinned. "So you're an existentialist."

"More a philosopher of existence and nothingness," he said. "I want to tell you about Helen's discovery."

"Please do," said Josephine.

"Humans have two conscious orchestras playing that are separated by milliseconds, separate moments of consciousness for each stimulus separated by a blink of the mind's eye. Sentio is the first orchestra, playing to our senses with smell, sound, color, taste, position, vibration, motion, shape, and number, and occurs twice as fast as Cogito, the second consciousness."

He paused at Josephine's arched brow. He wanted to simplify Helen's paradigm for her. "The Sentio orchestra plays after a sensory packet is received. The Cogito orchestra chimes in later after the same sensory passes through a filter where language-based processing is engaged. Helen believes that most people perceive sensory after it has passed through the Cogito filter. Sensory altered by language processing, not the pure sensory of Sentio."

"Intriguing," Mary Elizabeth said, "that someone might be able to experience infallible knowledge, objectivity from sensory data projecting into the immediate perception of Sentio."

"It is more than intriguing; it is ingenious," said Poulou. "Helen reported that after she tuned into Sentio—unfiltered sensory—her IQ doubled. I believe it."

"You said Sentio is twice as fast as Cogito, so that makes sense," said Mary Elizabeth.

"Yes, and Helen experienced everything in slow motion at first. She said that the Sentio frame rate is twice as fast as the mind's eye viewing speed, so it took her a while to adjust and to experience the world through Sentio."

"Oh, my!" said Josephine. "She experienced things faster than she could see them in her mind?"

"Yes," he said. "Then she wrote her book on intentialism where she made her claims and assertions from her experience of Intentio dwelling in Sentio."

"Please explain Intentio," Mary Elizabeth requested.

Poulou turned his chair toward her and crossed his legs as he leaned back. "Intentio arises prior to Sentio and just before the sensory packet is displayed in consciousness," he said.

"Intentio arises automatically with all incoming sensory?" asked Mary Elizabeth.

"Yes," said Poulou. "And Intentio rides parallel to the incoming data, a mirror image of the sensory information, searching for similar info packets in the Sentio and Cogito memory files, and then the new packet is determined to be important for one of three reasons: life or death, freedom or bondage, and pleasure or pain. The Americans named the reasons: life, liberty, and the pursuit of happiness."

"How interesting," said Josephine who appeared to compete with Mary Elizabeth for Poulou's attention.

"It is interesting," he said. "Intentio becomes selective attention in the consciousness window where it can be directed by free will and where it delivers our sense of being like a spotlight on a stage. It travels about twice as fast as Sentio and four times as fast as Cogito. When it moves through your memory files, it does appear as a super-conscious entity, and it is involved in matching and pulling relevant files for display in consciousness, your mosaic files for interpreting ink blots. It is not involved in a plot, an id *coup d'état* of your ego."

"That is unbelievable," said Josephine.

"Believe it!" Poulou said raising his brow. "Helen figured all of this out by her own observations, and she calls her philosophy, the Philosophy of True Freedom. Those bastards at Freiburg . . ."

"Why did Helen's work fail to reach mainstream philosophy?" asked Josephine.

Poulou shook his head in disappointment. "A footnote."

8

"Helen's work has been published as a footnote where it remains overshadowed by the all-male-boy-club philosophers. They snubbed her because she could think in ways they thought only accessible to men. Ironic, isn't it? They rejected her because she was too much like them," said Poulou.

"Sad," Mary Elizabeth said and lowered her head. "I experienced the same discrimination at the university in Berlin. The all-male-boy-club philosophers attacked my work."

"Sorry," said Poulou in an apologetic tone. After a few seconds, he flitted a smile at Josephine, then continued. "Helen suggested that consciousness could be experienced and measured in Sentio, Cogito, or both—and that we perceive our sense of being whenever Intentio settles in Sentio or Cogito, whether spontaneous or self-directed by free will. She could not prove her assertions, but she knew they were true. Remember; Intentio hovers on an identity mission then it lands in consciousness where it can be directed by self-will."

"Self-will?" asked Josephine. "Is that the same as free will?"

Poulou took a sip of brandy. "Self-will, free will, your will, my will . . . they are all the same if you ask me."

"Oh." Josephine lowered her eyes.

He continued. "When humans developed language-based thought, we redirected our attention to focus on building a language-based civilization with human-made laws and a new definition of freedom."

"What was the original definition of freedom?" asked Josephine, her head cocked sideways.

"True freedom is being free from bondage or control, free to live and act based on free-will decisions made for the greater freedom of all as experienced through Sentio with no need for language-based definitions," Poulou answered.

"So, we have forgotten all about Sentio, which has led to the enslavement of our attention or Intentio to Cogito existence," frowned Sister Josephine.

"Yes, enslavement," said Poulou in a sad tone. "We can use free will to redirect attention, but if true freedom is not on the menu in Cogito, then we are stuck without freedom."

"I understand," said Mary Elizabeth. "Our Intentio goes to where our institutions have conditioned and confined it to go."

Poulou emphasized the significance of Helen's claims. "Remember, Intentio knows no age, sex, race, color, gender, or creed. We experience these phenomena as part of our sense of being when our attention wave visits these memories or visits the experiences as they become new memories. Intentio interacts with consciousness to yield our sense of being whether it arrives in Cogito or Sentio, pre-reflective or reflective consciousness. Intentio by itself is nothingness."

Josephine's jaw dropped. "Nothingness?" she asked. "Surely it is something."

"It is like a light shining on something," Mary Elizabeth responded with enthusiasm. "The spotlight on a stage."

"Yes, exactly, and that was my small contribution to Helen's philosophy. *Me and Nothingness*, remember?" Poulou said. "Intentio, or the nothing being, is the one thing we all have in common. The thing that is identical in each human being and that we should share mutual respect for is nothing, the nothingness behind Intentio."

"*How do I know that I exist? Because I can direct my attention, with my selective attention agency within consciousness,*" Mary Elizabeth recited a quote from Poulou's book.

"Thank you," said Poulou. He appreciated her remembering and added, "For example, if a word pops into my head, then I can decide to think of another word through my ability to direct my attention with my agency of free will. Where we direct our attention is where we sense our being-ness. Addictions and passions steal our ability to self-direct our Intentio; they are a sad form of determinism."

"Explain?" requested Josephine and crossed her arms.

"In addiction Intentio gets drawn to the Sentio and or Cogito tracks focused on the release of pleasure," Poulou said. "The drug addict is enslaved by the need for a fix just as the jealous tyrant is enslaved by his need for wealth and power. Every incoming sensory packet for the addict or tyrant gives rise to Intentios trapped in a vicious cycle that know no freedom until and during pleasure release, which only makes matters worse for the next go-round."

Mary Elizabeth wrinkled her brow. "The demands of our institutionalized existence have enslaved our Intentio to Cogito."

"So we are like the addict or tyrant, but in a nicer way," concluded Josephine.

"Yes, you understand. At one time Helen believed she was addicted to language thinking," he said sadly. He got up from his chair and walked to the kitchen.

CHAPTER

9

"**Can you explain about** gender, specifically with children?" asked Josephine, moving to the edge of the sofa when Poulou returned from the kitchen with more brandy.

"Who said anything about gender?" Poulou asked, taking his seat.

"I'm just curious," said Josephine.

"Does this have anything to do with your villa mate, with the initials *JP*?" Poulou had picked up a masculine vibe from Sister Phillips.

Josephine shook her head no, but the blush on her face said otherwise.

"A child's gender defining begins at birth. The pleasure tracks are already there when the conditioning and institutionalization begins. Subtle things like gender-specific toys—dolls and toy soldiers that seem natural for either girls or boys—reflect the differences in the pathways for pleasure and nothing more. Intentio simply follows the easiest path to pleasure, causing the little beings to want to play with trucks or dolls to experience pleasure. Their selections and actions give us and them a sense of their gender as a byproduct; it tells us about their pleasure tracks."

Josephine nodded and Poulou smiled. He liked Josephine even though she reminded him of an English spinster.

"With puberty the masculine or feminine tracks take over and open up like a highway for Intentio to flow toward pleasure," he said, and glanced at Mary Elizabeth. "Teenagers learn to use the tracks for pleasure. I used mine every day as a matter of fact. Then I would redirect my attention toward homework and mundane things."

"What about arousal?" asked Mary Elizabeth.

Poulou leaned back in his chair, thrilled that she had asked. He thought for a moment about puberty when the arousal lights are always flashing. "Arousal appears as a flashing light to Intentio, which checks out the opportunity for pleasure. If it gets a go sign, then the pathways toward the pleasure center light up as the touch stimulation begins. Attention generates intention and then action until a pleasure release occurs. Once the joyride begins, the process moves forward and is hard to stop unless one's hand is redirected for a greater purpose, perhaps by the voice of his mother reminding him to finish a chore."

Mary Elizabeth and Josephine's faces filled with blood. Poulou turned his head away and lowered his eyes for a moment, remembering his lost pleasure. The silence grew until Mary Elizabeth asked for a demonstration of free will.

"I can think of a glass of brandy right now as we are talking. My free will redirects my attention from our conversation toward the form of a glass of brandy in my memory files. I leave you and our conversation and experience my sense of being in my reflective consciousness. Well, I don't really leave you. I focus my selective attention on the brandy glass while your material presence continues to generate an Intentio and image in my Sentio. I can imagine the brandy in the shot glass as a reflective conscious event that occurred earlier tonight through my memory files. Or I can look at the glass of brandy in real time on Helen's desk and experience it as a pre-reflective conscious event."

"I wonder how many reflective conscious events Helen

can hold at one time," pondered Mary Elizabeth as she stood up and stretched.

"Please, don't leave," Poulou said. "Helen is a singular case. She has a powerful Sentio and a lot more nothingness than me or you." He chuckled and continued, "Let me finish my explanation for Sister Josephine."

Mary Elizabeth sat down.

"Think about a teacher writing words on a board. For example, *the red fox*. Pre-reflective Sentio simply projects the experience of the senses: the chalk, the smell, the colors, and the forms of the letters. But remember Helen believes most of us experience our sensory after it is processed by the filter and then later in Cogito."

He paused. Josephine's eyes seemed to be in deep reflection.

"Remember, Intentio opens relevant Cogito memories and images that are labeled with *red fox*. The files are pulled for quick review and reflection while Intentio remains active. It can move faster than consciousness, and it can be split, reduced, or merged into focus."

"Thank you. That helps. And I believe you said that before," said Josephine, snapping out of her reverie.

"Well, some things are worth repeating," Poulou responded.

Mary Elizabeth added, "I think I'm beginning to understand Helen's view of consciousness."

"Mary, you wondered how many reflective conscious events Helen could hold at one time," said Poulou. "You mean like me observing me, me observing me observing me . . ."

"Yes."

"I imagine three or four, but I've never asked."

After a minute of silence, Poulou noticed the sisters were looking around the room and seemed bored.

"One other important point to remember is that Intentio is never time-stamped. I guess because it is nothingness," he smiled and winked at Mary Elizabeth. "All of our memories get time-stamped, but Intentio by itself remains free of time. Perhaps one day I will jump through the Sentio of Eden into eternity through the narrow gate as Helen has suggested," said Poulou, molding his hands to form a passage.

Josephine gave him a peculiar look, and Mary Elizabeth turned her eyes toward the door. After a sip of brandy, Poulou changed the discussion to his favorite topic.

"Personally, I enjoy good Sentio as much as I can. I enjoy erotica and finding the right sensory tracks to deliver maximum pleasure."

"What about the danger of becoming a deviant?" asked Josephine.

"I know all about the danger of overdoing it. So I mix things up."

Josephine's mouth opened. Mary Elizabeth stayed composed and joined the conversation.

"I must admit that I enjoy a little reflective erotica for pleasure every now and then," said Mary Elizabeth. "I have watched the young fishermen in Pierre and—"

She was interrupted by an outburst from Josephine. "Yes, I do too!" she confessed. "Sergio, the carpenter, is engraved in my—"

"Ah, the therapeutic effect of a confession. I hope that this does not ruin your pleasure track, Josephine Joseph." He kicked up his feet onto the table and began to reminisce as if he were talking to his schoolboy friends. "I play my favorite memories over and over. I have learned to conduct my two orchestras toward pleasure as well as the greats: Tchaikovsky, Mahler, and Rachmaninoff. They do not fool me; I know what they were doing. As a teenager . . ."

He trailed off for a minute to enjoy the memories of his youth, and the three sat in silence. Then he finished his thought. "The mind of our youth is such a beautiful thing." He stared at Mary Elizabeth with this final assertion.

"Do you believe that we are all bi?" asked Mary Elizabeth.

He paused to consider. "Oh, yes, of course, we are all bi-Sentio. Helen shared with me that she had reached pleasure while holding a female in her consciousness. I admit that I have not been able to do so with a male. I think that those tracks are inhibited or gated and would require a lot of effort to release in my case."

After looking at Josephine's pale face, he realized that he should have left Helen's pleasure tracks out of the discussion. He hurried to end the bi-Sentio discussion.

"And then there is the question of anatomy. Although it is not destiny, it is relevant for reproduction and the survival of our happy lot, the sexes." Poulou pulled on his chin hair. "Sentio esthetics is important for the most efficient somatosensory dance." The sisters' faces glowed with astonishment. They glanced at each other as he went on. "The sex hormones play a role in ramping and regulating the pathways toward pleasure. The tracks are there for either gender, but their priority is procreation."

He turned to look around to make sure that Helen and Sister Phillips had not returned. The sisters did not acknowledge his vague reference.

"Yes, but the female tracks are different," said Josephine. "Our arousal buttons are different. A brush of my hair, a male's soft whisper against my neck, a nice firm rub to my lower back, or a romantic story might give rise to my Intentio for pleasure."

"And a female's attention is more easily distracted from pleasure," said Mary Elizabeth.

"I think you mean redirected, or the tracks are gated differently. Perhaps a male's tracks toward pleasure are better insulated or less inhibited. Perhaps the problem is cobwebs or that it is dependent on the amount of pleasure for the effort." Poulou paused and considered. "We experience a measure of sexual pleasure that is handed out differently for male and female tracks."

"Yes, so what you are saying is that if I find the right tracks, then I can feel the release of pleasure as a male. I think I might like it." Josephine turned her amorous face and passionate eyes toward Poulou.

He got the feeling she planned to use him later in her reflective conscious pleasure experiment. "No," he said. "You need to do your male Sentio track experiments with a reflection of a female in your consciousness; do not put me in there."

Mary Elizabeth smiled, but it did not reach her eyes. She leaned toward Poulou, her blue eyes piercing him. Her countenance screamed dominance, and he was surprised when he felt fear grip his chest. Her raging eyes said that she wanted to take him for a ride on one of her male pleasure tracks. When he broke free from her eye contact, he crossed his legs in reflex and then smiled at the thought; he was trying to protect his phenomenological virginity.

10

The door to Villa #4 opened, and Helen and Sister Phillips entered through the foyer with commotion and loud laughter. Helen took off her coat, made her way to the sitting room, and produced a little belch, giving a hand wave for pardon.

Poulou, Mary Elizabeth, and Josephine sat in silence with surprised expressions.

"Have you had a nice chat?" asked Helen as she dropped into her seat seemingly ignored by all.

Sister Phillips joined Mary Elizabeth and Josephine on the sofa offering them a swig of brandy. They shook their heads in refusal.

Helen wasted no time after Sister poured another shot for her. "What have you been talking about?" she asked in a loud voice.

Mary Elizabeth and Josephine sat wide-eyed and motionless. Poulou looked at her but waited until she had turned up her shot glass to respond. "We have been talking about sex—correction . . . pleasure."

The sisters' eyes stretched even wider. Helen almost spat out her brandy then shook her head. "Of course you have," she smirked at Poulou. "It's all you ever want to talk about. I want to talk about something more important for the moment."

"What on earth could that be?" Poulou asked, giving the sisters a silly smile.

"I am concerned about how to reveal my compass to the orphans and the community at large."

"What about the world?" asked Poulou, chuckling.

Tickled for some reason by Poulou's silly behavior, Josephine produced a burst of laughter at his comment about the world. The guffaw escaped her lips just before her hand covered her mouth. She lowered her eyes from Helen's glare.

"First things first," said Helen. She downed the rest of her brandy and then cast a side glance at Josephine. She wanted her sisters to understand why the compass was necessary. "The use of profanity will indicate liberation. Man will live free together while cursing the existence of his fellow man. This will become the rite of existentialism: the idea of a freedom that abandons everything once thought moral and civil." She peered down her nose at Poulou, the closet existentialist, and stirred him to speak.

"I prefer Socrates' simple understanding, where knowledge is virtue and ignorance is evil," he said in a conciliatory tone.

"Existentialism provides a new way for man to avoid repeating history," Helen said, and laughed at her suggestion before continuing. "Man will create his story venturing forward and never looking back, and the seeds of existentialism will soon be flowering in America. Have you heard the music they are playing? The synthetic sound has spread to America from the exies in Hamburg."

"Helen, can you explain what it is about existentialism that you do not like?" requested Mary Elizabeth.

Helen sat up a little straighter and clasped her hands in front of her. "Okay, I will. Existentialism has created this idea that man can be free from institutionalization. That is impossible. Man is institutionalized by the very language he uses to create thoughts in Cogito. What is freedom? Men are redefining the meaning of the word every day."

"What *is* freedom?" Josephine asked, and then shot a grin at Poulou.

Helen noticed her sisters seemed to have been affected by Poulou. "The newest definition of freedom is the experience of doing what you ought to do because you want to. What you ought to do is determined by the institutions, which use language-based propaganda to enslave the masses and make them strive to live as slaves of existence. The horrible truth is that most people believe they are striving for true freedom."

Helen shook her head in disgust.

"I chose to teach the orphans English because of the modicum of success that the Americans had two hundred years ago with the English language. But even they have redefined freedom; no one is safe from the bondage of language-thinking existence. The politicians and lawyers, owned by the dictators, will always find a way to manipulate language to enslave the masses. The Americans have fallen under the control of the closet dictators, the business owners who want to rule their employees and the world." After pausing for a moment, she lamented, "Pictorial language showed promise but fell short."

Poulou downed another shot of brandy and eagerly jumped into the discussion. "Helen, you are the compass for the orphans. They need not look any further."

She responded, "When man can see the world through the Sentio of Eden then he can experience the compass that points toward greater freedom for one and all." Helen paused. She wanted to make her point that each man will find greater freedom for all through his own connection with nature through Sentio. "Freedom does not work if we are blindly following someone else's vision for freedom."

"Yes, but man has free will. He does not have to follow the compass," said Poulou.

"I know that," Helen responded quickly. "Man's free

will is not free, and we will show him true freedom. We will provide the opportunity."

Poulou looked down at his empty brandy glass and suggested, "So the Sentio of Eden becomes the magnetic field for the pure Intentio that points to Eden's north, for greater freedom for all. Intentio serves as the needle of your compass pointing and driving man toward this freedom. I presume that the consciousness of Eden is only a temporary and fleeting experience."

Helen nodded.

"Man simply has to experience the consciousness of Eden while connected to others and to nature," Poulou said. "The divine Intentio will emerge and direct his consciousness toward the path of greater freedom for all, and if man follows this path, then he will live a true essence life."

The sisters clapped with enthusiasm.

"That was a marvelous explanation," said Josephine. "I think I'm finally beginning to understand!"

Helen let out a snort and clenched her hands together so tightly that she felt pain. How many times had she explained this same idea to her sisters? How many times had Josephine either not understood, or worse, mocked her? She erupted out of her seat, raising her hand in the air but stopped short of making a fist when she realized it was her gloved hand.

"First," she said, "humankind needs the Cogito scaffolding to understand the compass: the antithesis of existentialism. "Second! One requires a sensitivity experience, like my experience at Munchausen's, and later in the Black Forest. Third! The sensitivity for the experience will fade if one returns to mundane existence."

"Fourth," mocked Poulou.

The sisters ignored him, and Helen took a moment to calm down. She thought about how important it was to remain sensitive after being reminded by her glove. "The renewal of sensitivity has been on my mind ever since my first compass experience. The orphans rejuvenated my sensitivity, which led to my second compass experience. The orphan children provide a strange form of love that I have found very sensitizing."

The sisters nodded in unison.

"Yes, the intimate touch of hand holding, hugs, or just looking into the children's eyes becomes extraordinarily sensitizing," said Josephine.

Helen paused. She thought of the human need for freedom in order for one to reach his or her full potential, and how love, Sentio, and freedom seemed connected, dependent upon one another. Strange.

"Humans have weakened their Sentios by ignoring them. They have lost the vision for freedom. The words *freedom, capitalism, franchising* . . . they mean the same thing to the greedy while the masses strive to find freedom from institutional existence. Their governments have grown into inefficient institutions with insurmountable barriers to common people. Their bureaucracies serve the few with the passion for power and wealth."

Mary Elizabeth chimed in. "I understand what Helen is saying. It's easier for governments and closet dictators to make us love our servitude by making us believe that we enjoy freedom. This was my subject of interest while I served in Berlin, the truth behind western democracy."

"Good, Mary Elizabeth," Helen said. "They make us love our servitude by making us believe that we enjoy freedom while their will for power and pleasure grow malignant."

"If humans have to live together and they cannot find freedom, then what can they do?" asked Poulou.

"The compass experience can deliver true freedom and true essence for those who want it," said Helen.

"But you cannot deliver your compass through Cogito. No one will understand," said Poulou. "You cannot create a compass with words. A compass points to something real, like the North Pole. When I use my magnetic compass, I do not intend to visit the North Pole. I might be heading to South Africa and then north to the French Riviera."

"I understand," said Helen. "I'm going to deliver the compass through our sunset christening ceremony. I will explain how I experienced Eden—the phenomenon of Eden is still out there—and teach the orphans and people of Pierre how to experience the compass through Sentio by revisiting the same sunset as was seen in Eden and can be seen over Andorra today."

"Helen, you're claiming that God gave man the compass to navigate a life in Eden, and man lost sight of the compass when he left," Poulou said. "For God's sake . . . what have you been drinking?"

"Yes, that is my claim based on my experience," said Helen.

"All of the great thinkers rejected this assertion."

"I know that. I was in the café with you."

Poulou shook his head and mumbled, "Man cannot consciously reflect on how the world would appear in Eden."

Sister Josephine acted as though she wanted to say something, but didn't. She bit her fingernails as Helen smiled and continued her explanation.

"Human Sentio is conditioned and inhibited. We need to free Sentio and restore its sensitivity in order to have the pre-reflective conscious experience that gives rise to the Intentio of providence, the needle of the compass of Eden."

Josephine raised her hand again, and Helen waved her off and pressed her point about the compass.

"That is why man lost his compass in the first place, and the same reason the great philosophers did not believe in its existence." She made eye contact with each Sister and Poulou before continuing. "Their Sentios were weak. You need a healthy and sensitive Sentio for the pre-reflective compass event and a Cogito that will allow the experience rather than slamming the door shut by telling you the compass does not exist."

"Okay," Poulou said. "I think I understand." He shook his head sideways and downed another shot of brandy.

Helen continued, "If I can deliver a sensitivity for Sentio through the sunset experience and deliver the right language to unlock Cogito, then each person might stumble upon the compass experience through nature." Helen said with enthusiasm. "I cannot wait to deliver the compass experience at our christening ceremony on Friday."

"Eureka! Eureka!" Poulou exclaimed with a thick tongue. He sounded drunk. His spittle sprayed into the air as he spoke. "Operation True Essence. Let Mary Elizabeth spearhead the sisters in discovering how to deliver your true essence and true freedom with a superior argument over the existentialists' argument. You will save humankind from the idea they are enslaved by Cogito existence, and you will not have to deal with this messy compass of Eden idea."

"That is a great suggestion," Helen agreed. She could tell that Poulou was drunk and about to fall asleep. "Mary Elizabeth, I want you to start educating the sisters about philosophy. You can tutor them at the library in Pierre."

After Poulou closed his eyes, Helen waved to Mary and whispered that she was simply appeasing him. She did not like his Operation True Essence suggestion.

Poulou opened his eyes and gestured for Sister Phillips to refill his glass. Then he held up the shot of brandy as the sisters stood and headed to bed. He downed the shot, took off his shoes, and stretched out on the sofa.

"Oh, Sentio, Sentio! Wherefore art thou, Sentio?" Poulou slobbered. "*I am here*, said Sentio with Intentio. One last toast to Operation True Essence." He had no brandy left to drink.

"Goodnight, my brother. I love you," Helen said.

"Me too," he mumbled. "Don't mess with my phenom-enal . . . virginity."

"What?" Helen asked as she covered him with a blanket and kissed him on the forehead.

"You know what I'm talking about." His voice trailed off as he passed out on the sofa.

After turning out the lights, Helen wondered what on earth Poulou had told her sisters.

11

"**Yes, we can take** her," Helen said into the phone.

"Thank you. You're a godsend, Reverend Mother. We'll have her there by Monday," the jubilant constable of Balley Bunion said. "I think I know, but please remind me. Where is your place?"

"Our campus is atop Mount Essence overlooking Pierre, France."

"I know Pierre, best trout fishing in Europe."

"Call me when you arrive, and we will meet you in Pierre."

"We'll have her there Monday morning."

Helen hung up. She had accepted a six-year-old Irish girl. She shuffled the paperwork together and stored the child's file in her cabinet. *Our first orphan named Jacki,* thought Helen. She gazed out of her window to see if the dark clouds had disappeared. The big day had arrived, and she was excited.

She stepped out of the school building onto the balcony porch for a better view. The winter sun remained high above the horizon; the sunset was at least two hours away. After scanning the sky, she twirled in joy: the big clouds had set sail and cleared the wild blue yonder.

Down the porch steps to the terrace, she went behind the school building where cheery sounds stirred. The campus had come to life. The children screamed in joy from the play area. They were running races, jumping rope, and swinging in the last warm sunshine of the day. The world could be at war, and the children would play. *Such happy beings.*

The white and baby-blue flag of Essence flapped overhead as Helen retreated to hide on the other side of the stairs. Two yellow-headed girls approached the terrace. One encouraged while the other hopped down the flat stone walkway.

"Step on a crack and break the Reverend Mother's back," repeated the lead girl with enthusiasm and as her sister hopped closer to the terrace, her encouragement grew. "Carry on. Carry on. One more . . . you did it! You did not break the Reverend Strangeglove's back." The cute little English girls embraced and ran back to the play area.

Helen maintained her private surveillance and restrained her laughter until they were long gone. They looked so much happier than when they had arrived. They had come into the world in a post-World War II life raft. Many of the children had lost their parents to disease.

Looking toward the playground, she saw more smiling faces. They no longer looked like forlorn beings. They had begun arriving two weeks ago, and already the orphanage bloomed with little children from Austria, England, Ireland, France, Germany, and Spain. The headcount had reached fifty as of the day before, all between the ages of five and fourteen. Hope beamed from their innocent faces as they engaged in the freedom of play.

Two of her sisters stood on watch in the distance: Sister Josephine and Sister Celia, one of the Catalan gals. They watched the children like shepherds.

The vibrations of the children's jumps pulsed through Helen's feet as she stepped onto the playground. The sensations caused her to pause in remembrance of the journey that had delivered the birth of Essence. She returned to where the flag waved beyond the children's view. She got down on her knees and leaned to touch the base of the pole with her lips.

The cold metal tasted bitter while her sweet memories from the construction phase of the mountain campus returned. Tears of joy welled in her eyes and traveled down her cheeks, dripping onto the smooth stone: one by one then two by two. She closed her eyes in reflection.

The conception of the orphanage had begun long before the first turn of a shovel nine months earlier. She thought back to the moment when the journey began. In a log cabin among the Black Forest evergreens, she had seen the vision of the grand orphanage for freedom during her compass experience.

After a couple of deep breaths, still on her knees, she wiped her tears with her sleeve and removed the precious letter from her coat pocket. The correspondence from the Geneva Post War Committee granted the sisters the authority to take in orphans from all over Europe and raise them to young adulthood.

She returned the letter to her pocket and looked up toward the sky in gratitude. Her ten-year odyssey had produced a beautiful campus for children to play, grow, and discover greater freedom. She paused to compose herself, unwrinkled the sleeve of her long black glove, and was reminded she had lived as a holier-than-thou philosopher addicted to Cogito.

With renewed confidence, she rose to her feet and walked toward the playground. Soon she would disclose to the world that she had found the compass of Eden. She had waited ten years for this moment to present her vision of freedom. Her only regret was that Poulou was not here to enjoy the moment with her.

She walked with a spring in her step and approached her sisters, heels clicking against the flagstone announcing her advance. The sisters turned and shared cordial greetings.

Careful to avoid eye contact, Helen didn't want to reveal her tears. She peered ahead watching the children swing then leaned her head toward Josephine.

"How did the afternoon practice go?" she asked.

Josephine explained with enthusiasm that the children had done very well. "They are ready for the ceremony. They have practiced their march up and down the steps and around the terrace many times. They know to wait for your hand wave. They are a sweet lot," Josephine added.

"Thank you. I share your confidence. We are ready," said Helen.

She sniffled a bit from her residual tears and asked Sister Celia, "How long have they been at play?"

"Almost an hour," said Celia, then reached to hold Helen's right hand. Celia's warm, gentle hand squeezed softly, and Helen experienced her intention for comfort. She met Celia's love-filled eyes and angelic face and admitted that she had shed tears of joy over the birthday of Essence. Celia shared her mutual joy.

Josephine lifted her rosy cheeks and pointed toward the snow-covered mountaintops, the stage for Andorra's sunset. The sun had progressed in its descent, and Helen felt a squeeze in her stomach as time grew short. She let out a deep breath, relaxed, and enjoyed the magnificent scene with her sisters.

The moment passed, and a west wind blew up from the valley and almost lifted their veils. They turned and crouched to resist the strong wind. The children screamed and huddled together for shelter.

"Wow!" said Josephine. "That gust came out of nowhere."

"Sisters, let's ring them in. It is too cold for play," said Helen.

"Yes, Reverend Mother." Josephine pulled her long whistle from around her neck and blew two sharp sounds followed by a much longer, continuous note—the rally tune for her troops.

Thirty-seven disturbed faces turned like contortionists with their mouths open, their eyes locked on the source of the whistled sounds. They joined together in a chorus of screams, released playful embraces, and ran down the hill.

Their little heads, blacks, browns, strawberry blondes, brunettes, carroty-tops, and yellow-mops—converged on the sisters as fast as they could run. The cute little beings, all younger than eight, raced to be the first in line.

"Put on your brakes!" shouted Josephine as she held out her arms. But it was too late.

Two boys tumbled and fell, and another little one reached for Helen's skirt. He slipped and fell, striking the ground with a thump. The child appeared unconscious until he blinked. Helen reached under his arms to tickle him, sensing that he was pretending. The little boy opened his eyes and began to wiggle with excitement.

"*Non! Non!*" he exclaimed through his laughter.

His cute, toothless grin reminded her that he was one of her precious six-year-olds, Jean-Paul, the little Frenchman.

"*Est ce que tu vas bien?*" Helen asked if he was okay as she knelt and helped him up.

"*Oui*, yes," Jean-Paul said.

After standing, he turned and looked at her with the saddest blue eyes, and she felt his yearning for his mother and a desire to jump into her embrace. Instead he turned and ran to get in line. Helen held back her tears, remembering the loneliness she had felt when she was orphaned at six.

Josephine instructed the children to line up and count off then led them single file across the playground to the Big Bell Chapel. Celia pulled the heavy front door open, and the children marched into the gathering area. The pine wood floors and the beams overhead warmed Helen's heart; she loved the wood-and-stacked-stone facility.

"Children, let's find a place to sit and calm down," Helen instructed.

The cooks prepared dinner in the kitchen to the left, and the older children played with cubes, spheres, and cylinders in the back right corner with Sister Cecelia. The fire roared from the giant stone fireplace in front and warmed the entire room. The younger children took their places at the four long dinner tables. Helen stood in front, a pillar of silence, and waited.

12

Helen held her finger to her lips for a moment. "Quiet! Please, quiet! Thank you. Everyone look at my face." She smiled and continued. "I am proud of you. We will have so much fun tonight. I want everyone ready for the christening ceremony at sunset, so I need you to rest and calm down. One of the sisters will be here soon to lead you in some geometric and arithmetic games."

The children lowered their heads at her announcement, perhaps not excited about the educational games. Helen loved geometric games; she wanted the children to experience the shapes and forms of sensory consciousness.

She looked for the other sisters as she waited for Sister Serelia, her math teacher. Sister Celia and Sister Josephine went to gather wood for the fire. *Where is everyone?* she wondered.

The children could not stay still for long. They began to fidget and then the touching began.

"Keep your hands to yourselves," Helen reminded them.

The children's eyes darted at one another. She felt them gawking at her. She had no formal experience with teaching children and knew they could sense her deficiency. A hand went up.

Helen pointed to the little girl. "Yes, you may speak."

"I think that I might require a refreshment and something for this dreadful breeze coming through the door," said the precocious English girl. "My name is Alice."

"Okay, Alice, you can come over here in this chair closer to the fire," said Helen.

Alice walked over and jumped into her seat and crossed her arms as Helen and the children watched.

"We will get some water from the kitchen after everyone has had a chance to warm and calm," said Helen with a gentle pat on Alice's shoulder.

Another hand went up and then another. Helen encouraged the children to have their say in English. "One at a time, and please tell everyone your name."

"I'm hungry and hot," said a German boy who stood up tall and smiled all around.

"What is your name?" asked Helen.

"My name is Edmund."

"Thank you, Edmund. You speak English very well," said Helen. "Please take Alice's seat by the door if you are hot. Next."

"I'm bored," said an Austrian girl. "My name is Eva." She stood and twirled, pulling at her curly brown hair.

"Me too!" agreed another, twisting her curly red locks with her finger. "My name is Heidi."

"Thank you, Heidi, we will have something for all of you to do very soon," said Helen, looking about for Sister Serelia. She needed help. Then their polite requests turned to examining questions.

"Why do we have to be calm?" asked an Irish girl. "My name is Miriam."

"Why are you wearing a black glove on one hand?" asked a little French boy standing on his chair.

Helen recognized him. "Please get down, Louis."

He smiled, jumped down, and sat in his chair.

Another question about Helen's glove preceded an

outburst of laughter. She couldn't repress her grin after strange glove remarks made by the cute yellow-headed twins.

Then . . . mutiny.

Several children wanted to use the bathroom, and when Helen hesitated to grant permission, they began to make their own way. She rushed to stop them and turned the tykes back to their chairs.

"Wait a minute; everyone sit down!" Helen knew that the children's questions were disguised to test her limits. She did not want to suppress their intention for freedom with discipline, but she needed to create a boundary for safety. She looked to Josephine for help.

"Where are the other sisters?" asked Helen, with her arms stretched between two tables.

"They went to put on their long johns for the ceremony."

"Please, Sister Josephine, could you take over for me? I need to check on Sister Phillips. She should have returned from Pierre thirty minutes ago."

Josephine jumped to the task. She grabbed her whistle and gave two forceful blows. The children covered their ears. Helen felt their pain as the shrill sounds stifled her too.

Josephine threw up her right hand and puffed with authority, "Alberto, Susan, James, and Louis, sit down! Children, listen up! We will take turns using the bathroom, and then we will all get some water. No one moves without permission."

The children no longer needed to use the bathroom, just as Helen had suspected. Josephine gathered a small party and led them to the kitchen for water while Celia directed the others to bring their chairs around the fireplace. The children leaped at the opportunity. They dragged the heavy, metal chairs to the fireplace, producing painful screeches and shrieks every step of the way.

Helen left the horrific noise and strode outside looking for Sister Phillips. After a few minutes in the cold and no sign of Sister, she proceeded back inside and made her way to the kitchen.

"Is everything okay?" asked Josephine.

"I hope so. I am worried about Sister Phillips."

"I know she had to pick up several items at the grocery. She will be here soon."

"Thank you, Sister Josephine. And thank you for, you know . . . ," said Helen, not wanting the children in line to hear that Josephine had rescued her from them.

The compliment brought a pretty smile and nod from Josephine.

Helen leaned back on the table, took a deep breath, and enjoyed the joyous sounds of the cooks preparing dinner.

13

Mrs. Ophelia, the main cook at the orphanage, interrupted the flow of water to fill three large pots. Several additional thirsty children had queued for a drink. In all the commotion Edmund, Alberto, and two others had slipped in front for a second turn. Josephine spotted them and directed them to the end of the line. She tickled Edmund to make her point. Then the children began to tickle each other.

The laughter turned into screams of "Stop it! Stop it!"

Heidi was on the floor in the fetal position guarding her loins from Louis. Helen watched in silence from her perch, leaning against the table.

"Get up, you two," Sister Josephine said. "Louis, get off your knees. You will rub holes in your pants."

"Can you tickle someone to death?" asked Heidi as she stood.

Sister Josephine threatened to blow her whistle, and the tickling stopped. After a moment, Josephine wheeled around toward Helen with the most curious twinkle in her eyes.

"Reverend Mother, please tell me again about the compass of Eden. I wanted to tell you something last Sunday when we were talking with Poulou, but I forgot. I think it was important."

Caught off guard by Josephine's request, Helen stood up straight. She had explained the compass of Eden to her many times.

Josephine gave an innocent little smile. "I want to hear what you are going to say at the ceremony."

Helen cleared her throat and began to explain once again in a slow and composed voice. "When God created man, he gave him a compass with which to navigate Eden in total freedom. Then God cast man out of Eden and blocked his reentry with a flaming sword and the cherubim. You know the story."

Sister nodded.

Helen went on. "I recently experienced the compass for the second time in my life. I told you about it. It was just last week while watching the sunset over Andorra with the sisters and the orphans during the rehearsal for our christening ceremony."

"Oh yes, how wonderful," said Josephine.

"My true sensory consciousness, my Sentio, returned to the sensitivity level of the first conscious moment in Eden when man's pre-reflective sensory consciousness began. Andorra's sunset looked like Eden to me during that moment, my state of grace. The texture of the blue sky emerged like oil on canvas and was displayed in my consciousness; words cannot convey what my sensory experience entailed. Nor can I explain the vivid, surreal experience of non-object things like oranges, pinks, violets, and purples."

"How odd that you experienced such a vivid sunset, and I did not," Josephine responded with a consternated expression and leaned over to lift the last child in line for a drink.

Helen turned her eyes from Josephine's disappointment and gazed toward the ceiling beams that formed a cross in the dining area. She waited and regained Sister's attention after the child finished her drink.

"I experienced the compass after my Eden moment. I closed my eyes. My Intentio had emerged as a contemporary with Eden's sensory experience, and it ran through my mind."

"Did you say *intendio* or *intentio*?" Josephine asked.

"Intentio, the wave of attention and selective attention. This Intentio was special. I recognized it immediately, as I had experienced the same almost ten years ago. It had a super-attention power and acted as the needle of my compass experience."

"Intentio is such a cute name. I like it. Did Shakespeare use the name in *The Merchant of Venice?*" Josephine asked in a playful tone.

"No, Shakespeare did not use the name. You must be thinking of Cicero or Poulou."

Sister Josephine arched her brow and puckered her lips. "Do you mean that for every sensory event of consciousness there is a little Intentio that rises up and runs through your mind? That explains why I have all these weird thoughts and feelings that come out of nowhere."

"Yes, for every sensory experience that reaches consciousness there is also an Intentio that begins a thorough examination of the matter for your own good."

"You mean like when a light turns on?"

"Intentios, or attention waves, stream from all of our sensory experiences—touch, light, sound—and we redirect and focus our attention waves thousands of times a day. Many of the children have not learned to focus common attention waves, but that is another matter entirely."

"Poulou told me about Intentio," Josephine smiled.

"Husserl and Brentano pioneered the understanding of Intentio, and I studied under Husserl."

"I know," said Josephine with a hint of indignation.

Helen lowered the tone of her voice. "I am trying to explain to you about the uncommon Intentio that arose in Eden: the needle of the Compass of Freedom."

Josephine gave a look of understanding and nodded.

Helen continued. "Where the Intentio of Eden flowed in my mind was where I experienced my sense of being during the compass experience. The powerful attention wave ran through my conscious memories leading me on a visual journey and revealing every moment in my life when I had discovered or failed to discover a new freedom—a motion picture of my lifelong journey of bondage and freedom."

"But how did you know which scene reflected freedom and which did not?" asked Josephine.

"Whether I had experienced or simply projected the possible experience, Intentio led me into the greater freedom scene and delivered my sense of being there."

"What is the sense of being? I forget."

"For example, during my first compass experience, when I was trying to decide whether to stay in the Black Forest or move to Paris with Poulou, the Intentio of Eden lit up the grand seventeenth century architecture of the Hotel de Crillon, the Eiffel Tower, and the *Arc de Triomphe*—my favorite memories of Paris. My freedom scenes were in bright colors, and I sensed my beingness within those scenes."

"Your beingness in the future?"

"Yes, the future is part of you, whether you like it or not, as is your past and present. You are your past, present, *and* future, which can change within the limits of your finitude. And you can experience your sense of being in a possible future."

Josephine pursed her lips.

"The scenes of when I grew up in Freiburg that led to bondage were displayed without color," Helen explained. "Intentio did not linger in the scenes from my dark past. It was obvious to me that I was being directed through the colored scenes toward greater freedom."

"They have made televisions that can show color, did you know?" asked Josephine.

"Please, Sister, let me go on," Helen said with a small sigh, then reminded herself to show patience towards her Sister. She noticed Josephine's face had lengthened, and she felt a pang of guilt. Helen apologized and acknowledged that the subject matter was difficult. "The compass is critical for finding greater freedom for all," Helen said emphatically.

"I know," Josephine told her. "But I want to make sure that it doesn't backfire."

"I appreciate your concern. I have waited ten years to share my discovery with the world, and I am ready."

"I understand," said Josephine.

"My most recent Intentio movie began nine months ago at the groundbreaking ceremony for Essence. The scene reflected my happiness and excitement. A new scene appeared that was neither resolute nor familiar to me—a fuzzy scene. I experienced my sense of being in the future for a brief moment then."

"Your sense of being in the future?"

Helen looked at her. "Yes, the future. We discussed this. All of our sisters appeared to be praying in the chapel, dressed in those silly-looking white and baby-blue habits that some of the sisters saw in that magazine from Paris. I do not know why they were praying. I would never condone such public behavior. Then the bright-colored scene faded." Helen sighed, feeling drained. "Intentio moved with great power through my mind. I could not redirect it with free will. That is how I knew that the Intentio produced by my Sentio experience of Eden was divine and that it was the needle for the Compass of Freedom."

Josephine seemed deep in thought for a moment and then spoke up. "We are condemned to free will, aren't we?"

"Yes, we have free will. But today's Cogito menu for free will does not include freedom. I refer to the free will choices available in Cogito as *self-will* or *institutional will*. For many years, I struggled to find freedom with the best Intentio that I could muster. I saw my missed opportunities during my compass experience, and I do have regrets."

"We all have regrets," Josephine observed in a soft voice.

"I know," Helen said. "But I have had no regrets since my compass experience. I experienced true free will after I saw my freedom visions. I wanted to use my free will to follow the compass's path to greater freedom. Without the compass, human beings will remain forever lost in their life-boats, forced to use self-will as a paddle on the sea of language-thinking existence."

Sister Josephine had placed her elbow in her hand then directed three fingers to support her chin. Helen waited to see if Josephine was going to say something, but she remained quiet.

"I have seen the path to greater freedom for all men through a renewal of Sentio. That was my compass of Eden revelation in the Black Forest. That is how you and the others will be able to experience the compass of Eden, too." Helen gave her final words of revelation: "Seek ye first the Sentio of Eden and all will be given to you."

She leaned back against the table and waited for a response. Applause? Praise? Something? But Josephine offered no feedback and remained flat-faced in her thinking pose, her eyes reflecting critical thought. With her arms folded across her chest, Helen turned her attention to the children who had begun to sing.

Josephine spoke in a soft tone. "I remember now what I wanted to ask." Helen turned to meet her eyes. "How do you know what Eden looks like?"

"Oh, I have seen it before," she responded as automatically as a tap to the knee.

Josephine squinted at her skeptically.

I have seen it before. The words echoed in Helen's head, and she realized the fault of her exposition. Such an assertion probably sounded crazy to Josephine. Doubt squeezed at her chest. *But what else could it have been? The vivid sunset had to be the sunset of Eden.* Helen almost laughed aloud but then found herself fighting the urge to cry. She bit her lip to quell her anguish. The silence grew louder. In those few seconds, her mind fired with rapid thoughts of self-assurance, an attempt to calm herself.

It does not matter if I can or cannot see Eden. I know that I experienced the compass of Eden.

Despite her best efforts, her heart sank. She had no sensory evidence to corroborate her story and no actual photographs of Eden for genuine comparison. No matter what she saw, how could she prove to herself or anyone else that it was Eden? No one in recorded history had seen the place. She realized her testimony sounded ridiculous. She did not want to be compared to the writer who claimed to have seen something like Eden on an LSD trip. The critics of her compass experience might say she had hallucinated, but she knew in her heart that it was not a hallucination, and she did not need proof.

Meanwhile, Josephine had picked up a little strawberry-blonde girl to drink from the faucet. The thirsty little girl slurped and gulped from the stream of flowing water. Helen could not have prepared herself for what came next.

"Yes, Sentio," Sister Josephine looked at her with a wry smile. "I know that the children would love to see Eden, even if we can't go there to visit, just to see it would be nice." She put the little girl down with an unmistakable glee sparkling from her eyes.

She was making light of Helen's compass story.

Helen felt anger rise within her, and her thoughts raced. Her face flushed as she searched for an area of comfort in her mind, salvation from this dreadful feeling of betrayal in the pit of her stomach. Josephine had a knack for fault-finding, and she seemed to enjoy bringing others down with her cynical view. Stinging with resentment Helen thought to herself, *I will show her and the world what Eden looks like.*

Helen pivoted away from Josephine as her chest tightened into a large knot of disappointment. She walked out of the kitchen toward the front door with her head tilted down and her gloved hand against her bosom. She heard Josephine's voice join with the others in song, the cheerful melody discordant with Helen's thoughts.

What on earth are they singing about? Her mind fired. *How about some arithmetic games, something quiet!*

She sat on the windowsill near the front of the room and continued to ignore the singing. She reconsidered the idea that her Intentio, the needle of the compass, arose from the pre-reflective Sentio experience of Eden. She knew that it was the truth, but she had no way to explain without sounding crazy.

Damn!

After a deep breath, Helen looked down at her long black glove. The glove produced an internal smile, and she relaxed. She had relapsed to her old obsessive thinking, so she focused on the beautiful blue and green colors painted on the walls. The canary yellow kitchen ceiling delivered her attention to Sentio, and then the melody and the children's voices rejuvenated her. She peeked out the door and saw the sun's advance toward the horizon. She needed to put on her whites for the ceremony.

14

Winter filled the air as Helen walked out of the chapel, made her way across the straw-covered ground, and walked around the dormitory to Villa #4. She entered through the back door then went to her bedroom and changed into her long, flannel underwear. She pulled on her ceremonial white habit and fixed her veil. After a quick look in the mirror, she exited in a hurry following the sidewalk to the terrace.

Sister Phillips had just arrived; Helen was relieved to see her and approached the back of the wagon. "What took you?"

She did not respond and tended to unhooking Marcel. The mule had pulled the wagon from Pierre filled with food, clothes, a case of brandy, and one bottle of champagne. As Sister Phillips lifted the mule's harness, Helen made eye contact with her.

"What took you?" Helen repeated.

"I had to fix the right rear wheel. It came loose."

"We need to hurry. The men from Pierre can help us unload the wagon after the ceremony."

Helen lifted the case of brandy and dashed to the barn almost sixty meters away. She did not want the brandy on display. She found a discreet place on the top shelf of the tool cabinet then closed the door and took a seat on the bench.

After several deep breaths, she relaxed and realized

she had not thought about the compass since sitting on the windowsill.

Sister Phillips led Marcel into the barn, leaned over, and pulled on his front leg.

"Is everything alright?" asked Helen.

"No, I think Marcel picked up a rock in his hoof." Sister held his flexed leg and probed with her finger.

"I'll see you on the porch in a few minutes," Helen said. "Don't forget to pick up the bottle of champagne in the wagon."

When Sister did not acknowledge, Helen turned back around. "Oh, there is blood," she murmured. A red trail had wrapped around Sister's finger as she dug into Marcel's hoof. A small rock fell. Marcel pulled his leg away and yelped then stomped while Sister tried to steady him.

The mule's distress and Sister's blood gave Helen a queasy feeling. She sat back down on the bench. Sister Phillips lifted the mule's leg and released it after a quick wipe of his pad. She looked up toward Helen with sorrow written all over her face.

"Marcel began to limp at the halfway point. He made the last half-mile in pain," Sister Phillips said, and reached to caress his leg. "I should have stopped, but I was in a hurry to get back."

Helen raised her gloved hand to her forehead and hoped that her queasiness would pass. She was afraid to speak for fear that she would retch.

"Thank you, Reverend Mother, for staying with me," said Sister.

Helen resisted her gag reflex, and the knot in her throat relaxed.

"I am thankful for you, Sister," Helen said, and took a breath.

Faint human voices carried into the barn with the wind. The sounds of human footsteps turned Sister Phillips' head, and the chorus of hard leather heels striking the cobblestones drew near. The sound of the heel strikes reminded Helen of troops in retreat during the war. When an excited French female's voice exclaimed, "*L'Essence est belle!*" she knew the guests had begun to arrive and could see the townspeople on the road.

"The visitors from Pierre are arriving for the christening ceremony. We need to hurry," she told Sister Phillips, who had moved near Marcel's head. Her eye twitched, and her face looked as white as the tunic of her habit.

Helen walked over to comfort her, gently rubbed her arm. "Do you remember how well you performed at our rehearsal? You were wonderful. Just do it again. Take a moment to rest, but be quick. We can't be late."

"Thank you, Reverend Mother. I will be right behind you."

Helen proceeded out of the stable to the road where she fell in line behind her builders as they walked toward the orphanage. The builders from Catalan were accompanied by their wives and the mayor of Pierre. Helen smiled as they turned to greet her. She enjoyed seeing them and their pretty wives. She greeted all ten as they walked. The builders looked so handsome and tall, gentlemen dressed for a ceremony rather than a day's work.

She smiled to herself, remembering how the builders bickered and argued every day when they were erecting the structures that would become Essence. They seemed to need to argue. She remembered how she had served biscuits and tea every afternoon to remind them to be civil to one another.

Helen looked up from the road and gazed around at the campus. In the end the builders had proven to be master craftsmen. They cleared the land and built everything with little more than mountain stones and cedar pines. She could see how their arguing had served a purpose, fueling the enterprise of building—Marx's dialectic.

Sergio, a handsome young carpenter and a favorite of Helen's, said "There is your perch, Reverend Mother," referring to the second-story porch with the large awnings and cedar rail that overlooked the flagstone terrace. The porch faced west to capture the beautiful sunsets of Andorra. Helen could see the workmanship required to make the porch safe with I-beams and double-pillar support underneath.

She turned toward Sergio and the others with a smile broad enough for them all. She shared their pride. She had designed the balcony porch with tonight's christening celebration in mind. She was glad to have the makers of her vision present for the occasion.

She continued to walk with the builders to the center of the property where they all paused to enjoy the full breadth of the scene: the four mountain villas; the school building; and the Big Bell Chapel building—so named by the children—with the bell tower, kitchen, dining, and gathering area, was connected by a hallway to the adjacent dormitory building. They turned slowly, taking in the fruit of their labors against the evening sky. Helen hugged each of the builders and felt reciprocal gratitude from the warmth of their strong embraces. Last, she embraced the mayor, and he prolonged his hold for longer than she wanted while he announced to everyone her list of accomplishments.

A cheap trick, she thought. She had no choice but to stand in his clutches until he finished. She noticed the builders' wives staring at her glove.

The cold wind of Andorra began blowing again, and the sun dipped below the pine trees. It was almost time.

"Excuse me, I need to get ready," Helen said, and broke from the mayor's hold. She headed toward the chapel.

"We will see you on the porch," the mayor said and followed the builders toward the terrace. They went to start the bonfire.

In the chapel, the cooks were mixing flour into dough.

The children had stopped singing and were seated at the tables.

"Is everyone ready?" Helen asked without waiting for an answer. She hurried to her changing room, slammed the door shut, then retrieved a bottle of cherry brandy from the medicine cabinet. She held the bottle in her gloved hand and took a big swig then leaned against the door and waited for the warm tingle to spread from her toes to the top of her head.

She took a seat at her dressing table and looked at herself in the mirror. She tried not to think: *It's the crazy lady who claims to have seen Eden.* She smiled at her reflection, amused at her thoughts. Her brown eyes glistened, but she looked pale. Her bushy eyebrows made her face look gaunt. She repositioned her habit and veil to pull tight on her skin and then trimmed her brow with small scissors. She practiced a modest smile and liked what she saw after only a dab of blush on her cheeks and a brush of gloss on her lips. She wanted to induce a pleasing sensory for the attendees. She took off her black glove and pulled on two long-sleeved white gloves for the ceremony.

She felt energized and ready to lead her community as she exited the changing room. The Sisters of Freedom and the children had gathered near the front door, waiting for her. Everyone looked ready.

"Just a minute. Children, get your jackets and put them on," Helen instructed before opening the door.

They marched in two lines from the chapel to the school building and up the steps onto the porch. She led several little ones to measure the sun's angle from her mounted sextant. She lifted Alberto and then Louis for a look, explained that the earth turns at fifteen degrees per hour.

Alberto frowned, and Louis asked, "But what time is it?"

"It's almost time to begin."

She smiled at Louis who jumped from her arms and ran to join the others. Helen figured twenty minutes before it would be time to begin. She turned and gave notice to her sisters, and Sister Josephine directed the children to sit against the school building and rest.

The moment gave Helen a chance to appreciate her creation. Her vision had become real. She savored the sensory experience and looked down at her neighbor community. She turned toward the valley and saw the nine new gas street lamps, lining the pre-war cobblestone road that ran through the border. For more than a mile the road twisted from Essence, Andorra, down to Pierre, France. A parasol approached in the distance as the visitors continued to parade up the mountain. Then she gazed up toward the heavens. The sky was a vivid blue with lacy white clouds floating above the tall mountain pines, like full sails gliding on the Mediterranean Sea. The view took her breath away and made her dizzy. She leaned on the rail, restoring her balance.

All of her sisters had gathered close behind, huddled and shivering under their black and white habits like penguins. Helen suggested that Sister Josephine fetch Sister Phillips from the barn. "We need to begin the ceremony soon," she said.

On the terrace below, the crowd moved closer around the bonfire. The builders gazed up and spread their hands above the flames, waving toward Helen and the sisters. She bowed her head, turning in small increments to address the crowd, giving smiles to her friends from Pierre, Andorra, and Catalan. She waited for the final minutes to pass.

Helen directed some of the older children to take positions in the stairwell. Josephine approached in full stride, and several paces behind her Sister Phillips stopped to pick up the bottle of champagne from the wagon.

Helen took one last deep breath; the long-awaited ceremony was about to begin.

15

The cheery-faced and athletic Sister Phillips hurried with a skip and a bounce to join the group. In her haste, she stumbled and found herself teetering on one foot on the edge of a step as the crowd *oohed* in fear of a fall. She righted herself, and the crowd gave a collective *ahh*. She climbed over the children, up to the porch, and set down the bottle of champagne.

"Are we ready?" asked Sister Phillips, twirling in excitement. Helen widened her stare and let out a deep breath before nodding. Sister Josephine blew her whistle to gain everyone's attention.

Helen wasted no time. She made a Moses-like gesture, and with her outstretched arms and white-gloved hands, she parted the noise and silence fell in between. After a quick turn toward the children, their giggles from the stairwell ceased. With the crowd's attention, Helen directed her voice toward nature's large iron-pigmented rocks that surrounded the terrace like an amphitheater.

"I offer no pretense, no special introductions, and no acknowledgments. We embark upon our journey together as each one becomes we. Thank you for coming."

Helen called on Sister Phillips for her overture: a recitation prepared for the celebration.

Sister Phillips stood out among the Sisters of Freedom. Helen had chosen her because of her gentle giant nature. She stepped up between Helen and Josephine, towering one head taller than Helen and two taller than Josephine. She looked down toward the terrace then up toward the sky.

As Sister Phillips began to speak, she sprayed some brandy spittle on Josephine's veil. She raised her hand to wipe up the droplets, and Helen gave a gentle tug on her shoulder to bring her back to her task. Sister squared her broad shoulders, and words began to roll from her tongue in Catalan.

"Please, use English," Helen reminded in a soft voice.

Sister Phillips began again in English with an Alsatian twang. "Essence is the quality that makes something special and without which it loses its identity. Our orphanage carries the name Essence as a reminder of our duty to keep essence true. If one follows the compass of Eden, then one can lead a true essence life."

Applause rang out from below, and Helen waved her arms for quiet so Sister Phillips could continue.

"The majestic Pyrenees Mountains of Andorra reach toward the sky and touch the clouds. Our glorious stage turns at sunset into a light show with bright colors: yellow, orange, pink, and violet on a light blue canvas sky. The beautiful sunset lights a spiritual fire on the horizon, illuminating wispy clouds for smoke. The sunlit fire warms the beings who stand in wonder of nature's full glory. And as the horizon's firelight dims, it leaves behind the essence of mountaintops lingering into early darkness and forever in the mind of *the one*."

The uncontrollable spasm of an aborted sneeze interrupted Sister's words. Helen's slap on the back arrested her diaphragmatic convulsions. Sister Phillips placed her fist near her solar plexuses and thumped twice, apologized, then continued.

"If we can block out our past and future for a moment then we can agree. We live as amazing beings that be. Each of us has our own philosophy to deal with life together and alone. We live for intimacy in relationships and in communities. Yet we think alone.

"When one climbs the mountain toward her finitude, she notices others on the same journey and reaches out to join them, and one becomes we. We experience a bond that we had not been aware of until we joined together on our journey. We share the primal drive to find a new and greater freedom for all.

"Let's take this moment to enjoy our sunset experience together as we begin our journey toward greater freedom for all at Essence."

The crowd erupted in loud applause. Sister Phillips bowed a second time as the thunderous ovation went on. When the noise began to quiet, some of the visitors started to disperse. Helen sent Sister Josephine to spread the word that the ceremony was not over.

The grocer, the shoemaker, the baker, and several others began to unload the food and donated clothes from the wagon. Helen waited for their return.

The smell of baking bread wafted from the kitchen and captured the attention of the orphans who clung to the steps. Helen could see the questions on their faces. Someone murmured, "Can we eat?"

She whispered, "Just a minute. We are not ready." When the grocer and his helpers returned from the chapel, Helen spoke to those assembled below. "My voice is weak, so please give me your focused attention." The visitors moved closer together and raised their faces toward her. "Thank you, Sister Phillips, for the moment of transcendence delivered by your thoughtful words and strong voice. We have teamed with the people of Pierre to bring hope and the water of life to the weary and thirsty. We welcome and offer love for the world's orphans to whom the compass of Eden has been bequeathed.

"I stand before you on this balcony porch looking out

in remembrance with a different view than that seen by Charlemagne over 1300 years ago. Darkness, thunder, and lightning filled his consciousness. Our collective consciousness will soon witness the most beautiful sunset ever."

Then with sudden gusts, the howling wind of Andorra raised the awnings. The gales almost blew Helen over. She steadied herself with the help of Sister Josephine. Those below crouched on the terrace and huddled near the roaring bonfire. The children pulled their coats over their heads and clung to the porch in fetal positions.

Helen resumed her speech while trying to stand, "I know that it is cold and a little windy. Please, stay with me."

The wind was too strong. She could not rise. Sister Mary Elizabeth came forward like a flying buttress opposite Sister Josephine. They supported Helen and stopped her veil from flying away. Helen whispered her thanks then continued to address the crowd.

"If you are a visitor to the area then you are in for a special treat. In just a few minutes we will experience a spiritual light show like no other. With brilliant and velvety colors on the master's sky, the sunset will direct our attention to an orange ball with texture and warmth.

"Sentio, your sensory consciousness, will yearn to reach out and feel the ball to warm your playful heart. Cogito, your language-thinking consciousness, will ponder my words while Sentio remains captive by the fiery ball's advance toward darkness. As the last visible light fades, we will experience the fusion of nature's full glory through our Sentio and Cogito blend."

The temperature was falling fast. Helen paused and rubbed her gloved hands together.

"Please join me in observing man observe nature while we ride Sentio and reflect. To experience this moment, we each must observe ourselves as individuals approaching our finitude, our end. We are the *one* before the one can become *we*. One's Sentio must realize that the one is not alone. So please, let's join hands."

Helen nodded and signaled with a wave, and the sisters and children walked down and encircled the terrace, beckoning the visitors to grasp their hands. The visitors obliged, and the entire group connected. At that moment the wind of Andorra subsided, and the air grew still.

"Each of us awakens in this world to different circumstances. Our Sentio realizes that she has been orphaned in a life raft in a great Cogito tragedy. She must reorient herself with the compass that points her toward greater freedom.

"We, the Sisters of Freedom, have found the compass that was lost in Eden. We had hoped to share our finding, but for reasons beyond our control, we cannot share our discovery today." Helen paused and glanced at Josephine to acknowledge she was right. If Helen had explained that the pre-reflective Sentio experience of Eden was necessary to experience the Compass of Freedom, she would've sounded crazy.

"Instead I ask that we feel our connection to each other, as if we were in Eden, as we experience the mountain sunset with a heightened sensitivity. Once the enchanting Andorra delivered the consciousness of En Dor. Someday our orphans will deliver the consciousness of Eden—for you, me, and the world—and a new vision of freedom. Our new orphanage will carry the name Essence as I christen this most glorious creation of love; a place for orphans to see the compass pointing toward freedom as they begin their true essence lives."

A ruckus of applause followed. The builders stomped their feet and clapped their hands. Helen felt a warm glow and waved at them. Sister Phillips broke the bottle of champagne over the balcony rail. The sound of breaking glass brought screams of surprise from the children and greater applause from the visitors.

Helen held out her arms once again. "We will embrace

our intimate neighbors of Pierre, and we will not stray from our commitment. We will bring true freedom to the world together, Essence and Pierre."

When Helen finished, everyone joined hands again and turned toward the sunset. The terrace and balcony began to glow with the joy of beings connected by the most beautiful sunset that Helen had ever seen. She could not believe the texture of the orange sun and the violet clouds that danced on the purple stage above the snowcapped mountaintops. The magnitude of the moment approached a climactic finale.

Spellbound, the visitors watched as the horizon's firelight dimmed. The twilight faded into darkness while no one moved or spoke. They savored the experience in connected stillness.

CHAPTER

16

A halo had formed above the sisters' veils as the lanterns were lit. Helen exchanged smiles with her sisters and turned toward the visitors who held white candles and passed the flame from one to another until all were lit. Their twinkling eyes told the story and no summary words were needed.

Helen turned to her left to thank Josephine then to her right to share words with Mary Elizabeth. She was grooming Mary Elizabeth and wanted to take advantage of the splendor of the ceremony to make sure that she felt accepted. Mary Elizabeth stood smiling and waved toward some visitors who acknowledged her with candlelit smiles.

"Sister Phillips did a wonderful job," Helen said as she and Mary Elizabeth held hands. "The simplicity of her words—with no reference to prior values, religions, or institutions—set the stage for the being experience that we just shared."

"I could not agree more, Reverend Mother. Holding hands was the defining moment for me. What a beautiful experience and such a powerful way to connect with our community," said Mary, her face aglow.

Moved by her testimony, Helen hugged Mary. As they embraced, tears streamed down Mary's cheeks. Helen tried to wipe Mary's cheeks with her handkerchief.

"You, Reverend Mother, have transcended being and

time with this single experience. I feel a connection to my brothers and sisters from the beginning of time and my future brothers and sisters until the end of time."

Helen knew all about Mary's dark past: a former assistant philosophy professor in Berlin during the Third Reich and a former holier-than-thou woman. She had accepted Mary as a Sister of Freedom as a favor to an old friend from her youth in Freiburg, and now she was happy for Mary Elizabeth.

Then Helen asked, "Could you feel the connection to nature?"

Mary smiled with moist eyes and replied in a soft tone, "Yes. The great philosophers of sensualism brought this connection to my awareness, but you delivered the experience through my Sentio."

Helen retreated to her own glowing Sentio as she greeted some of the visitors with Sister Josephine by her side. Josephine estimated that about three hundred had attended the dedication including a mysterious, beautiful lady with an entourage and the co-prince of Andorra.

Several guests had climbed up the steps to offer Helen their congratulations and support, including the prince. She accepted his praise with reverent modesty and respect. She embraced him and expressed her gratitude for his support, and after giving his blessings, he departed.

She greeted the grocer and his wife then turned toward the stairwell and noticed two men kneeling on the landing with their arms outstretched to clear the way as a beautiful lady approached. Helen felt the urge to kneel. She removed her gloves out of reflex and genuflected toward the lady. She recognized the woman as the one who had supported her in Geneva at the hearings for Essence. The woman reached out, grasped Helen's hand, and pulled her up from her knee. They shared a warm embrace then pulled back, and the lady peered deeply at Helen with her beautiful and sparkling blue eyes.

"I am honored to be here."

"Thank you for coming," said Helen.

The lady gave a look of joy and confidence. "Your sunset experience created a singular and true essence moment for one and we to discover our common bond for freedom. I will never forget this experience. I am so proud and happy to be a part of Essence."

Helen looked on with no words to add. She knew that the lady understood the message of the christening ceremony and her purpose for Essence. They embraced once again, then everyone watched as Her Grace stepped down with pure elegance and gentility.

As the lady left the mayor approached from the stairwell and gave Helen a farewell hug. "That was incredible, Reverend Mother." He departed to Pierre with a large smile and a bounce in his step.

Helen gave her last hugs with European grace and made her way off the porch. Sister Phillips went to ring the big bell, taking several little boys to help with the task. Helen instructed them to ring seven times, and they vibrated the campus sending echoes of joy far and near.

The builders from Catalan met Helen on the terrace and apologized because the furnace pumps had stopped working yesterday. "We should have the new Magnus-pumps in by next Monday, Reverend Mother. The generators work, and you have light," said Sergio. "I'll be back in the morning."

"Thank you, we will make do," said Helen. She had a plan in mind to make the best of it.

She turned her attention to the play area where the children had formed a long queue for dinner. The older kids had taken the front positions, and the line stretched from the playground to the chapel. Helen noticed the small children shivering at the end of the line holding candles dripped with wax. She ordered them all into the Big Bell Chapel at once. It was too cold for them to be outside any longer.

The children ran to the warmth of the chapel and found their seats where they were served stew, bread, rice pudding, and milk by the sisters. Helen searched for Sister Phillips to congratulate her on her oration.

"She went to check on Marcel," said Josephine.

After everyone was seated Helen went to her changing room. She put on her long-sleeved black glove for the last time and poured some of her brandy stash into a small glass. Cut with spring water, the shot of brandy warmed her chest. She enjoyed another shot as the warm tingle spread through her body. She relaxed and took a slow deep breath.

Fifty orphans, fifteen nuns, and five support staff will be thinking, feeling, and living together. We must rely on our hearts for heat pumps to keep one another warm.

She returned to her bishop's chair near the fireplace in the main room, warm and glowing. She propped up her feet on a stool and relaxed.

"I have one more announcement," she declared to the group.

"The Reverend Mother has another announcement!" exclaimed Sister Josephine.

The children grew quiet and looked toward Helen.

"Actually I have two announcements. First, you have earned a special treat. I am proud of you. Mrs. Ophelia has prepared lemon cake for desert."

The children shouted their thanks and clapped.

"Second, we will need to sleep together for a few nights here in the chapel until the new pumps are installed. We will use our hearts and bodies to keep each other warm," said Helen.

The children sat still for a moment until it dawned on Heidi and Eva. Helen could see their enthusiasm as they shouted, "A sleepover!" Excited, high-pitched screams followed as the news spread from table to table.

Helen smiled knowingly, "Yes, a grand slumber party.

We have plenty of wood for at least two weeks. Enjoy your dessert. God bless, and sleep well."

The children grew noisy again. The little girls ate the warm bread while the little boys devoured the lemon cake. It did not take long for their fingers to spread the icing in the most and least likely places as the treats disappeared into anxious bellies.

Sister Josephine herded a group of little boys into the kitchen to wash their sticky hands. After a minute she called for Helen. Sister turned the faucet backward and forward with a sputter as Helen looked over her shoulder. "The water pumps must be frozen," said Josephine.

"Use the spring water and towels in my changing room," offered Helen.

After a quick cleanup of the lemon cake, the children rushed down the hall to the dormitory building to collect their bedding and then raced back for the coziest positions. They snuggled together while the sisters tucked them in.

Heidi and Eva begged Sister Josephine to tell them a story. The children lay together with full bellies and wide eyes. Their angelic faces glowed all around the fireplace, charmed by the tall flames and roars from the burning wood. Sister Josephine began to read a story aloud from her seat near the hearth.

Helen enjoyed Josephine's theatrics when they were not directed at her. Josephine had studied drama in London before she joined the order. Her fall from her holier-than-thou eminence had been a soft one—nothing like Helen's or some of the other sisters'.

"I'll huff and I'll puff . . . "

Sister Josephine rose from her chair and breathed through her nose while pushing out her cheeks like a trombone player. Then she gave a big blow. A slew of giggles arose from the children.

"Do it again. Do it again," the little boys asked.

She blew several more times, and then Louis stood and joined her, giving his own blows. The little Frenchman regularly sought attention; he reminded Helen of Poulou.

Sister Josephine finished her stories by telling one of Helen's favorites, "The Pied Piper of Hamelin," and towards the end of the tale little eyelids began to droop. The children started dropping off one-by-one. At half past nine all of the children were asleep until the loud snoring sounds from Sister Phillips filled the sleepy chapel and woke some of them. Several concerned children ran over to check on her.

"What's wrong? Why is she making that sound?" asked Edmund, his voice filled with concern.

Sister Phillips had rolled over on her cot with her head tilted backward, and her jaw relaxed. Helen reassured Edmund and the other children that nothing was wrong after repositioning Sister Phillips' head on her pillow.

"Think of her snores like ocean waves beating against the shoreline," suggested Sister Josephine as she ushered the children back to their pallets.

In sleeping bags and mattresses pulled from their rooms the community drifted off to sleep. Helen moved over to a rocking chair near Josephine. She reached out with her right hand to thank Sister for her caution regarding the revelation of her compass experience.

"I almost made a foolish mistake today. Thank you, Sister, for bringing the fault of my testimony to my attention."

"Reverend Mother," Josephine said, "I knew you felt passionate about your experience. Sometimes it takes someone else to help you see that your message needs to be refined, lest mankind make a fool of you, me, and the children."

"You are so right," Helen said, looking into Sister's gleaming blue eyes. "I want us all to work together so that we can deliver a new vision of freedom for the world."

Josephine smiled, nodding in agreement, and then

asked, "Where is your brother? I hoped he would be here. He is so much fun."

"He had to attend an important meeting about his women's undergarment business," Helen smiled. "Maybe he is right. We will need to overcome the fallacy of existentialism to free Intentio so our followers can experience the compass."

Helen and Josephine squeezed each other's hands once again before letting go and drifting to sleep.

17

After Sergio installed the new heat pumps, life gained a semblance of normalcy at Essence. In the early dawn, Helen rocked in her chair gazing out from the screened-in porch of Villa #4. Facing east, she could see the valley horizon as the sun rose. The yellow-orange ball peeked between the tall pines, which were far enough apart to create a sunrise vista and a view of the white-capped mountaintops in nearby France. The wispy clouds swirled above the trees on the winter blue sky.

Sunrise was different than sunset. It produced an Intentio that delivered Helen's attention to the present, mundane reflections, needs, and desires for the day. Whereas, the sunset delivered the Intentio for past reflections and future reflections where she could experience her vision for freedom. Feeling the chill in the air, she pulled her shawl over her shoulders, and as the beauty of the moment passed, she began to reflect on the tasks for today. There were so many things she needed to do at the school.

The redstarts and squirrels came up to feed on her bread crumbs. A rabbit then a blue bird came near, nudging the pinecones and poking at the leaves to get at the feast. Rocking softly, Helen thought about how she would deliver her vision of freedom to the orphans. She needed to give the children the Cogito scaffolding for freedom.

The sound from the percolator brewing in the kitchen interrupted her thoughts, and then Josephine came out and shared a morning greeting and handed her a cup of fresh coffee.

"Thank you," Helen said.

"It's hot," said Josephine.

Helen took a sip, "It's good," and resumed a slow rocking motion. Josephine turned up the electric heater then took her seat at the small breakfast table.

"Would you like some sugar?" Josephine asked, stirring her coffee.

"No, thank you."

They watched in silence as a little chipmunk came out of his hole and jumped around a tree stump then a blue bird swooped down and scared him away.

Helen looked over at Josephine and broke the silence. "I'm happy to see that the children have established a routine in their new home."

"They are getting used to things; they thrive on a routine," Josephine said. "I love to watch them after breakfast when they march together to the school building."

"They are so cute," Helen said. "How do you think the kitchen staff have done adjusting to all of the new children?"

"Mrs. Ophelia and her cooks continue to amaze me. They have prepared great lunches, and you know how delicious dinners are. Breakfast remains my favorite, oatmeal with fruit and raisins." Josephine took a sip of her coffee.

Helen smiled. "I meant to tell you how much I have enjoyed your bedtime stories. But I think we should begin no later than quarter past the hour after the last bell ring. It will give you plenty of time, and we can have the children in bed by 10:00 p.m."

"I'll make the announcement this morning. I love acting out the stories."

"You have a great talent."

Josephine smiled.

Helen talked about the curriculum again to make sure the children were getting enough sensory stimulation. She emphasized the rudimentary physical sciences, geometry, and physics.

Josephine reassured her about the children's sensory education and reported most of the children had learned to speak English very well. "Sister Amelia has done a wonderful job teaching them."

Helen took a sip and gave a gentle nod of appreciation, "You understand why I chose English as the preferred language for freedom."

Josephine nodded.

"Next Monday I will give the children a talk on freedom."

"Oh good, I love your talks."

They grew quiet for a moment and watched some blackbirds walking along the porch steps searching for crumbs. The birds flew away as the big bell began to ring.

When the echoes from the rings faded, Josephine asked, "Do you still want the bell rung at 7:00 a.m., 3:00 p.m., and 9:00 p.m. on Saturday?"

"Yes, I want the bell rung to deliver the sensory to generate an Intentio that gives the children direction for their busy days, so they will understand how the compass of the mind works," Helen said. "So that someday they will experience the Intentio from the Sentio of Eden, the needle of the Compass of Freedom."

Josephine gave a polite smile. "I think I understand."

"Who's ringing the bell this week?" Helen asked. "I've noticed the energetic rings."

"The cute little Sister Anna Marie. She's a feisty one and enjoys giving a forceful tug on the bell."

"Oh yes, Poulou took a liking to her," Helen said, and followed Josephine's gaze toward the clock on the wall.

"Time to get ready," said Josephine.

Helen took her coffee cup into the kitchen as Josephine hurried upstairs.

I FREED A THOUSAND SLAVES, AND I COULD HAVE
FREED A THOUSAND MORE IF ONLY THEY KNEW
THEY WERE SLAVES.   —*HARRIET TUBMAN*

Early Monday morning Helen read her favorite quote,
closed her book, and stepped out of the school building onto
the balcony porch and into the cold air. She hurried down
the steps and walked to the chapel, pondering her topic of
discussion. She had already introduced the idea of consciousness to the children, and the younger children demonstrated
an aptitude for her philosophy. She wanted to advance their
understanding as quickly as possible. She wanted to engage
the children in a discussion about internal freedom.

The cold wind blew up from the valley, and she ran
through the straw-covered ground toward the morning sun,
hoping for a little warmth. She found herself skipping on the
flat stone sidewalk then rushed to open the door. Inside the
chapel, the large roaring fire brought immediate relief from
the cold.

The cooks were cleaning up after breakfast, washing
dishes in the kitchen, and two of the sisters folded linen in
the hallway outside the laundry room. The children had

remained seated after breakfast, giving their attention to Sister Serelia who stood up front.

Helen looked at Sister Serelia and gave a nod. "Let's go ahead and get started."

The chapel grew quiet as Helen took her position in front. Sister Serelia, a handsome woman, gestured, and the children stood up at their chairs.

"Good morning, Reverend Mother," said the group of sixty children, ten new orphans since the christening. They stood at attention beside the four long dining tables.

"Good morning, one and all. Please be seated." Helen said. "I have something very important to discuss with you today. Can anyone guess what it is?" The children took their seats then silence filled the room. "I'm going to talk about freedom."

The children's faces lengthened and their eyes rolled. The older children in the back lowered their heads.

"Who knows what freedom means?" she asked.

The faces remained frozen in silent perplexity. Sister Josephine spoke softly, "Alice, you know what freedom means."

Alice shook her head and looked down.

Edmund stood up and blurted out, "Freedom means money. I am going to have so much money someday that I am going to buy the world."

The children laughed out loud.

"Don't laugh," Helen said. "To some people money provides a hope for freedom, and money can be a means for freedom, providing the necessities for existence, but it can also enslave and take away your freedom."

Heidi and the twins began to giggle. "I can't help it Reverend Mother," said Heidi. Helen understood the girls were tickled because Edmund continued to stand.

"Thank you, Edmund," Helen said. "You may sit down."

Several more hands raised into the air.

Helen pointed at Louis who got up and tried to stand on his chair until Helen shook her head. Louis turned forward, and said, "Freedom means everything is free, and you don't have to go to school."

The older kids joined in with rowdy laughter.

Helen smiled. "Enjoy and laugh, but calmly, please. Thank you, Louis."

Heidi added, "Freedom means pretty clothes and diamonds."

"Oh, how nice. Thank you, Heidi."

Alberto spoke, "Freedom means toy trucks and tractors and a mountain of sand to play on."

Helen nodded. "Yes, play is a great way to exercise the muscle of freedom."

"How about dolls and doll houses?" Miriam said. "They are freedom too."

"Yes, they are. Thank you, Miriam," said Helen with an affirmative nod.

The children grew quiet.

"Freedom means not being here. I want to be with my mother," said Jacki.

The children's faces lengthened in sadness. Helen looked around giving consoling looks. All of the children could relate to Jacki's yearning for her mother, and Helen reassured them that their mothers would want them to find freedom: greater freedom for one, and for all.

"Freedom is not a thing," Alice said. "It is an experience in your mind after an opportunity and a choice you make that can lead to greater freedom. Only time will tell if your choice of action leads to greater freedom."

Helen grinned and nodded at Alice. She wanted to keep the discussion on internal freedom rather than external freedom and the latitude of nature. Alice's comment came at the perfect moment.

"What Alice says is true if freedom is a possible outcome

from the choice you make, but what if it is not?" Helen said. "What if freedom is not on the menu in your mind or what if the meaning of freedom gets redefined?"

"Get another menu," exclaimed Louis.

Alice crinkled her nose. "Then you can't experience true freedom because even if you make a free choice decision your actions will not produce freedom," Alice said in a confident tone. "So you may think what you are doing is going to produce freedom, but it really isn't."

"Excellent!" Helen said. "Did you know that in America years ago there were slaves who did not realize that they were slaves?"

The children shook their heads in astonishment as though they could not believe such a story.

"Americans are strange," Eva said. "Their slaves do not know that they are slaves. How weird."

"It's true," Helen said. "And now you have begun to see how important your vision for freedom will be for finding freedom. I am going to share my ideas, and I hope to help you experience a vision for freedom that few people have ever experienced."

The children's eyes widened as they sat quietly. Helen smiled and walked around making eye contact with those sitting up front.

"Freedom starts with a fundamental process in your mind, your consciousness." Some of the children made a face at the suggestion. "Does everyone remember the way we think of our consciousness?"

Edmund stood. "Sentio, Intentio . . . I can't remember."

"Cogito," said Alice.

"Intentio, Sentio, and Cogito," Helen said. "Does everyone remember the story about the flashlight?"

"Do you mean the camping story?" Louis asked.

"Yes," Helen smiled at Louis. "At night when you are in your tent with the dimly lit lantern, you can see, smell, hear, feel and even taste your surroundings, and that is what we call Sentio. When you turn on the flashlight and shine the light on an object, your light becomes Intentio, attention or selective attention, the spotlight that allows you to see clearly whatever you point at. If something crawls in your tent, you will direct your light toward the object. Why?"

"So you can kill it," said Edmund.

The older kids chuckled.

"Well, first you want to know what it is, right? It may be a puppy or your friend." Edmund nodded, and Helen grinned at him as he sat down. "So Intentio is the light from our flashlight and Sentio is the consciousness where all of the things in our surroundings inside the tent are projected for you to experience. When we turn on our flashlight, we experience what we shine the light on, correct? Where our light shines is where we experience our sense of being."

The children nodded with puckered lips.

"So where is Cogito?"

Their mouths flattened, and their eyes darted around the room for an answer.

"We forgot," said Louis.

"Cogito is when you open your book and shine the light to read, remember?" Their heads bobbed up and down in agreement. "The light shines on the print and the words and sentences come off the pages and play in your mind creating a whole new world. Intentio, the light, shines on the words of language and allows your sense of being to be experienced in the meaning of the words while you are reading. Cogito is our language-thinking consciousness—whenever or wherever language is used."

Helen paused for a moment and pointed at the table. "How many of you can tell me what I am pointing at?"

"A table," exclaimed the children up front.

"How many of you saw four wooden legs supporting a flat brown piece of wood?"

Silence returned, so she gave the children a moment to consider her point.

"Just as you are listening to me speak now. You are using Cogito. But first you must hear my sounds through Sentio, which create the words for Cogito. So I want you to start focusing on the actual sensory experience in Sentio and give it your attention rather than the language-based interpretations in your mind."

The children scratched their heads, and Alberto raised his hand.

"Yes, Alberto."

"I'm getting tired," he said. "My mind is hurting."

"Just a little more," said Helen.

Sister Serelia stood up. "Children, you are doing wonderfully."

Helen looked at Sister. "Just a few more minutes." She turned toward the children. "So Intentio is the light. Who gets to choose where the light shines?"

"You do," said Jacki.

"Yes!" Helen smiled. "So that is the fundamental upon which all freedom is experienced. You have the ability to move the light of Intentio in any direction within Sentio and Cogito."

Helen feared that the children's Intentio was already enslaved to Cogito, perhaps addicted to language-based consciousness as she had been. But she was going to find a way to free them. First she needed them to understand the Cogito scaffolding for how to obtain internal freedom.

"Next week we will talk about the problems with Cogito and language versus the truth of Sentio and nature. How passions and addictions can imprison the light from your flashlight, and how despite experiencing your basic freedom as the director of your flashlight, you could still be a slave of existence."

"Can we go outside of the tent?" asked Louis.

Helen smiled and looked around at the children's faces alit with the idea of going outside the tent. "We will talk about going outside of the tent next week. Remember what I said: others will try to control where you shine your light and demand you use your flashlight where they desire. The world may limit the flashlight to only the books they want you to read or the thoughts they want you to think. And your light will grow dim if it is not recharged by the sunlight of Sentio."

"What is the sunlight of Sentio?" asked Alice.

"Nature, human love, warmth, food, sleep, exercise, rest, health, and avoiding passions and addictions."

The answer came out of Helen's mouth like a reflex; then she realized from the children's weary faces that she had given them too much information. She just needed to tell them one more thing and turned to Sister Serelia. "Intentio gets its power from Sentio. I want the children to be thinking about a suggestion I have for strengthening their Sentios."

Sister Serelia nodded and Helen stepped forward.

"Imagine what it would feel like to be kissed or embraced by your brothers and sisters, for one reason and one reason only: to restore your vision of freedom and theirs. You would endure this because I believe that it will give you a new vision of freedom. You want to be free, and you want others to be free. The only way to find freedom is with a vision for freedom. Correct?"

"Yes!" said the children in unison.

"Individually, we yearn to find greater freedom for one and all. We are on a journey together, and our need for freedom unites us. We must keep our Sentio healthy and our Intentio free. Do you believe that you can do this? Give and receive hugs and kisses?" asked Helen, looking around at the children's furrowed brows.

"Yuck!" said Alberto.

"Double yuck!" Edmund shook his head. "No kissing!"

Several children giggled and others laughed aloud at Helen's suggestion.

"Freedom is strange," Alice spoke. "I thought the desire for freedom would make us want to be alone and independent. But I understand without others you would not learn the interesting places that they have found: new freedoms to experience with your flashlight—Intentio."

"Wonderful, Alice," Helen said, and motioned for Sister Serelia; she had finished her discussion for the day.

"Let's have a grand applause for Reverend Mother," said Sister Serelia.

The children jumped to their feet and produced generous applause. Their attention toward Helen beamed from their eyes and expressions of gratitude.

"Thank you," Helen said with a big smile. She could not believe how bright and aware the children were.

As they streamed out of the chapel, Louis appeared to be trying to impress Alice.

"No," Alice said. "You are not supposed to leave your tent after dark."

"Yes, I know," Louis said. "But let's say that you could leave. Where would you shine your flashlight? At me?"

"On the trail so that I would not fall," Alice said, and joined several children in laughter as they marched off to class.

Helen smiled to herself at Louis, her little Poulou. Josephine approached and reassured Helen that the children would begin the hugs tomorrow after breakfast.

"Sister Josephine, soon we will all be free from the bondage of Cogito," Helen said. "I want the children to understand that the hugs are voluntary. I want them to understand what it means to give consent because I believe that consent is part of the magic of their sensitizing love."

"And they will," said Josephine.

CHAPTER

19

The honeymoon of Essence and Pierre was short-lived. It took less than three months for the tavern owner in Pierre to stick his nose into the goings on at Essence. Helen left a message of her suspicions of malevolence with Poulou's secretary and waited for him to return her call.

Two days later he called. "Hey, I got your message. What did he ask?"

Helen paused. She was upset that Poulou had taken so long to return her call. "I'm not going to tell you what the tavern owner asked of me."

"I'm sorry I did not get back with you sooner," Poulou apologized. "What did he ask? Please tell me."

Helen was glad to hear his voice. She sighed and gave in. "He wanted me to try and pick the winning horses in some races in London last weekend."

"Well, did you?"

"Of course not."

"What could it hurt?"

"What if my picks won? I would never hear the end of it. The tavern owner shows no respect for me or the other sisters. He wants to buy Essence. He wants to turn our campus into a tourist resort. He said that someday he will make the Sisters of Freedom an offer we cannot refuse. He believes that we would sell Essence. No respect."

"I think he is attracted to you," said Poulou.

"Never in a million years," Helen replied. "He is a thin-lipped misogynist."

Poulou sighed. "I will deal with the tavern owner but not now. Later."

"The tavern owner worries me. What if he finds out we are not real institutional nuns? I think I know what he would do."

"Oh Helen, he is not going to find out. We have that covered with the two retired sisters at the motherhouse in Vichy. Sisters Lena and Lenina will take care of the tavern owner."

"I'm nervous."

"Did you take off your glove?"

Helen paused and looked at her left hand. "Yes."

"Good. Stop worrying and relax; I'll call you next week. Got to go. I am trying to merge my company with a silk manufacturer in Hong Kong. See you soon, my love."

"Love you," Helen said and hung up.

Ever since his visit, Helen had grown fonder of Poulou in a powerful way in her Sentio reflections. Her Intentios would automatically pull up his reflection when she was alone, having fun, or anytime for that matter. The images of him made her smile and gave her a tingling sensation of pleasure. At times she felt like a smitten teenager when it came to Poulou and other times as his essential lover in an existential world.

The week passed quickly, and Helen stayed busy. On Monday morning while sitting in her office, she heard a loud banging on the door. Without waiting for the door to be answered, the burly tavern owner with stubbles on his chin and scruffy sideburns barged in. He looked hungover.

"Good morning," said Helen with surprise.

He approached her desk with a smirk on his face. "I have some bad news," he said.

"Bad news?" Helen wrinkled her brow and glared at him. "What on earth are you talking about?"

He stood in front of her desk, stretched out his arm, and handed her a letter. "Forty citizens have signed the complaint over the bell rings."

Helen looked at the letter with an internal sigh of relief. She thought he had discovered that they were not real nuns. She reviewed the illegible signatures with a squint. After a long moment of reflection, she lifted her eyes into his gaze and offered a compromise.

"Okay, we will stop the nighttime chimes and no more tolls on the weekends." She pushed the letter back toward him.

He picked it up. "We want all the rings stopped." He placed the letter in his pocket and added, "The vibrations from the clangs have loosened the mortar of the tavern's foundation."

Helen smiled politely and shook her head to disagree. The two stared each other down for several moments, Helen expecting him to say more. Instead, the tavern owner grumbled and stomped out of the office.

Helen was baffled at the man's scandalous audacity. The mortar of the chapel had not loosened. *Why had the bell triggered ill will from the owner?* She thought that it might have something to do with his Intentio that arose from the sounds of the bell—he did not like the reflective experiences visited by his Intentio.

After the tavern owner's visit, the whispers began about the bell and Essence. Helen heard them when she visited Pierre on Wednesday. The tavern-dwellers had begun to fling insults and gossip about the sisters and the orphans. Sister Phillips reported hearing unpleasant gossip about Essence's bell when she visited the grocery on Thursday, and the grocer predicted that things were about to get ugly.

Late Friday afternoon while in her office, Helen received a call from the mayor. The grumblings of a civil war between the long-standing tavern and Essence had gained his attention as well as the attention of the Pierre Town Council. Helen explained how she had compromised and bent over backward in an attempt to satisfy the tavern owner. She told the mayor she would not stop the daytime bell rings. The children needed them.

After her talk with the mayor, Helen tried to call Poulou. *Where was he?* She needed him for his diplomatic assistance. The next day, she left messages at his office in Paris and even sent a telegram to his home, but no response. He should have returned from Hong Kong; he was long overdue. She waited and waited but no Poulou.

After another week of bell ringing, the tavern owner threatened Essence with an injunction during a nasty exchange over the phone. Helen hung up, furious. But she was able to calm and consider her options after watching the sunset from her office. She did not want to concede the bell rings, but she needed to know what was going on in the tavern. *What were they saying about Essence?* She needed to know if they had figured out that they were not real institutional nuns. The existence of Essence could be in jeopardy.

She considered using a French underground tactic she had heard about from her roommate at the Munch, Sparrow, the little dynamo of a woman who had rescued more than one hundred prisoners from the Gestapo. Helen remembered Sparrow telling her about a covert operation in a piano bar, how she had become a barmaid and infiltrated Goebbels' operation in Berlin.

Helen discussed her idea with Mary Elizabeth during dinner the following Thursday night. Mary Elizabeth thought her idea was brilliant, so Helen passed the word to her most trusted sisters, Josephine and Celia, about a meeting she wanted them to attend in her office after the children were in bed.

Around ten o'clock that night, Sisters Josephine and

Celia walked into her office with polite but nervous smiles. Helen sat at her desk, and Mary Elizabeth stood with a solemn face to her right.

"Please sit down, Sisters," Helen said, trying to put them at ease.

They sat on the wood bench in front of her desk.

"I have a special mission that I need you both to do for me," Helen said and then explained the entire situation.

The sisters listened quietly with wide eyes, their mouths open.

Helen stood up behind her desk. "We have named the undercover mission: Operation Liberty Bell."

With a half-smile Sister Josephine asked, "Undercover . . . do you mean like spies?"

Helen walked around to the front of her desk and looked down at her sisters. "Your assignment, if you choose to accept, will be to infiltrate the tavern and gather as much intelligence as possible."

Sister Mary Elizabeth moved forward. "We need to know if the tavern owner knows that we are not real nuns."

"Yes," Helen reiterated. "We need to know."

Sisters Josephine and Celia sat quietly, not offering a word.

"I know, Sister Josephine, that you played the role of an undercover agent on stage in London," Helen said. "Do you think you can do this?"

Josephine responded with concern. "I did not play an undercover agent. I played an assistant inspector in *Lupin Meets Sherlock Holmes*."

Helen smiled, looking into Josephine's eyes. "That is close enough. Will you do it?"

"I guess so," said Josephine.

"I will too," Sister Celia said. "I think I might enjoy joining the revelry of the tavern. It sounds dangerous and exciting."

"Thank you, Sisters. You will be fighting on the front lines for freedom," said Helen.

Josephine smiled at Celia then asked Helen, "Won't they recognize us?"

Mary Elizabeth chimed in, "Without your habits you will be unrecognizable."

Helen added. "Mary Elizabeth will procure a couple of skirts and tops. She has your sizes."

"Oh," said Josephine.

"It will not be dangerous," Helen reassured her. "The outfits will be conservative."

Helen dismissed the sisters and instructed them to keep the mission secret.

"Practice for Operation Liberty Bell will begin tomorrow night after dinner, here in Helen's office," Mary Elizabeth reported.

Helen did not want to frighten them, but she intended to send them into action tomorrow, Friday night. She had reserved a room at the hotel in Pierre.

Josephine and Celia hurried out of her office and down the steps.

Helen looked at Mary Elizabeth. "I hope that we are doing the right thing."

Mary Elizabeth looked at her with a smile of reassurance and nodded. The plan was set.

Operation Liberty Bell.

Helen smiled thinking about the name for their under-cover operation as she heard Josephine and Celia hastening up the steps to her office. They entered through the door, and Helen suggested that they try on their clothes. Mary Elizabeth handed them their outfits and led Josephine and Celia down the hall to change in the second-grade class-room. While they were gone, Helen put on a gray skirt and white blouse with a gray scarf around her head and dark sunglasses.

Josephine and Celia came back, and their eyes opened wide, appearing surprised to see Helen dressed like a spy. She explained that she was going to tag along as a spotter and wanted to go through the dress rehearsal with them.

Josephine smiled at Helen. "You look nice."

Celia nodded to agree.

"Thank you," Helen replied. "And you both look con-vincing. Josephine, fluff up your hair a little more."

"Yes," Mary Elizabeth said as Josephine back-combed and mussed her hair.

"That is better," said Helen.

Sister Josephine acted like a former barmaid and approached Helen as if she were a man. Her practice performance produced smiles all around. She acted as a displaced, burned-out tart who liked to drink and party, and Sister Celia playacted as her psychic friend who could read palms and perform numerology.

Helen observed them while Mary Elizabeth played the role of the tavern owner, asking tough questions of the sisters. "Where are you from? What are you doing here?"

Josephine proved very convincing, delivering their cover story about being on a trip from Geneva to Barcelona, and Helen was satisfied. Then Helen gave a few pointers to Celia about numerology. "Power numbers impress men; they love the numbers seven and nine."

Celia nodded. The sisters appeared ready, so Helen gave them the news: they would move tonight.

"Tonight?" Josephine said with surprise.

"Yes. You will be staying at the Hotel Crillon in Pierre tonight and tomorrow."

Celia squeezed Josephine's hand.

"You can do this," said Mary Elizabeth.

Helen gave them hugs, and then presented their code names: Raphaella Weil and Gabriella Arendt. Josephine and Celia looked at each other.

"I like Gabriella," said Josephine.

"Fine, you can be Gabriella, and Sister Celia you are Raphaella," Helen said. "We need to get going. It's getting late."

Off they went. Helen handed Josephine and Celia a carpetbag filled with a change of clothes, money for food, and personal hygiene items. Then she grabbed her purse and walked with her sisters as they slipped down to Pierre under the cover of darkness. When they entered the hotel, Josephine picked up the room key reserved under her code name, Gabriella Arendt. She seemed convincing as Helen watched from the guest lounge.

Josephine and Celia followed the bellhop to their room

while Helen followed at a safe distance. After her sisters were inside the room and the bellhop left, Helen knocked on their door and Josephine answered.

"Who is it?"

"Sister, it's me. Open up."

Helen entered the hotel room, looked around and found an atomizer. She pulled a bottle of brandy from her purse and filled the crystal bottle and sprayed her sisters until they reeked of alcohol.

"*Ooh!*" Josephine said. "We smell like alcoholics."

"Remember your code names," Helen said, and shared embraces. "Call me."

Josephine and Celia snuck out of the room and down the stairs as Helen peeked out of the door. They looked so excited. She waited until they had time to reach outside and then exited down the fire escape.

The sisters walked up to the tavern while Helen watched from across the street. The tavern vibrated with loud music, and the bass vibrated the sidewalk. Josephine shook her head at Celia as they entered. Helen knew what they were thinking. *No one could hear a bell or anything else inside there. The tavern owner's claim about the Essence bell was preposterous. His own juke-boxes vibrated the foundation.*

Helen returned to Essence and waited. Time seemed to stand still, and she worried about her sisters. She did not hear a word for 24 hours and almost went to get them on Saturday night, but Mary Elizabeth talked her into waiting.

Josephine and Celia finally returned to Essence early Monday morning. Helen saw them approaching the terrace and breathed a sigh of relief. She had been waiting in a rocking chair on her balcony perch since the sunset. They walked up the steps to the porch. Sister Josephine seemed upset as Helen let them into the school building. It was 2:00 a.m. by the time they sat down in her office, and Sister Josephine started talking.

"Those men called our Sister order a bunch of gypsies with veils. I heard them with my own ears. An older fellow with one eye, he called us the witches of Endor."

"Oh, the one-eyed man. I know him. His name is Ogie. He seems harmless," Helen said. "He came to our christening."

"Well, Ogie said that we had a compass pointing to hell and that we liked to inflict pain with our big bell," Josephine said. "They called it the bell from Hell."

"I wanted to slap the tavern owner," Celia said. "He urged several of the men to complain about Essence. But I must admit he does have cute blue eyes and nice hands. I read his palm, and I told him I saw trouble in his future with a woman of the veil."

Helen smiled at Celia.

"And that's not all," Josephine said. "Some of the dwellers told the merchants to keep an eye on the orphans. They suspected we sent the children into town to steal from them. Can you believe their mendacity?"

Helen shook her head. "Are you certain that you were not recognized?

"The butcher thought he had met me in London," said Celia. "But no, Reverend Mother. With our hair down and thanks to your makeup, we fooled them."

"And are you sure they believe that we are real institutional nuns?"

"I know they believe that we are real nuns," Josephine said. "They wished we were not for reasons that make me blush."

"Oh, I see," Helen said. "Thank you, Sisters."

Helen gave a sigh of relief. She hugged Josephine and then Celia.

"You both did wonderfully. You may go and get some sleep. Please put your habits back on before the children see you."

"Yes, Reverend Mother," they replied in unison. They changed clothes in the classroom.

"Where should we leave the outfits?" asked Celia.

"Leave them here in my office," said Helen.

She followed her sisters out of the office and down the stairs. She heard them talking and giggling about the tavern as they walked holding hands. Helen stayed back and paced on the terrace for a while, her mind busy thinking about Josephine's words: gypsies with veils. She journeyed to #4 but was unable to sleep, so she walked back to her office.

Her Sentio and Cogito tracks were lit up and delivered the feeling of a hot poker in her chest—hot rage. She rocked on the balcony porch until dawn and then went straight to Pierre to find the mayor. She wanted to let him know about the ugly gossip promoted by the tavern owner.

Of all the buildings in Pierre, the tavern was located closest to Essence. Helen had to pass by the French Tudor structure on her way to and from town, and daylight revealed the truth. When she approached the three-story, rundown structure with a rickety porch, she averted her eyes. She was disgusted by the thought of the tittle-tattle going on in there.

Once in Pierre, she walked around town and tried to calm down. She visited the mountain stream for some soothing sensory. She gave all her attention to the force of the cold water running over and reshaping the smooth rocks; for several minutes she watched and noticed the sound of the rushing water relaxed her entire body. She looked up toward the trees and listened to the chirps of a red bird. After relaxing for a few more minutes, she walked back to town and saw the mayor near the library.

Thank goodness he was up early. "Mayor, do you have a moment?" Helen yelled and ran to catch up with him.

"Of course, what can I do for you on this beautiful morning, Reverend Mother?"

He looked directly into her eyes, and she remembered his long embrace before the christening. She felt blood rush to her face.

"You look upset. Are you okay?" asked the mayor.

"I am upset. I am furious," said Helen.

"Tell me, what is wrong?"

"The tavern owner caused a brouhaha when we first commenced and began ringing the bell three times a day. I thought that the matter had been settled after I agreed to stop the nighttime ringing, which upset his clientele. Now he has threatened me with an injunction."

The mayor listened as he stood straddled between two steps. "You told me this on the phone two weeks ago. So what happened?"

"They want no part of Essence. So what do they want?" asked Helen, placing her hand over her forehead. She did not want to mention Operation Liberty Bell.

The mayor shook his head. He did not know the answer. "I need to go, Reverend Mother. Come by my office next week, and we will talk about this injunction. Oh, I see that your left hand is better—no glove."

Helen hesitated and wiggled the fingers of her left hand. "Yes, much better, thank you."

"Good, I'll see you next week," said the mayor.

Helen returned to Essence, still furious. She needed to talk with Poulou. Finally, late that afternoon, Poulou's secretary responded to Helen's message that she needed him. The secretary explained he had left the country on a vacation to South Africa, and she had left a message for him to call her as soon as possible.

It was late that night Poulou rang. Helen explained Operation Liberty Bell while he listened in dead silence. When Helen finished, he paused and sighed.

"I think that the tavern guys have committed a racial slur by calling you and the sisters gypsies with veils," he said. "I'm sorry that I can't be there to punch the owner for you."

"I wish you were here."

"I'm sorry Helen, but my undergarment modeling and advertising division had not prepared for the shortage of waifs in the world. I had to give my full attention to a couple of prospective French models for our newest line of panties."

"Of course you did," Helen said sarcastically. She was upset Poulou had not been available for Essence when she needed him, but understood he needed to gallivant to improve his sensibility. *Damn existentialism.* She bit her tongue and softened her tone.

Poulou suggested that Helen make an alliance with the owner of the main attraction in Pierre.

"That young, good-looking fellow, Javier, owns the Paradise Tour and Tackle shop. You'll checkmate the tavern owner and the town council," Poulou said and went on to explain his idea in detail.

Helen liked his suggestion and appreciated his wisdom. Before they hung up, Poulou expressed his love for her and promised to return as soon as he could. Helen apologized for being upset and expressed her gratitude for his assistance. And said she loved him. Helen had a strong desire to be with him intimately like a lovesick teenager, and she believed that Poulou could sense her desire. After they said good-bye she could hear him listening, but she was afraid to say what she was feeling. She hung up the phone and stared out of her office window, shaking her head. She had fallen in love with Poulou.

The next day Helen went to the library in Pierre to look for newspaper articles about Javier, the owner of Paradise. She studied his history and business and devised a plan: a win-win merger. She wanted her sisters and the orphans to work with Javier at the restaurant and lodge during the summer. The boys and girls from Essence would benefit from the horseback riding and mountain hiking tours, perhaps even the rafting, and Helen wanted a good reason to bring the fishermen to Essence for her sunset experience. She would trump the tavern owner and further her mission of freedom for all. Her new plan was set.

22

Two days later Helen talked Sister Marie into accompanying her to pay a visit to Paradise. Poulou had recommended using Marie to appeal to Javier's Sentio. Anna Marie Simmons Antoinette, Sister Marie, knew how to use her female attributes to get just about anything she wanted from a man. Poulou reported that he had fallen victim to her, so Helen decided to bring Marie with her just in case.

Helen and Marie enjoyed the view on their walk from Pierre to Paradise. Fly fishermen came from all over the world during the spring and summer. The white water mountain stream ran around the western boundary of Pierre and provided the best trout fishing in Europe. The Paradise Outdoorsman Tour and Tackle shop was a sprawling log cabin structure located at the end of town behind the island of pine trees. The lodging cabins were nestled near the base of the mountain where the stream widened.

"Men get so excited catching fish," Marie said then turned, smiled at Helen, and added. "You look nice in the blue and white colors."

Marie had found the new habits in a Paris design catalog and talked Poulou into ordering them for the sisters to match the flag at Essence. Marie had surprised Helen with the new attire, knowing she would love the colors.

The new habits with their duckbilled veils created smiles

of joy for many of the forlorn children, so Helen permitted the sisters to wear them. She had also seen the sisters wearing the same colors in her vision of freedom, when she saw the sisters praying together.

"You look nice, too," Helen said, quickening her pace. "So many men . . . I bet there are over thirty men wading by those rocks where they are catching fish." She knew by the vibes in her Sentio that this would be a great merger for Essence.

The fishermen gave excited looks at Marie's pretty, young face framed by her blue and white wimple. Several men lifted their catch with smiles that even Helen had not enjoyed before, and she felt her face blush at her female arousal buttons lighting up, her heart pounding. She grabbed Marie by the arm and hurried through the front door of the lodge.

"Wow, this place does look like paradise," Marie said. "The mountain stone fireplace is beautiful, and the Spanish tile floor is gorgeous—ivory."

Helen spoke up after making sure they were alone. "Javier, the owner, is a self-made man from Lisbon; he became an orphan by circumstances of the Spanish Civil War." Then she added, "He is single."

Helen only mentioned that to encourage Marie to use her female attributes if necessary. Marie smiled, understanding.

"Hello? Is anyone here?" Helen called out.

Helen and Marie snooped around while waiting. There were rods and reels and spools of fishing line. On the other side of the lodge, the live bait gave off a dreadful smell, like the recycling garden at Essence.

"Look, the hats and fishing jackets are on sale," said Marie.

"I'll be right with you," came a baritone voice from behind the counter. Then a tall, handsome man with beautiful blue eyes and long brown hair stood and looked down at

Marie. His eyes met hers, which were giving him more than a flirting glance. The mutual stare lasted a long moment.

Helen could see that they were mesmerized. Neither could get out a word. Helen interrupted their Sentio connection for fear their Intentios might merge.

"You must be Javier," Helen said. "I am the Reverend Mother Helena Moyen, and this is Sister Marie Antoinette from Essence. We have come to ask you for a favor. A big favor."

Javier jumped over the counter, causing Marie to back up as he almost fell into her. He grabbed her hands and pulled her upright with a broad, apologetic smile.

"Yes, of course, Reverend Mother, I attended your christening ceremony a couple of months ago. I will never forget that glorious sunset. Thank you for a wonderful experience."

"Thank you," said Helen.

"What can I do for you, Reverend Mother?" he asked, his focus still on Marie. He pulled a couple of Coca-Colas from his cooler. Marie accepted while Helen politely declined.

Helen moved closer to Javier and explained that she wanted to work with him to bring his fishermen to Essence for a sunset experience. His brow arched and mouth twisted into a question mark.

"That sounds great," he said. "I would do anything for Essence. But I am not sure how that will work."

Helen could see that the poor fellow was distracted by Marie. She took the little attention that he gave her and told him exactly what she had in mind. After some back and forth, she convinced him of her plan.

They forged a deal that would allow the sisters and orphans to work at Paradise for the spring and summer. Javier looked at Marie while shaking Helen's hand to confirm the deal. Marie smiled and turned away with bashful eyes.

"I can't pay them much," Javier said.

Helen smiled. "The experience will be our payment."

Javier took Marie's hand and led them on a tour of the shop and the restaurant next door. He showed them his rental cabins and horse stables. They met Maggie, his bookkeeper. The tour finished on the pier where Javier and Marie stood next to each other, almost holding hands. Helen excused herself but stayed within eavesdropping range. She heard Javier promise Marie that he would help out in any way that he could, and Marie gave him a hug and whispered something in his ear.

Helen interrupted again. "Thank you, Javier. Marie and I need to get back to Essence."

"I'll see you this weekend," said Javier as he waved good-bye.

Marie and Helen departed for Pierre. Helen reached for Marie's hand and squeezed as they passed by the fly fishermen casting and jerking their fishing lines. They hurried back through town. Helen was curious about what Marie had whispered to Javier, but she didn't ask.

When they got back to Essence, Helen went to her office to reread Sister Marie's dossier file. Marie had joined the sisters after a life-changing experience. Sister Marie Antoinette was the former actress, Anna Simmons, a beautiful starlet with the greatest celebrity. Petite with dark brown hair and brown eyes, she had once lived and paraded in metropolitan Paris.

All of her beautiful attributes were not enough for Anna, who believed that she was holier-than-thou. Her arrogance resulted from anger and inner despair. She became famous for her unhappiness, displayed publicly in piques of bad temper captured in the *Paris Gazette*, complete with pictures.

On one occasion Anna got drunk and upset, took off all of her clothes, and jumped into the Fontainebleau. In her fit of rage, she told her agent to go screw his own essence and leave her alone. Then she fell into the drunken abyss. She awoke a few weeks later to discover that she'd been betrayed and robbed by the love of her life, her boyfriend, who was also her agent. He had taken everything except her name, which remained for the gossip column of fallen fame.

After being stripped of her possessions, Anna lost her identity. Then she discovered a new-found sensitivity for nature and began the journey to create her true identity, her true human essence. She read about the Sisters of Freedom, joined at the motherhouse in Vichy, and took the name Marie Antoinette. She had learned that Marie Antoinette's last words on her walk to the guillotine were *Pardon moi*, because she had accidently stepped on the executioner's boot.

Sister Marie Antoinette joined the Sisters of Freedom as her living statement to the world: pardon me, but not as an apology. For Sister Marie it was simply an awareness that her prior human essence was the result of institutionalization and not based on true essence. The freewheeling decisions she had made as Anna Simmons were part of the gig that she had been programmed to play, just like the other Marie Antoinette. Anna Marie Simmons Antoinette was now grateful to her agent for the wake-up call.

Helen had read the file many times. Each time it had the same effect; she felt connected to Marie's journey for freedom. She knew Marie was destined for greatness.

CHAPTER

23

Eden's sunset stage over Andorra's gray, rock-faced mountains with their evergreen ground cover awaited another day's grand finale. On the balcony porch, Helen rocked in her front row seat and scanned the horizon as the sun moved into position. Josephine came up the steps, looking cute in her baby-blue and white habit, and sat in the chair beside Helen. They shared smiles, and Helen noticed Josephine's eyes were red.

"Have you been crying?" Helen asked.

Josephine sniffled. "Yes."

"What is wrong?"

"Oh, nothing." She gazed toward the horizon then turned toward Helen. "Jacki hugged me earlier today, and I started thinking about it. . . . She asked me to be her mother."

Helen reached to hold Josephine's hand as she shared her tears. "What did you say?"

Josephine choked on her words and took a moment. Helen handed her a handkerchief. "I told her that her mother's Intentio would flow through me to her, and then Jacki began to cry, and we hugged for the longest."

Josephine began to cry again, and Helen squeezed her hand. "Sister, I know what you can do. When you experience Jacki in your Sentio, say to yourself: *I will let the Intentio of her mother flow through me to deliver love for Jacki.*"

"I will."

"And at our sunset experiences when you are holding Jacki's hand, use the moment to let her feel her mother's desire for Jacki's freedom flow through you to her, delivering her love for freedom."

"I will."

Helen and Josephine held hands and leaned back to resume their rocking motion capturing a beautiful twilight moment.

"Our first Sunset dinner will be tomorrow. The fishermen are coming from Paradise," said Helen.

"I can't wait," Josephine said; her sadness had lifted. "I think that it is going to be a great success."

"I hope that the children and the fishermen will experience the Compass of Freedom."

Josephine looked at her and nodded in encouragement.

CHAPTER

24

Marie moved with excitement when Javier showed up early with a couple of strong, young men who carried the four tables and chairs from the chapel to the terrace. After Marie directed them to move the tables to her liking, she covered them with some beautiful white and blue cloths and placed lanterns and candles as centerpieces.

Helen waved with approval from her balcony perch as the fishermen began arriving. Sister Serelia led the children from the dorm to the terrace where they formed a big circle and waited to begin the festivities.

Helen made her way down the steps and suggested the entire group share embraces to begin the ceremony. She wanted everyone as sensitive as possible, especially the fishermen, who seemed reluctant to share hugs with the sisters and children as a sensitizer.

Javier approached and hugged Helen to break the ice for the first embrace, and then he shared an embrace with Marie. The other fishermen followed Poulou, who had returned from South Africa earlier that morning. They hugged the Catalan sisters first and worked their way around the circle. Helen enjoyed Poulou's sensual embrace until he tickled her, and she pulled back and gave a subtle *not now* look.

"Let's get started," Helen announced. "We need a big circle."

After joining hands, the group turned and faced the horizon as the sun made its final descent. Helen wanted to reveal her idea about the pre-reflective Sentio of Eden as the driver for the divine Intentio of the Compass of Freedom, but she refrained because she knew the idea would be rejected, preventing the possibility of the compass experience.

Instead, Helen hoped to deliver the experience to her followers first and explain the phenomenon later. She instructed and guided them with her words—a Cogito and Sentio blend—for an individual and collective sunset for freedom experience. Their faces beamed with wonder and delight as she finished speaking.

The grand finale followed as the orange glow on the horizon disappeared, and the direct sunlight gave way to twilight. The fishermen grew silent as Helen encouraged everyone to close their eyes and reflect on the experience, hoping that someone would have a compass experience. After several long moments of reflection, Helen signaled, and Sister Josephine played the accordion, producing a French-café ambiance. Marie lit the candles, and the children escorted the fishermen to their seats at the tables as they had practiced and then took seats next to them.

The Catalan gals in the kitchen had spent the entire afternoon preparing the five-course feast. The sisters served the fresh trout caught at Paradise with broccoli, carrots, beans, and warm bread. Sister Phillips poured wine for the men. Once the eating began, the party erupted with laughter and jovial stories from the fishermen. They bubbled over with cheer, hugging and bouncing the children on their knees. Marie, Celia, and Cecelia sang the song of liberty, "Fight for Freedom," and danced, kicking up their feet while berry pie was served for dessert.

As darkness fell, an old fisherman named Bud, a huge man a head taller than Javier, got up and began telling a story to the children. He acted out the story like Sister Josephine, and the children were enthralled by his theatrical display and deep husky voice. With wide eyes they watched and listened as he performed *The Old Man and the Sea*.

"He struggled for three days and three long nights to pull the whale-sized marlin into his dinghy. . . . He held tight to the fishing line hooked deep in the throat of the monster fish . . . until the twine ripped through the skin of his hands and the bleeding ensued. . . . He anchored the line around his body while his boat drifted far, far . . . out into the sea."

Bud pulled and twisted his body as if he were wrapped in the fishing line, then he leaned, reached beneath his table, and pulled up quickly with a loud roar, causing the children to scream and scaring Helen and Mary Elizabeth. Then Bud began to whisper.

Helen gave a sigh of relief and shook her head at Mary Elizabeth after Bud's theatrics. It really was an interesting story. *The Old Man and the Sea* was about a man who had fallen on bad times. *Then he catches the biggest marlin of his life after fighting the fish for three days and nights. But on the way back to port, the fish is eaten by sharks, leaving the old man with just a skeleton.*

The children's eyes grew larger and larger. Helen looked over and saw Poulou enthralled by the story, with Jacki on one knee and Louis on the other. He seemed to be having more fun than anyone. Helen smiled at Mary Elizabeth, who also noticed Poulou and produced a grin. They continued to stroll around, observing the festivities.

At bedtime the children gave the men final hugs and bounced on their knees one last time then encircled the terrace and sang, "You Are My Sunshine," a beautiful ending to a wonderful experience.

The fishermen gave compliment after compliment as they departed, and Helen felt proud and grateful to deliver such a sensitizing experience. Poulou hugged her, and she thanked him for giving her the idea to form an alliance with

Javier. She embraced him again and felt a warm tingle in her chest and a strong desire to be with him intimately. He gave her a big grin then hurried toward Pierre, having to be in Paris in the morning.

"Call me," Helen cried.

He turned and waved. "Tomorrow evening. I want to hear if anyone experienced the compass."

After the men left and the children were in bed, Helen rocked on the porch with Mary Elizabeth, wondering if anyone had experienced the compass. Mary Elizabeth remained cautiously optimistic.

"I hope the men took time to reflect after sunset as I instructed."

"I saw them closing their eyes," said Mary Elizabeth.

"I know that someone will experience the Compass of Freedom soon," Helen said. "I did earlier tonight."

"What did you see?"

"The same as last time."

"Our sisters in Prayer?"

"Yes," said Helen.

25

Helen gave her blessing as Javier put the sisters to work as cooks and servers at his restaurant that summer. The sisters prepared the delicious fish caught daily during the week for the fishermen's evening meals at Paradise, and every Saturday on the terrace at Essence, the sisters served them the special five-course meal after sunset. The orphans helped Javier, taking lures and live bait to the fishermen, and the older kids learned to act as guides for the Paradise hiking tours.

One month after the merger of Essence and Paradise, the community had grown into one big, happy, tourist economy. Helen greeted the mayor and the tavern owner, who apologized for past misstatements. She accepted their apology and a key to the city with jubilation during a ceremony held for her and the children at Paradise Tour and Tackle Shop.

The following Saturday, Helen's sunset celebration began and ended with joyous hugs and kisses from the orphans. At the end of the celebration, most of the men shed tears. The fishermen gave generous donations and made promises for a better next time.

Helen had observed the orphans as they interacted with the fishermen and realized that their freely-given hugs, kisses, and handholding were the catalyst for sensitivity. The fishermen seemed able to experience the sunset through a more sensitive consciousness. Helen considered that it was an important realization that the intimate touch of a stranger, a little orphan being touching a fisherman, could have such a powerful effect on their sensitivity.

Hoping that someone would have a compass experience, Helen followed up with all of the fishermen and solicited their feedback regarding the experience, but none of the men reported the compass experience. Neither her sisters nor the orphan children had experienced the compass. Some of the children had made claims, but they proved to be false. Helen began to doubt that anyone would experience the compass.

After the last Saturday of the season and no reports of a compass experience, Helen sat in her office alone and reconsidered Poulou's suggestion. She contemplated taking on the task of redefining true essence by providing a language-thinking argument that would prove that existentialism and the existential freedom was a fallacy—Operation True Essence.

At one time in her life, Helen thought man would stumble upon the Compass of Freedom if provided the Sentio of Eden experience as she had experienced in the Black Forest. But now she doubted that would ever happen. She knew the Eden experience was fleeting, and the fishermen would lose their Sentio sensitivity gained at the sunset dinner experience. Once they returned to the existential world, they would be forced to use language-thinking for existence.

Helen thought about what she had observed during the sunset celebrations and concluded that existential language-thinking inhibited man's search for true freedom. She needed to free the fishermen from existentialism, and then she could deliver the Compass of Freedom.

CHAPTER

26

Helen and Mary Elizabeth met in her office the following Monday morning.

"We need to deliver an explanation in simple, philosophical terms that is clear: a new understanding so that all humans can find true freedom and live true essence lives," Helen said. "So humankind will not be misled by the false true essence and false freedom of existentialism."

"I think that may be possible," said Mary Elizabeth. "I have reflected on what Poulou taught me and what you've taught me. I would like to start a philosophy study group."

Helen smiled. She had a better idea and explained it to Mary Elizabeth. Two days later, Helen called an emergency meeting for all of the sisters at Essence. She had developed a plan with Sister Marie and Mary Elizabeth.

Helen met with her sisters in the Big Bell Chapel after the children went to bed on the night of the autumn equinox. After the duckbilled sisters were seated, Helen started the meeting with a happy greeting.

"Quack! Quack!"

Cordial laughter followed. Then she stepped up onto the hearth, requesting everyone's attention. She had Mary Elizabeth and Marie stand just in front of her facing the other sisters.

"Please, quiet," Helen said, and waited until she had

everyone's attention. "We are all philosophers, whether we like it or not. Each of us has to live together and alone in search of meaning. We all need a compass to find greater freedom in life. The only way to experience the compass is through the Sentio of Eden, but man needs to understand how to see freely through his Sentio, to see without the doubt created by existential beliefs stored in his Cogito. I believe existential thinking has prevented the fishermen, and perhaps even you and the children, from experiencing the compass."

The sisters' expressions grew serious, and Helen paused giving them a chance to seethe about existentialism.

"I have directed Sister Mary Elizabeth to head up Operation True Essence, our new priority mission to find a way to free man from his existential thinking and existence. Sister Marie Antoinette will be her assistant. Are there any questions?"

Helen gave a stern look to discourage questions. She did not want to be too specific about their mission. She did not want to institutionalize or condition her sisters.

Nonetheless, Sister Phillips piped up with a question. "What is virtue? Is it like true essence? Some of the children were asking me."

Helen looked away to conceal her grin then assured the group, "Sisters Mary Elizabeth and Marie Antoinette will help you find the answers to all of your questions."

The two sisters gave half-smiles and affirming nods toward her and the sisters.

Helen stepped down, and Mary Elizabeth moved forward on her cue. She stepped up onto the hearth with a countenance of authority and confidence. "We will start next week. Monday night after the children are asleep we will walk to the library in Pierre to begin our research," she explained. "Sister Marie, would you like to say something?"

Helen noticed the other sisters shrank in Mary Elizabeth's presence. Her voice was terse, almost harsh, as she spoke.

Sister Marie Antoinette stepped up without hesitation as if she were going on stage. Her warm demeanor reached out and embraced her sisters. Her voice was soft and confident with excitement. "Helen once said that she wanted to deliver one slap across the café-dweller's impertinent face, and then she could rest in peace. No argument would be needed to hide her tears shed for the lives of little orphans and their adopting families, whose hopes were being destroyed by existentialism.

"I am here to say that we will win this war with a superior argument. The existential movement is a curse. The hoity-toity café-dwellers have created an existential freedom that is being used as a license by ignoramuses everywhere."

The sisters stood and clapped. Sister Phillips joined in with an uppercut fist pump.

"Yes! Quack! Quack!" said Helen, and then clapped.

She smiled on the inside after Marie's speech. She realized that Marie was somewhat confused about the mission. The existentialists had not created a new freedom, but that did not matter. Marie's enthusiasm was intoxicating, and that was just what the mission needed in a leader. Helen felt she had made the right choice in asking Marie to assist Mary Elizabeth in debunking existentialism. She walked over and whispered to Mary Elizabeth, "They are ready."

After a pause, she asked Mary Elizabeth to let Marie lead the sisters into battle. "I know that you understand philosophy, but if Marie can lead the sisters to find a simple formula that will free man from existential existence, then all men will understand. I have a strong feeling about Marie. If we give her some responsibility, she will blossom."

Mary Elizabeth considered Helen's words and acknowledged that Helen's feeling was similar to her own about Marie. She agreed to step down and support Marie as the group's leader.

27

On Monday night in early darkness, Mary Elizabeth gathered the sisters for a meeting on the terrace. As they prepared to go to the library, she addressed her troops.

"Existentialism poses a threat to the essence of our orphans unless we do something to stop it. I encourage each of you to consider your role in this mission, like a soldier on the battlefield for freedom. What you uncover here today will echo in orphanages everywhere for eternity. I will oversee your efforts, but I have decided to remain here to watch after the children while Sister Marie leads you into battle."

Suddenly, all eyes were on Marie, who no more expected the announcement than her sisters. Sister Josephine's mouth opened in surprise.

Marie's hands began to shake. *Why me?* she wondered, trying to maintain her genteel appearance. *Mary Elizabeth is the expert on philosophy. I'm not even sure what existentialism means.*

Meanwhile, the other sisters were invigorated by Mary Elizabeth's passionate words. Sister Jahn Phillips talked about how they would crush the existentialists. Marie listened as the group talked up the fight. She felt her throat tighten and drew in a deep breath to try to calm herself. All she had to do was lead the sisters to the library.

Marie swallowed with great effort and took one step, then another. She led the sisters in two columns through the darkness and followed the gas streetlamps into Pierre. She felt as if the success of Operation True Essence had fallen onto her shoulders. With the weight of this new responsibility, her legs felt weak and her palms sweaty as she led the dozen toward the library.

Sister Phillips gave Marie a swig of her brandy, and the two marched side-by-side. The warm liquid hit her stomach, and Marie started to regain confidence. She remembered how she had once been a starlet, a successful actress on the little screen in Paris. She picked up her steps and took the lead as she marched her troops into battle.

The group approached the library, the grandest building in Pierre. Sister Josephine shared the history of the building as they approached. Built in the seventeenth century, it was a replica of the French National Library in Paris. During World War II, it was used to hide many of the great works of literature from the Nazis. The impressive building had beautiful three-story, arched, multi-pane windows. The streetlights lit the three flights of gray marble steps that led up to the entrance.

Marie led the group through the double front doors into a huge room, where giant fans adorned the forty-foot ceiling. Row upon row of bookcases and shelves lined the walls, each filled floor to ceiling with books. The sisters stood awkwardly, unsure where to go.

It would be hard to get another book in edgewise, Marie thought as she looked around. Some of the books were so old that they would break apart at the bindings with the slightest touch, as Sister Phillips discovered.

"Please do not touch!" a voice rang out, startling the sisters. "That is the preservation and restoration section," the four-eyed librarian scolded. The slight woman leaned down from a tall ladder and pulled on the bookshelves to slide toward the sisters. When she climbed down she turned to face Marie.

"May I help you?" she asked in a sarcastic tone.

"Where is your philosophy section?"

The librarian laughed, rolled her eyes, then motioned with a wave of her hand. "Follow me," she said, "if you want to see our philosophy section."

The sisters followed single-file as the librarian marched them across the library, through a door, and down a flight of stairs to the basement. The librarian stepped down onto the dirt floor and then gestured toward the dirt walls that supported the stone foundation.

"This is where we keep all of the old philosophy books. During the war these books were in the National Library in Paris. The French underground brought them here for safekeeping. We have had no reason to dig them up. They have remained buried alongside the skeletal remains of the unknown dead."

"Where did the skeletons come from?" asked Marie.

"During the war the cathedral burned, the people in Pierre moved the skeletons from the church walls into the library basement. The French underground fellows dug tunnels for graves and buried the philosophy books with the skeletons," explained the librarian.

"You mean the books are buried in graves . . . in that dirt?" asked Sister Phillips with an incredulous tone. "How can we read them? Dig them up?"

The librarian looked at Marie. "Yes. If you want to read them, then you will have to dig them up."

"Thank you, we will find our way," said Marie.

The librarian went to a closet and returned with four buckets and several tiny shovels. "Remember, please be quiet for the readers upstairs," she said as she handed over the tools.

"These little shovels, they look more appropriate for building a sand castle or potting flowers," said Sister Phillips.

The librarian said nothing, turned, and ascended the

steps. She stopped on the top step and turned back, looking at the sisters. "If you need anything, I will be upstairs at the reference desk. There are summaries about the love of wisdom books in the handouts on the table. You will need a drop cloth to move your dirt if much digging is required, and perhaps a lantern or two."

After reminding them that the library would be closing in two hours, the librarian disappeared, shutting the basement door. The room boasted only two small lights strung 100 feet apart in a basement the size of a ball field. It was very dark.

"Love of wisdom books?" Marie said aloud as she looked over the handouts. "These reference handouts tell us nothing. I guess we will be digging. How odd, they buried the philosophy books with the critical content that we need in these graves, in the walls."

"All libraries are filled with the dead. They wait for someone to read their books so that they can come back to life," said Sister Celia.

Marie nodded. "I guess it is not so odd."

The sisters split up and began to look about. The walls of hard black dirt stood over eight feet tall.

"They've buried the books in graves of the unknown dead," Marie said, and began reading the labels over each grave as she walked about. "Socrates, Plato, Aristotle, Machiavelli, Bacon, Descartes, Pascal, Hegel, Kierkegaard, Heidegger, and Sartre. They've named the skeleton burial sites after the great thinkers."

"But Heidegger and Sartre are not dead. Are they?" asked Josephine.

"It doesn't matter. Their works are as good as dead, buried in graves," Marie responded tersely.

"For each of the 37 graves, a philosopher's name guarded the unclaimed skeletal remains and a philosophical treasure of Western civilization," said Josephine after counting the graves. "I guess it is an act of reverence to use unclaimed human remains to protect the dead philosophy books."

"Perhaps it is a peculiar reminder to let the dead philosophy remain buried with the mundane dead," responded Marie.

Marie knew that unearthing the books would be a colossal undertaking and filthy dirty work. They would need to wear old clothes. Human skeletons buried in walls like a human library. The sisters would have to dig with care to make sure they did not hurt the human remains and then recover the books and read and review all of the great philosophers' works from over the last 2400 years.

"I need to check with the Reverend Mother to make sure that this is what she wants us to do. With her permission, we will come back tomorrow evening with appropriate wear and begin digging," said Marie.

The sisters left in a hurry and returned to Essence. Marie hoped that Helen would call off the dig.

Helen and Mary Elizabeth conferred the next day during lunch, and much to Marie's disappointment, Helen gave her the go-ahead to begin digging. Marie informed her dozen after dinner that they needed to wear their old clothes. They would begin the dig tonight.

The sisters changed into their black and white habits after dinner and marched from the terrace back to the library with two lanterns, a drop cloth, and several boxes. They walked straight through the library down to the basement as the librarian looked on without interfering. Once in the basement Marie gathered her sisters for a pep talk.

"Sisters, it's time to dig, and let's not forget why we are here—Operation True Essence. We are here to find freedom and liberty."

Her sisters chanted softly, "Freedom, liberty . . ."

As their chants faded, Marie said, "We will keep three

active dig sites going at all times, four sisters for each site. Each dig team will have a name: Tom, Dick, and Harry. So choose a team and let's get started."

"Tom, Dick, and Harry?" Josephine repeated. "Weren't those the names of the tunnels dug by the prisoners of war who tried to escape to freedom from Stalag Luft III?"

"Yes, I read the names in the book by Paul Brickhill, *The Great Escape*," Marie said. "We are digging for freedom too, to escape existentialism."

The sisters split up and rearranged their teams several times until Marie designated herself, Sister Phillips, and Josephine as captains. Finally, the sisters settled into teams and began to dig with the handheld shovels. Sister Phillips suggested to her team, Dick, to use small pick motions with the shovel tip to break up the dirt. Josephine taught her team, Tom, the scratch-dig technique. Marie watched and then taught her team, Harry, how to dig by pushing down on the shovel blade and lifting.

CHAPTER

28

The digging continued, and Marie gave daily updates to Mary Elizabeth, who encouraged the sisters to complete the dig and gather the books as soon as possible. They dug for two hours every night, and the nights became weeks and the weeks mounted into months. During the coldest winter months, they couldn't dig because the ground was too hard. Now spring was in the air, and they hadn't found a single book.

On the night of Good Friday, Marie gathered the group around Dick's dig site and explained that Helen was upset with their lack of results. They needed to show something for their efforts.

"We need to find something before Easter," said Marie.

"We need bigger shovels and something to shore up the dirt," Sister Phillips said. "Our holes refill with dirt during the day."

"I know," agreed Marie, sharing the sisters' frustrations. "We need to find something soon," she reiterated. "I have made arrangements to stay all night if needed." The librarian had showed Marie a side window where they could exit after hours.

Sister Phillips turned and began to dig. "Look, here is another foot. That makes three. Has anyone found Dick's head? I can't find his head," said Sister Phillips, looking frustrated as she held the foot up for everyone to see.

"Keep digging," Marie said, and shook her head. "Let's all get back to work."

The sisters resumed digging. Marie watched her team and then walked over to Josephine's dig site. "Sister Josephine, how is Tom going?"

Josephine looked up and shook her head. The Catalan sisters turned and shook their heads. Marie went back to dig at Harry's site and dug harder and faster than she ever had, like a ground squirrel. She kept digging even though the dirt was falling on top and all around her. She remained determined and dug until she hit something, and shouted, "We got something! I found it!"

Marie pulled a canvas case from under the pelvis of their skeleton. Sister Celia dusted her off as the other sisters jumped for joy. Marie removed two books from the case. She cleaned off the book covers with her skirt. "Plato's dialogues," she said, reading the covers. "We found his dialogues!"

The sisters gathered around smiling and looking at the books under the lantern, and Marie began to read, mumbling the words to herself. Josephine picked up the other book and began reading out loud as the sisters laughed and danced with joy.

By early morning, Marie felt exhausted and dirty. She led her troops to bathe in the cold mountain stream near the tavern. The sisters enjoyed the mountain stream bathing, and Marie found it to be exhilarating and a reward for their hard work.

The next day in Helen's office, Marie told Helen and Mary Elizabeth of their discovery, and Helen smiled with excitement. "Keep digging," she said.

Three nights later Marie found Aristotle's treatise on metaphysics. She and Sister Phillips celebrated with brandy. After reading the first page of the book, Marie knew

Aristotle's work was the most important find of the dig, and she read through the book in less than an hour. It was such an easy read, and it made sense to her.

On the way home that night they stopped by the stream to bathe. Marie was so excited that she encouraged Sister Phillips to get naked with her. Marie wanted to experience Aristotle's sensualism, the experience of knowledge through sensory. After she warmed to the cold water, she tried to encourage the other sisters to join. "This is wonderful, Sisters. Come on in."

Sister Josephine and the Catalan gals looked on shaking their heads, fearing that the tavern dwellers were watching from above. The tavern lights flickered, and Josephine reported she saw a cigarette lit in the window when all the lights went out. Marie laughed at their concern. She felt free.

"Who cares? Let them watch," she said.

When Marie came out of the stream, she stood naked for a moment in the moonlight. Her sisters ran to form a screen as she dried and then dressed. The dozen made their way back to Essence, and Marie went to sleep feeling exhausted. She awoke refreshed after only four hours of sleep. Sensualism had reenergized her. She could not wait to share her news about Aristotle's work with Helen.

Later that day, Mary Elizabeth approached Marie in the hall during her break between first and second period. Marie smiled and was about to announce the Aristotle find when Mary Elizabeth produced a frown. Marie knew that something was wrong.

"No more bathing in the stream," said Mary Elizabeth, her blue eyes glaring into Marie's.

Marie was at a loss for words and had no argument to make except that she was sad to lose her freedom to bathe in nature's stream. "Aristotle would be sad," she said. "We found his treatise."

Mary Elizabeth reminded her that safety superseded

freedom, no matter what Aristotle wrote. Mary walked away, and Marie had a strong feeling that Josephine was the one who had snitched about the nude bathing. She felt betrayed.

After the children were asleep, Marie met her troops as they streamed out of their villas, and she told her sisters that they would not be able to use the stream for bathing.

Sister Phillips brought her eyebrows together, "That's okay. The water is probably too cold."

The other sisters shook their heads and pursed their lips. They did not care. Josephine's eyes widened, and she would not look Marie in the eyes, confirming that she was the one who had snitched. Marie bit her tongue to keep from saying something to Josephine that she might regret.

The group marched on the cobblestones down to Pierre. After an hour of digging, Marie made her rounds. She decided to ignore Josephine.

"Great digging, you are making a great contribution: Sister Celia, Cecelia, Amelia. You too, Sister Serelia, all of the sisters from Catalan," said Marie, turning her head from Josephine.

All nine of the Catalan sisters worked and moved in synchrony like twins, never complaining or saying an ill word. When one reached to wipe her brow, the others would stop to wipe their brows. Marie noticed that they were affectionate to each other as well, and their affection sensitized her.

After Marie completed her rounds, Josephine's team erupted as if they'd hit the jackpot. She looked on as Josephine counted aloud, pulling books from a large satchel. They'd found twelve books at the gravesite labeled Kierkegaard, books written by Nietzsche, Sartre, Heidegger, and Merleau-Ponty.

Marie could not help but feel Josephine's joy and excitement. She hugged her and apologized for being upset with her. Josephine forgave her and hurried to read the newest books. After reading until 1:00 a.m., they celebrated by wading in the stream, and Marie hugged Josephine again.

"I know that you were concerned for my safety."

Josephine smiled and nodded.

For the next three nights, Marie celebrated and enjoyed the new books, sipping on brandy and reading next to Sister Phillips as they lay on the drop cloth, but the books provided little insight for how to defeat existentialism. Another week passed. They'd read all of their books and needed to resume digging.

"That makes sixteen books that I have read," said Sister Josephine. "Not one clue has been unearthed so far."

"Sister, we found another book at Dick's site," Marie said. "And we are ready to open up a new group of graves for Tom, Dick, and Harry."

Josephine shook her head in frustration. Marie puckered her lips at Josephine. Complaining only made things worse.

As the groups took a break before moving to their new dig sites, Marie sat down and began to read, sharing the lantern with Sister Josephine who was reading the newest book from Dick's site.

Josephine finished another chapter and shook her head, "Nothing, no clue. Reading philosophy is agonizing. This guy, Kant, he never learned how to end a sentence," she complained.

Marie looked away and then back down at her book. She tried to ignore Josephine and focused on reading. After a few minutes everything got very quiet.

"What are we looking for?" Marie said in frustration as she read about phenomenology. "Are we searching for something real or just some idea that only exists in our minds?"

"We are chasing our tails, searching for nothingness. I am not sure what we are looking for," Josephine replied. "The only decent writer in the bunch was Nietzsche and perhaps Sartre, and they gave us no clue either."

"True essence is not a thing, and nothingness is not a thing, Sister. We need information, the truth," said Marie with newfound confidence, recognizing that they needed a place to begin their argument of dissension with existentialism.

"I thought that we were looking for Eden," said Sister Phillips after downing a shot of brandy. "Finding something is not easy when it's hidden in dirt."

Marie raised her forearm to her brow. *Eden . . . we are not digging for Eden*, she thought. "That is enough for tonight, Sisters," she said. Marie needed a new direction for the operation, and she was determined to find it.

29

The next night Marie made an announcement. "Okay, we can't find Eden or the compass by digging. But according to what I read in Husserl's phenomenology, we should be able to find the compass if we can recreate the consciousness of Eden. We will find the compass in our reflective consciousness of Eden."

"Did you say reflective or pre-reflective?" asked Josephine.

"Reflective!"

"Bravo!" said Sister Phillips. "Does that mean no more digging?"

"Possibly. I am going to redefine Operation True Essence. We must find a way for man to restore his Sentio sensitivity through language-thought and reflection. Man needs to be able to read his way to greater sensitivity so that he can experience the compass and live for true essence," said Marie.

Josephine shook her head fiercely. "That will not work. Man cannot language-think his Sentio into the sensitivity state that he enjoyed in Eden. Language thinking suppresses Sentio."

Marie shot a disapproving look at Josephine but knew she was right. After a moment Marie sighed and looked to the dirt floor for an answer, feeling defeated.

Sister Phillips grabbed her little hand shovel. "I guess we

will have to keep digging," she growled. Then she kicked her box of human remains toward the large pile of dirt.

After another hour of digging, Sister Phillips brought out the brandy and took a break with Marie. The two sat back and relaxed on the drop cloth as they shared the flask.

"Cogito ergo sum. I think therefore I am. What a beautiful saying," said Marie handing the brandy back to Sister Phillips.

Marie picked up another book and began reading. After just a few minutes she cried out, "We have a solution!" All digging halted abruptly and the sisters stared at Marie, excitement across their faces. Marie read aloud: "Descartes divided human existence into the mind, which thinks, and the body, which is made of matter. However, the idea of *I think* only secures the existence of the mind and leaves doubt about the existence of the body."

She paused for the others to digest the words then continued. The sisters had gathered around and sat in a semicircle in front of her and Sister Phillips.

"The existentialists added the proposal that human life is more than thinking. Human life is acting, living, and feeling. They suggest that everyone is born first into existence having been cast into a life raft in the middle of an ongoing tragedy called life. After existence one creates his or her true essence."

As Marie read, the excitement drained from the sisters' faces.

"It is not a breakthrough," murmured Josephine.

Marie grit her teeth and continued reading. "Essence is what makes something what it is, and without which it loses its identity. But it may not be true." Marie looked up from the book and tried to explain her thinking. "Existence is nothingness. Essence is nothingness without true essence. True essence came first. It was here before my existence. I know that it was. There is the breakthrough. That true essence came before existence."

"I think Marie is having a breakdown," muttered Josephine to Sister Phillips.

Marie heard the whispers and began to perspire. She tried again to explain. "The existentialists believe that one becomes the person that he creates after existence, and the creation of true essence is based on his freedom to act, where his free choice is driven by an authentic self who measures the impact of his decision on everyone else before acting on his decision. This is quite mad. How can anyone do this? Man needs a compass. The true essence compass had to come before existence," said Marie.

"What was that again?" asked Josephine, standing and stretching her legs. She seemed disinterested, but Marie answered in earnest.

"We believe that the perceived true essence of existentialism is, in fact, human essence that has been corrupted. It is simply existence packaged as true essence."

The sisters resumed their digging, clearly not convinced.

Marie walked back and forth around the new Tom, Dick, and Harry dig sites, thinking out loud. "Come on, we need to dig deeper," she said.

Josephine shook her head and mumbled, "I wish that Marie would keep her false discoveries to herself."

Marie ignored Josephine and wiped her brow with her handkerchief. "We must go deeper to get to where Sentio resides. Aristotle said that we have to get our hands dirty to find the answer. Keep digging," she said in a soft tone.

Sister Phillips gave Marie a perplexed look. "But where? Merleau-Ponty's grave or Heidegger's?"

Marie sighed. She was tired. "That is enough digging for the night. We have our progress meeting at 5:00 a.m. with Sister Mary Elizabeth."

The sisters packed up and headed back to Essence. Marie went to Villa #3 for a short nap before the morning meeting.

30

Marie awoke at 5:00 a.m. and ran to the chapel. She had overslept. When she walked in late for the meeting, everyone was seated in the chapel, staring at her as she entered. Sisters Josephine and Mary Elizabeth were sitting next to one another, and Josephine was leaning in close to Mary Elizabeth, who seemed disturbed. Marie watched from the kitchen, trying not to stare.

Mary Elizabeth cleared her throat and beamed her big blue eyes directly at Marie. "Tell me what have you and the sisters discovered this week."

Marie took her seat and thought for a moment before answering. She felt a knot in her stomach and needed something to drink. Sister Serelia handed her some apple juice. She preferred a chug of brandy in the morning with her juice. It made her think clearer, and it kept the jim-jams away.

After she downed the juice, she smiled at Sister Phillips who came over and filled her cup with brandy.

"Thank you," Marie said, and took a sip. She felt a warm tingle in her chest and turned to answer Mary Elizabeth.

"We are not deterministic nor do we believe in predestination. Everyone has to earn their true human essence guided by their true essence compass that points to greater freedom as experienced through their Sentio."

Mary Elizabeth smiled. Marie breathed a sigh of relief,

147

but she was concerned about what Josephine had been whispering to Mary Elizabeth. She worried that Josephine had undermined her authority by snitching to Mary about her false discovery.

Mary Elizabeth gave her another look, and Marie elaborated, "We believe that true essence is available to everyone despite the institutions of the world. But the darn existentialists have made it almost impossible to live a true essence life. They have blocked the Sentio of Eden with their silly language thinking. The idea that Cogito essence precedes Sentio true essence needs to be buried in our recycle garden."

"It is ironic that the existentialists were the ones who called out institutionalization," added Mary Elizabeth, "and now they are the biggest offenders—institutionalizing us with language thinking."

Mary Elizabeth gave her blessings to the group and waved good-bye after turning the group back over to Marie, who nodded and thanked Sister Mary. Then Marie announced that she wanted to lead the group in prayer. Some of the sisters had confided with her about being weak at praying.

"I want to take praying to a new level with our new philosophy. Just what do we believe?" Marie asked her sisters and took a drink from her cup.

"I forgot what Helen said about prayer," said Sister Phillips with an arched brow.

Marie shook her head and laughed. "I am the prayer expert. Prayer passes through space and time, toward a central goodness beyond our faculties, which I call God. If we can get a message to God, then all of our prayers for the wrong things in the past can simply be redirected to our new and better prayer request." Marie walked around to the front of the chapel as the digging dozen rested their heads on the tables. "Prayer remains forever, beyond time. We just need to give it a new purpose, a new intention for our updated want."

A concerned look crossed Josephine's face as she rose up then laid her head back down.

Marie continued. "We believe that the existential freedom to choose is based falsely on a freedom that does not exist nor should it exist for the safety of orphans. The orphan does not know about the wisdom passed down through generations of families. Most orphans would not know true essence if it bit them on the bottom. When the orphan acts freely based on existentialism . . . well, it can cost him his life and maybe his eternity. The existential freedom to choose capriciously is the great deception of our present-day human existence," said Marie, realizing that she had gotten off the topic of prayer. She looked at Josephine who was glaring at her.

Marie took another chug of brandy as the sisters got up from their seats and knelt, holding their eyes toward the floor in prayer while Marie continued to mix philosophy with prayer.

"Being is always experienced from the present moment's perspective where one lives at the vanishing or event point of her essence in the middle of existence, mundaneness." The brandy smoothed Marie's words and removed any doubt from her voice as she delivered her favorite quote to end another session. "True essence cannot be played on minds that have no idea what true essence is."

The sisters cheered and clapped after Marie's last words for inspiration. Josephine barely clapped and looked fed up as she stood from kneeling and led the Catalan gals to their morning teaching duties.

"Tomorrow is a holiday, so there will be no digging tomorrow night," said Marie.

"Hurray! Hurrah!" said the sisters, raising their arms in the air.

The next morning Josephine surprised Marie by standing to speak before she had a chance to start preaching. "Helen has always said that true essence can only be lived by following the Compass of Freedom as experienced through the Sentio of Eden. Thus our entire operation for freeing man from existence has become another philosophical Cogito experience." Josephine shook her head. "The digging has unearthed nothing."

Josephine's words stirred internal questions about Operation True Essence, and Marie recognized some truth in her words. Over the previous week, Marie had the recurring thought that she would make a great discovery: finding the right Cogito to deliver the Sentio of Eden. She just wanted a few more nights of digging, so she gave no response. But Josephine would not let it rest and demanded an immediate hearing before any more digging.

31

Josephine took her demand for a hearing to Helen, who at once called for an emergency meeting in the Big Bell Chapel.

After the children were in bed, the sisters convened, and Josephine vocalized her complaints about the mix of philosophy and prayer. She said Marie had gone too far. Several of the Catalan sisters joined in with tears and displayed large blisters and calluses on their hands in front of everyone. Helen looked on and shook her head several times in disbelief. The Catalan sisters had never complained before tonight. Marie knew that Josephine had pulled them to her side.

Helen voiced surprise at how far off the operation had ventured. She stated that she knew at the onset that it was a nearly impossible task, but that did not warrant anarchy.

"The great philosophers were not able to deliver: Husserl, Heidegger, and Sartre all failed," said Helen.

Marie felt the urge to close her eyes, and then Helen announced, staring at Marie as she spoke. "Operation True Essence has gone astray. You cannot mix philosophy and prayer to deliver true freedom. Kierkegaard had tried to use faith, and he failed. It will not work."

Marie knew Helen was making reference to Kierkegaard's book about the need for a leap of faith, *Either/*

Or. But Helen misunderstood how she intended to use prayer for freedom. She wanted to say something, but Helen continued.

"Our philosophical dig has become an allegory for mankind's failed attempt to simply explain in plain language what it means to be and how to live a true essence life. Based on my observations, Operation True Essence has failed. It is done."

It took a moment for Marie to experience the devastation of Helen's words. She covered her face with her hands and began to cry and shake; her head bobbed as she jerked. Helen walked over to her, sat down, and placed her arms around Marie.

"Your digging did produce some good," she whispered. "We needed the scaffolding of existentialism in order to appreciate the Sentio of Eden—the acting, feeling, and living side of being. Your digging produced the scaffolding. But now you have gone astray with your mix of philosophy and prayer. It will not work. We need to get back on track with the sunset experience and pursue the consciousness of Eden for the compass experience. My way is the only way to live a true essence life, through the experience of nature and increasing Sentio sensitivity for the Compass of Freedom experience."

Marie raised her head and considered Helen's words. Despite no measurable fruits from her labors, she still hoped that a better way to freedom and true essence would become evident. She did not want to remind Helen that her way had not delivered the compass for her or anyone else. She brightened at the idea that the dig had provided the scaffolding.

"Now we have the scaffolding!" exclaimed Marie as the meeting adjourned.

The digging dozen walked away with their heads down. Sister Pauli, who was new to the order, gave a lone smile to Marie then walked out with the others.

Sister Phillips comforted Marie with a chug of brandy

on the balcony porch. They rocked together giving support for each other's shame about their failure.

"We did not fail," said Marie. "We proved that the answer must come through Sentio."

Sister Phillips squeezed Marie's hand. "I know. We did some damn good digging. Those little hand shovels sucked— excuse my French. We could have freed humankind with some bigger shovels. If we could have dug another three feet or so, we would have found the damn compass."

Marie smiled and thanked Sister Phillips for sticking by her side.

"I wish that I had dug up Merleau-Ponty," said Sister Phillips in exasperation.

Marie hugged her shoulders. "Hang in there. We may have lost the dig, but I have another idea." She stood, patted Sister Phillips on the back, and left for Villa #3 to work out her idea.

Later that night, Marie slid a letter under Helen's door.

To: Reverend Mother Helena Moyen

Thank you for the opportunity! The hallowed compass that I seek will function as a north star that gives direction to one's human essence and allows one to create true human essence–the direction that humans were given before the apple form became a tasty language thought, to use your analogy.

The Compass of Freedom will direct one to live an authentic life of true human essence in the middle of existence. These are critical moments in one's life when the compass is needed to find meaning and greater freedom. If one has access to the compass, then he can freely choose the right path to become a great lover, genius, or both.

Pascal found the Sentio of Eden; he followed the compass. I can too and so can every human being.

Yours very truly,
Sister Marie Antoinette

Marie wrote the letter as a thank you note to Helen for her inspiration and consideration, hoping that she might reconsider the library dig.

32

The next day Helen told Marie to debrief the sisters with her revelations stated in her letter. Marie got excited and called for a meeting that night after the children's bedtime story. She wanted to share her post-dig reflections and findings. She had discovered some rather profound things after all was said and done. She felt proud and humble and was grateful for the opportunity to share.

After sending the children to sleep, Marie took the pulpit position in the chapel. As the meeting began, tears filled her eyes. A tremble traveled through her chest to her hands as she apologized and expressed hope for her own atonement for leading the group astray.

"Operation True Essence is over, but we have not lost the war," said a humble Marie with a quivering lip. "It appears that since the beginning humanity has been in a steady progress toward a greater consciousness of freedom. Sentio allows man to be free from institutionalization. Once Sentio comes back into man's awareness, the new freedom will triumph over everything.

"Humans come into existence already in the muck of life, and yet the muck and circumstances have not swayed man's individual search for meaning nor his desire for freedom." Her voice began to rise in excitement, "That should tell you Sentio is alive and well. It just needs resuscitation, an increase in sensitivity. From Spartacus to Martin Luther, we find a common theme: freedom!"

The sisters cheered as Marie provided new hope that their digging had produced something.

Helen stood in the back and spoke. "We all have the potential to experience the grand Intentio force of freedom if we can restore the sensitivity of Sentio to that of Eden." She walked up front next to Marie. Helen's eyes gleamed. Then Marie looked at her sisters and spoke, knowing that Helen might not agree with what she was about to say. It had dawned on her that prayer by itself could work. Forget about philosophy.

"First we need to make a specific prayer request, and then we need to tag all of our unanswered prayers over the last several years with the new request," Marie said with confidence. "We can apply our accumulated unanswered prayer cash for our new purpose. I am sure that God will understand. For example, at the very least the world needs someone with the same true essence ilk as Spartacus who can lead the human slaves of existence to freedom through the consciousness of Eden—"

"Wait a minute," Helen interrupted. "I do not understand how Spartacus can help us now."

In that moment Marie felt superior to Helen. She was amazed that Helen could not see. She answered her Reverend Mother with excitement. "If we can call forth a living man with a Sentio who can persevere through mundane existence and the thoughts of institutional existentialism, then he can lead the others to Eden. He will follow his compass and deliver the others. We only need one compass to find the way back to Eden. Don't you see? Once back in Eden, it will be easy for others to experience their own compasses for freedom. But the deliverer must be a strong leader like Spartacus to deliver the slaves of Cogito existence."

"Oh, I see," said Helen. She seemed quite impressed with

Marie's logic. "But I can't allow you to pray for Spartacus because we don't know for sure if his Sentio ever rose to the sensitivity required to see Eden. I'm not even sure that we should be praying."

Helen looked at Mary Elizabeth, who raised her eyebrows and nodded. Marie knew about Helen's recurring compass visions of the sisters in prayer.

Helen contemplated, briefly closing her eyes, then spoke. "Praying for a man with the same true essence ilk as Spartacus to free man from Cogito existence . . . well, I do not see any harm," she decided.

Marie jumped for joy. Sister Phillips produced a loud whistled noise, and the sisters clapped and yelled, "Hurray! Hurray!"

Josephine spoke up. "It might be easier to say new prayers rather than try to remember all the old prayers, which did not get answered."

Marie shook her head at Josephine. "We should not waste good prayers. God has already heard most of the unanswered prayers. Reusing them will save him time and make him more likely to answer our new request."

Sister Josephine looked baffled. Helen walked over and embraced her. Marie huddled with Sister Phillips, anxious to start the prayer vigil.

33

In the time after the dig, the prayer vigil produced nothing but feelings of entitlement among the sisters, as if God owed them something for their praying, and Helen felt responsible. After several years with more of the same, she left Essence and set out to build another orphanage so that her first graduating class of orphans would have a home as freedom instructors. Helen moved to the motherhouse in Vichy, Andorra.

Much had changed since that first year at Essence. Helen had given up hope of sharing her compass vision of freedom with the world. Not a single child, fisherman, or sister had experienced the Compass of Freedom. The children understood freedom but could not seem to keep their Intentio in Sentio long enough to experience the compass, addicted to Cogito.

After a year at the motherhouse, Poulou proposed to Helen. While she did not believe in the institution of marriage, she agreed instead to be his essential lover. Poulou celebrated their committed essential relationship by giving Helen and the Sisters of Freedom the Spanish castle that overlooked Lake Oberg in Vichy. Helen had been eyeing the gorgeous property with horse stables, a barn, and vineyard for the site of her newest orphanage. The beautiful facility was made of clay, stucco, and tile; it stood adjacent to the pine forest above the lake. The co-prince of Andorra had restored the estate one year before. The entire lot included more than four hundred acres of land.

On a pleasant autumn day, Helen sat back in the Jeep and turned her attention to the scenery as Poulou drove her on a tour, her curly brown hair blowing in the wind as he whipped over the rocky, mountain terrain then down through white sand on the man-made beach. They circled the entire property and stopped to view the wooden stakes outlining the foundation for the new school building.

"We will build a beautiful orphanage here," said Poulou.

"A stunning view of the castle," Helen sighed. "This is magical."

The two embraced and shared a tender moment, rolling in the purple heather like newlyweds. They rolled and rolled then stopped with Helen on top.

"Thank you, thank you," she exclaimed and stared into his baby-blue eyes.

Poulou took her breath with a deep kiss. He released her and shared, "I could not be happier."

"It's time for another trip to Eden. I need this." She stood and helped Poulou up. "I've begun to age again. Mundane existence has started to take its toll on my sensitivity," she explained as they made their way to the Jeep.

"You do not look a day over thirty," said Poulou after jumping into the driver's seat.

She smiled at his white lie. "I do not care about my appearance as much as I do my Sentio sensitivity," she said, telling her own little white lie. Helen believed that she needed the special sensitizing love of the orphans to renew her. In just two more weeks the children would come to stay at the castle.

"Come here, Beaver, and give me a hug." Poulou reached over to pull her next to him.

Helen looked up at Poulou's wrinkle-free face. He had experienced his own rejuvenation over the last couple of years but with so slow a transformation that he barely noticed, but she had. He looked debonair in his sunglasses. After a sensual embrace, Helen laid her hand softly on his shoulder as he cranked the engine.

They drove back toward the castle and parked. Poulou exited the Jeep to assist Helen, and she reached out to hold his hand. He jumped into the air, and Helen followed with her own leap. Before she realized, they were jumping and skipping their way to the veranda. With joyous laughter, they embraced and leaned on each other to catch their breath.

After a moment, Helen kissed her lover. "We make a great couple."

"I feel like a child when I am with you."

"Me too. I'm so happy," Helen said. "I hope the children are happy at Essence."

"Of course they are," Poulou assured her.

"I believe Mary Elizabeth is a great Reverend Mother, and I'm glad that Marie has moved into Villa #4 as her first assistant."

"They are a marvelous team," he agreed.

They approached the dining area and saw the table and place setting for two with candles already lit for a romantic dinner.

"Awesome, Pepé. I am famished," said Poulou.

Pepé nodded with a broad smile. "Gracias, Mr. Poulou."

Mrs. Ophelia had prepared their dinner, and Pepé stood in a white jacket holding a bottle of brandy, preparing to serve their meal. Pepé had come with the castle, and Mrs. Ophelia had moved from Essence to get things ready for the new staff. They were great company, and Helen had grown close to them.

Pepé poured Helen some brandy.

"Thank you," she smiled. "You may go. Take the rest of the night off. Go have some fun in town." Helen wanted to be alone with Poulou.

Poulou asked, "Pepé, could you turn on the music before you leave?"

He grinned and turned the channel to romantic favorites on the BBC. The soft music played and added to the amorous atmosphere. Helen got quiet as she enjoyed the pasta dish, the warm bread, and then the fruit salad.

Poulou smiled, "You were hungry."

She was thirsty too. The grape brandy was from the vineyard, and it was delicious. Poulou poured her a second glass, and she tickled his leg with her foot.

"I agree with you about Mary Elizabeth and Marie making a great team," Helen said. "But I received the most upsetting letter from Sister Josephine the other day. She wrote that some of the sisters might be using prayer to avoid work, and Essence looks run down."

"That sounds odd. Are they still praying for Spartacus?" asked Poulou, and then downed his glass of brandy.

Helen hesitated to answer, embarrassed by the proposition. She was upset that she had let the prayers go on this long. Then she recalled seeing the prayer vigil as a pathway to greater freedom during her last compass experience.

Poulou gave a lovey-dovey grin and winked. He rose, took off his shoes, pants, and shirt, then jumped into the hammock and began wiggling his toes.

"Boy, this feels good," he said.

Poulou loved to fool around in the hammock, which Helen had found quite awkward at first, but now she enjoyed the feeling of not being able to move while being loved by an aggressive and rejuvenated Poulou.

"Yes, the prayer vigil for Spartacus—I mean, the spirit of freedom—continues," said Helen, as she slipped out of her shoes and skirt then unbuttoned her blouse.

Poulou reached out and pulled Helen into the hammock. "Let's forget about Essence tonight. I want to embrace you under the stars."

They giggled and laughed, tickling each other. Poulou pressed against Helen, warming her arousal tracks, and she let her Intentio go. The hammock provided an unnatural coziness, and she loved the sensations of Poulou's skin pressing against her own. His forceful embrace gave rise to an Intentio that raced toward pleasure and was sustained by her own powerful to-and-fro attempt to escape his masculinity.

The hammock, the pendulum of pleasure, swung until her journey ended in a grand eruption of ecstasy; Poulou's *oohs* and *aahs* gave way to the finale, accompanied by a muffled scream—Helen put her hand over his mouth to mute his primal cry of elation. She did not want to disturb Mrs. Ophelia.

Helen released from the embrace, and Poulou sunk next to her. They enjoyed the aura of sexual satisfaction and stared at the shimmering moonlight that played on the surface of the lake. Poulou kept his arm around her in a relaxed embrace and maintained the hammock's slow swinging motion as darkness fell.

When the starlight grew bright, he broke the silence. "We are essential lovers. The love for freedom is the foundation for our essential relationship. All the other women were just for my sensibility."

Helen paused before responding. "You do not need to confess." She looked up at the starry sky and identified Polaris, the North Star, twinkling as if to get her attention.

Silence filled the air yet again.

When she turned her head, she saw that Poulou was sleeping. She pulled his arm from behind her, laid it across her bosom, and rubbed his warm, hairy skin. She found the moon and wondered why only she and Poulou had experienced the rejuvenation. As she drifted into sleep, Helen concluded the powerful effect of Intentio dwelling in Sentio must be the key and why she and Poulou could benefit from the sensitizing love shared with the orphans.

The next morning Poulou received an urgent call. His women's underwear business in Hong Kong had been hit by a financial contagion, spreading from Malaysia.

"I have to leave for a few weeks," he told Helen. "I will be back as soon as I can."

He grabbed some clothes and hurried to the Jeep. Helen followed, listening to his murmurs and grumbles. She did not understand the issue with his business.

"Be careful. I love you," she said, and gave him a good-bye kiss.

"I love you," he cried, and waved as he drove away.

After he left, Helen wondered: *How are we going to pay for all of this?* The castle, the new orphanage, the school, and Essence . . . the contagion thing sounded worrisome. She knew that her Cogito worry files would begin attracting her Intentio to revisit the same thoughts over and over. She directed her attention toward Sentio.

She focused on her pleasing surroundings and went down by the lake where Pepé joined her with his fishing pole. While he fished, Helen sat on a tree swing and played in the sand with her toes. Experiencing Sentio by the lake delivered Helen from obsessive thinking. Mrs. Ophelia brought a picnic lunch, and all three enjoyed a lovely meal. In the late afternoon, Helen returned to rest on the veranda and fell asleep.

She awoke and stayed up late rocking and thinking. She called and spoke with Poulou's secretary to see how things were going in Hong Kong. The contagion was more serious than first thought, spreading from country to country, moving through Southeast Asia.

The following morning, she received a telegram from Poulou: *The mission fund is running low. We are overextended. I'll call tomorrow.*

She did not understand. Poulou could send the most triggering messages of any man that she had ever met. At least he included that he was going to call her the next day to explain. She worried all day and did not fall asleep until after midnight. Early that morning, her phone rang. Half asleep she scrambled to grasp the receiver on the nightstand.

"Hello?" Silence followed. *"Hello?"*

The operator came on the line. "Collect call from Mr. Poulou Marcel. Will you accept?"

"Yes."

Without preamble Poulou warned, "We may have to sell Essence. You have some dead wood."

"What do you mean, dead wood?" asked Helen, still groggy, "What time is it? I was in a deep sleep."

"Sorry, I'm in a hurry, Beaver," said Poulou. "The Nikkei is about to open."

"What do you mean, dead wood?" she repeated.

"Sister Lena and Lenina," Poulou said. "I've got to run. I love you. I'll call you later."

"Wait! Sisters Lena and Lenina were your idea, remember?"

"We needed the retired sisters for our legitimacy. We had to have the motherhouse in Vichy."

Helen sighed. "Retired ex-gamblers you met at a gamblers anonymous meeting in Monte Carlo."

"They were real retired nuns who were recovering gamblers—addicted to slot machines. They were nice, and they
served a purpose."

"Yes, so what can I do?" asked Helen.

"We may have to sell Essence," Poulou repeated. "We
will figure this out. I love you."

"I love you."

Helen was upset by the news. She knew Sisters Lenina
and Lena were very ill. A couple of months ago, Sister Lena
had required transport to the Woman's Hospital in the
United States and had run up a big hospital bill. She guessed
Lena was the dead wood.

What can I do?

She rocked in her chair until dawn contemplating
her situation. By late morning she decided that she wanted
to maintain financial freedom. The praying at Essence
must end. If she must sell Essence, then she wanted to put
her best foot forward. She would sell the property to the
tavern owner or perhaps Javier. She had heard the rumors
that Javier turned to alcohol out of boredom during the
off-season—a hazard of owning a seasonal business—and
his life was in shambles. Buying Essence might turn his life
around. She accepted that she might have to sell Essence.
She would shine up the orphanage and focus on the castle.

In the afternoon, Helen notified Mary Elizabeth that
the praying must stop. She did not mention that they might
have to sell Essence. Helen did not want to worry the sisters
and the children. Mary Elizabeth took her order about
the praying without any show of emotion and told Helen
she would make the announcement the first thing Monday
morning.

CHAPTER

35

A dozen blue and white habits filled with pale, youthful faces engaged in calisthenics. The sisters jumped and reached for the sky maintaining their formation. With a smile Marie led her group and counted aloud with each jump, aware the Reverend Mother was watching from the balcony.

"Fifty-one, fifty-two, fifty-three…"

The front rows were in synch, but the sisters in back slowed. Mary Elizabeth turned her eyes from the staggering group and looked toward the mountaintops before making her way down to the terrace. She moved near Marie and waited until the counting stopped. The sisters took the moment to slow their breathing and cool down.

"Good morning," Mary Elizabeth garnered the full attention of the group. "What a beautiful day this will be for the beings at Essence. I have some great news from Vichy. The Sisters of Essence have been relieved from the duty of our prayer vigil for Spart—I mean the spirit. The freedom has been granted by our Sovereign Mother, Helen. We must wait for God to respond to our unprecedented request."

The Reverend Mother's words came as a shock to the group. The exhausted sisters exchanged fretful glances and looked toward Marie with uncertainty. She had spearhead-ed the prayer vigil and pioneered the use of reactivating centuries of unanswered prayers, but she too was stunned and could offer no explanation.

The sisters murmured, "Why?"

The Reverend Mother gave a stern look for her reply. She certified her words by taking down the praying sign-up sheet from the school door. Marie realized that she would no longer need to relieve Sister Phillips after her night shift of praying on Sunday or any day ever again. The prayer vigil was done. The sisters appeared in shock as they hurried to ready for school.

Marie went back to the chapel and finished her morning routine as if nothing had happened. At 7:00 a.m. she completed her task as the official big bell ringer, the morning rooster ring. She assisted two new disabled children in getting ready for school and sent them off for breakfast. Then she found the Reverend Mother in the school building outside the Office of Reverence.

Mary Elizabeth glanced quickly at Marie then began her morning walk-through of the classrooms. Marie pursued the Reverend Mother's footsteps and gave her room while she hoped for an opportunity to speak. Mary Elizabeth kept looking forward, avoiding looking at Marie. After the last room was checked, she turned toward Marie, who bowed and requested to speak.

"You have my permission."

"Reverend Mother, why should we stop praying now since there is no deliverer? We do not need freedom from praying. We need freedom for the world's slaves of Cogito existence. We need more focused praying for a deliverer."

The Reverend Mother stood tall and looked down at Marie. Her hesitation filled the tense moment with silence and calm. "I know that you are upset, Sister Marie Antoinette. The motherhouse in Vichy ordered us to stop praying and wait for a sign."

"But why Reverend Mother? Why was I not consulted?" Marie could not hide the frustration and betrayal she felt over this sudden decision.

"The Sovereign Mother has spoken," Mary Elizabeth calmly stated. "But if you must have a reason, then I will tell you. Helen gave the directive because of the deterioration in the physical appearance of Essence and an anonymous complaint."

"A complaint?" Marie asked in disbelief.

"Yes, some of the sisters may be involved in a prayer scam. Certain sisters seem to be arranging their prayer time in order to get out of their maintenance duties around the school. The praying must stop. That is final." With that final assertion the Reverend Mother turned away from an open-mouthed Sister Marie.

When Marie continued to stand there in shock, the Reverend Mother pushed on. "It's time to get to work. Your students are waiting."

Marie turned and left. On her way to her classroom, she saw the ivy growing above the windows. *So what? That should not matter.*

The big bell tolled for freedom.

Sister Marie could not hide her anger over the abrupt end of praying for Spartacus. She rang the Essence big bell very hard the next morning and continued with violent rings for several days. The Reverend Mother noticed but considered Marie's release of frustration to be harmless and perhaps therapeutic.

On the fifth of December, the Pierre town council meeting was held at the tavern instead of the library. The prominent members of Pierre gathered for their 7:00 a.m. meeting. The Reverend Mother Mary Elizabeth attended as an ex-officio member. As the meeting commenced, the clanging of the big bell filtered into the tavern.

"The Bastille holiday ended five months ago. It sounds like Essence is still celebrating, Reverend Mother," Ogie, the town council president, said disapprovingly.

Mary Elizabeth turned her head to look away from the one-eyed Ogie.

"I bet that's Sister Marie ringing the bell. I can tell when she's upset," remarked the tavern owner with a smirk.

Several members laughed loudly.

"It sounds like her," agreed the mayor.

Mary Elizabeth smiled and spoke after the ringing stopped. "I want to remind everyone that our sovereign mother, Helena Moyen, made an agreement with the town council that allows the big bell to be rung twice every day, and on occasion it tolls for a fallen citizen of Pierre. For the orphans at Essence, the big bell rings at 7:00 a.m. and 3:00 p.m. to signal the start and end of their busy day."

"What about the collapse of the library?" asked the tavern owner.

A deafening silence filled the room. Murmurs traveled through the air about the bell rings and the philosophical dig as causes of the library listing. The mayor tabled the discussion, but the tavern owner made sure that the topic would be taken up at the next meeting in January. After the meeting adjourned, the mayor told Mary Elizabeth that he would pay a diplomatic visit to the tavern owner and follow up with her about the library matter.

Two days later the mayor arrived at Essence as promised. "I am sorry for bringing up the big bell again, Reverend Mother. The tavern fellows are using the collapse of the library's foundation to their advantage," he explained. "They are making accusations. The timing for the loud bell rings could not be worse."

The mayor took in a deep breath and looked downward in reverence as he continued in his apologetic way. "Some of the merchants have joined the tavern owner in making disparaging comments about the bellicose ringing of the big bell."

The Reverend Mother sat with perfect posture and showed no concern. "Sit down, Mayor. Catch your breath. So many are trapped in existence by their own vices. If the drinkers could make the journey to freedom, then they would understand why the big bell is rung twice every day. The big bell guides our children at Essence through their day like a compass."

The mayor began to speak, but Mary Elizabeth's mind focused on her analogy of the big bell as a compass.

The bell rings are like a compass, thought Mary Elizabeth. At that moment, she understood Helen's compass experience analogy. *The sensory from the sounds of the bell rings give rise to an Intentio that serves to light up the Sentio and Cogito pathways toward greater freedom in the morning and then greater freedom in the afternoon for the children of Essence.*

She smiled. The big bell did not provide the Intentio of providence; it provided the Intentio of Essence, guiding the children throughout their day.

She returned her attention to the mayor and was considerate of the mayor's diplomatic position. After some back-and-forth, she agreed to a compromise. "Okay, I will tell Sister Marie Antoinette to tone down her morning rings for the sake of the merchants," Mary Elizabeth said, and walked the mayor out of her office and down the porch steps.

"Thank you," he replied with a head bow and a quick farewell. He exited through the play area, waving to the children and catching a ride on the wagon pulled by Marcel. Mary Elizabeth returned to the school building with concern about the big bell. She went back to her office and signed out. She needed to talk to Marie.

She walked down to the first floor and looked through the open door at Sister Marie teaching her first-grade class how to read. She had the children sitting in a half circle.

"Jacob, it's your turn to read."

Mary Elizabeth observed from the hallway for a minute before she knocked and beckoned Marie with her finger. "Sister, could I see you for a moment?"

Sister Marie turned and acknowledged the Reverend Mother's request. "Jacob, I want you to continue reading. I'm listening. I'll be right back."

Marie met Mary Elizabeth in the hallway, keeping one eye on her students. "Yes, Reverend Mother, what is it?"

"You must tone down your ringing of the big bell in the mornings. I know that you are upset about the prayer decision. But those men from the tavern who blamed us for the collapse of the library have complained again."

"But the orphans need the big bell," insisted Marie.

"I know that, Sister; just tone it down. Don't pull quite so hard on the rope," the Reverend Mother instructed, frustration creeping into her voice.

"I will. I mean, I won't," Marie agreed, then returned to her place among the first graders. "That was very good, Jacob. Now, Eliza, let's hear you read where Jacob left off."

The Reverend Mother smiled. She enjoyed watching Sister Marie teach the children to read. She stimulated and captivated the children's Intentios. She shared love through her instruction, and the children responded, obviously delighted by her company.

37

On December 18, during a quiet celebration dinner in the chapel for Helen's birthday, Marie had a private discussion with Helen, after which she understood the seriousness of the threat to their Essence. With hope, Helen asked Marie to give her full support to Mary Elizabeth during these trying times.

Following her discussion with Helen, Marie sought out Mary Elizabeth and invited her on a walk to Pierre later in the evening. She wanted to apologize for the bell-ringing incident and discuss her thoughts about Essence. Mary Elizabeth accepted her invitation.

"Happy birthday to you, Sovereign Mother," the children sang in a final farewell to Helen.

Marie and the children gathered around and followed Helen and Poulou to their Jeep, sharing hugs and kisses with them. When Marie embraced Helen, she felt so much love for her. Helen's vision of greater freedom for all had delivered the most wonderful form of love she'd ever experienced. Marie whispered to Helen that she would find a way to save Essence. Helen smiled at her and got into the passenger seat of the Jeep.

Helen gave final waves to the children as Poulou pulled out slowly and turned toward Pierre. The children ran after them for a moment until Josephine blew her whistle. Marie helped Josephine usher the children to their dorm rooms.

Then she joined Mary Elizabeth near the chapel to begin their walk to town.

The temperature had fallen to near freezing, but Marie was unaffected by the cold. She looked at Mary Elizabeth and smiled at her shawl and long coat. Marie wore only her habit and a wool scarf. She reached to hold Mary Elizabeth's hand, and Mary's fingers were freezing cold as they began the walk to Pierre.

"God is going to answer our prayers with a deliverer for the slaves of existence. Existentialism will soon be kaput, finished. I can feel it. The deliverer is nigh," said Marie, squeezing Mary's hand.

"I hope you are right. I get so angry at the existentialists at times," Mary Elizabeth said. "They are playing their music in Pierre on the jukebox, that exie band."

"I know. I've heard the songs played when walking into town. Sometimes I wish Helen had slapped that café-dwelling chap. Maybe it would have put a stop to all of this."

Marie smiled at Mary Elizabeth as they continued toward town, enjoying the beautiful wreaths and garlands decorating the streetlights, reminding them that Christmas was near.

Mary Elizabeth sighed. "I wish the dig had been more successful, but it was necessary, as Helen said. You showed great leadership, despite the adversity and the outcome."

"Thank you," said Marie. Mary Elizabeth's words comforted her. She still battled feelings of failure when it came to the library dig.

Then for some reason Marie's thoughts turned to God's clock and to infinity. She had estimated there were thousands if not more infinities in a single eternity. She smiled at Mary Elizabeth, shared her revelation, and then added. "God is above time, but he still looks at his clock."

Mary Elizabeth adjusted her shawl and gave no response.

It was hard for Marie to tell if Mary Elizabeth understood because she was shivering. Marie squeezed her cold hand again, producing a warm smile from Mary Elizabeth. Marie returned the smile and shared her excitement over Christmas and talked about the joy she experienced earlier in the children's eyes. Their looks of wonder had warmed her insides. Mary Elizabeth seemed in deep thought as they rounded the final turn toward Pierre. Marie turned her head from side to side and noticed that the air stood still in an eerie stillness. Not a single breeze.

Marie glanced toward the tavern and noticed people walking toward a peculiar bundle under the last gas lamp near the main street, drawn by distinctive squawking sounds of distress. She released Mary Elizabeth's hand and ran toward the cries with Mary Elizabeth hurrying behind. As Marie reached the last streetlight, a crowd had gathered, and a young lady peeked into the bundle.

"Oh my gosh!" she exclaimed. "It's a baby."

Others looked on with concern as the squawking sounds grew weaker. A large group of people leaving the tavern joined the growing crowd. Another woman picked up the bundle and moved directly beneath the streetlight for a better look.

Marie felt compelled, her focus driven by a strong attention wave with such power and clarity, impossible to ignore. She had to rescue the tiny baby and pushed through the crowd. She slipped between two, tall men standing in front, approached the woman holding the bundle, and reached her hands out. "Let me."

The young lady carefully handed over the baby. Marie removed the small cloth around the infant and inhaled sharply.

"He is so teeny," Mary Elizabeth said sadly. "He has little more meat on his bones than a fertilized embryo."

Marie looked stricken. "I know."

Marie had played a nurse on a TV show in her former life. She knew the end of this scene—this orphaned preemie would soon be dead. She'd never seen anything quite like it— or him. She maintained a face of gentility and asked everyone to pray. The crowd knelt and joined hands. They recited the Lord's Prayer as Marie gathered the little body against her heart, cupped in her hands. She warmed his tiny little body against hers, scared to hope that he would stay with them.

On the third time through the Lord's Prayer, his limp form gained tone. Many continued to pray while others waited in a heavy silence. After what felt like an eternity, the tiny life began to squirm, his cries more robust. Marie's tears of joy streamed as its tiny arms and legs flailed. The others wanted to see, but Marie protected him from their pawing eyes. She removed his damp garments and wrapped him in her scarf against her bosom.

Something inside Marie clicked as she looked into his little squinting eyes. She was ready to give her life for him. In that moment Marie became his mother.

Mary Elizabeth thanked everyone for their prayers and asked the grocer to bring Dr. Frankl to Villa #4. Marie rushed on ahead up the road toward Essence. She hurried up the steps through the villa door and roused Josephine from the kitchen.

"Please Josephine, bring a warm towel to my bedroom."

Marie went straight to her room. After a few minutes Josephine brought a large white towel and placed it around Marie and the baby. Marie explained to Josephine about finding the baby and heard commotion downstairs. Mary Elizabeth opened her bedroom door and in walked Dr. Frankl, a handsome man with salt-and-pepper hair who looked like an angel carrying a black bag. He looked so calm and confident.

He approached Marie and reached to feel the baby's head and then wrapped the baby in the warm towel and laid him on the bed. He examined the infant on her bed, talking to him as if the baby could understand. Dr. Frankl had survived the war, where he learned to take care of preemies with no modern conveniences. He shared his story with Marie while examining the baby.

She knew he was trying to ease her fear. *What an amazing bedside manner.*

He comforted Marie and the baby and responded to her as the baby's mother. Dr. Frankl could find nothing wrong, not a single pathologic anything.

"A perfect little preemie. He is a tough little fellow," Dr. Frankl said, and folded his stethoscope into his bag.

Marie hugged Dr. Frankl with tears rolling down her cheeks and whispered, "Merci, Thank you."

Dr. Frankl's moist blue eyes lowered into her gaze. He smiled, nodded, then turned toward Josephine, and pulled something from his black bag. "I'll come by in the morning with some formula and show you how to feed him. Here's a dropper. He needs about 15 ml of water per hour, three droppers per hour through the night."

Josephine nodded and smiled at Dr. Frankl, took the dropper, and thanked him.

"Keep him on his back when he sleeps," he said, and made his way out the door.

Marie followed, thanking him again with an embrace, and returned to find Josephine had fashioned a diaper out of a handkerchief. She wrapped the baby in the towel and then handed him to her. Marie rocked the small baby, cradling him close to the sound of her beating heart, which seemed to comfort and strengthen him. Josephine sat on the bed near her, whispering soft lullabies.

The glorious news traveled to Helen and Poulou who traveled to Essence the very next day. They met with Mary Elizabeth outside of Marie's room. Helen peeked her head through the door and saw Marie holding the baby against her bosom.

"He's the one," Marie said as Helen and Poulou produced angelic smiles from the doorway.

Helen hugged Mary Elizabeth and then Poulou for a long time. Marie watched with a smile as her own eyes filled with tears. She stayed with the baby in her room, afraid to expose him or herself to the others for fear of the flu. Dr. Frankl had warned Marie earlier when he brought the formula that the influenza might rear its head in Pierre and that her baby's immune system was immature.

Helen stood in the hallway for almost an hour waving and grinning at Marie and her baby. Then she gave a final smile filled with love and gratitude, and Poulou gave the same with a salute of his hand, as they said farewell then departed down the stairs.

After saying good-bye, Marie held her fragile baby close and rocked him. She knew that he was still in danger and wouldn't let him out of her arms. When she needed to drink or use the bathroom, she would hurry while Josephine relieved her.

For the next three days the little baby fought to live. Marie fed him formula and enveloped him in warm human touch intended with love. The Sisters of Freedom maintained a vigil downstairs, and Josephine stayed by Marie's side helping her care for the baby. Dr. Frankl also had warned that the baby could take a turn for the worse with no warning, so Marie and Josephine kept close watch over him never letting him out of their sight.

On the third night Marie got up to rock the baby who seemed fussy. The clock on her desk showed it was 2:00 a.m., and Josephine sat up awake in her chair. Marie was rocking him when his breathing stopped for no reason. He turned pale and went limp in her arms. Fear stabbed her in the heart. She reacted quickly, blowing through his nose several times then rubbing his back while holding him tightly against her chest. It seemed like an eternity as Marie rubbed and prayed. She felt air moving out of his nose. He had started breathing on his own, the pink color came back to his face, and his blue eyes twinkled.

Afterward Josephine hugged Marie; they both cried. Seeing the baby's body so pale without signs of life for those moments had been devastating. Marie couldn't sleep after the episode and stayed awake holding the baby, encouraging him to breathe with soft whispers conveying her love for him and her need for him to live.

Dr. Frankl came around at sunrise and called the episode an apnea spell, which is often seen in babies that are premature.

"Can it happen again?" Josephine asked Dr. Frankl.

He said it could until the baby grew and became stronger. Till then they just needed to watch him.

The days hurried by, and every morning Josephine read warm letters from the caring people of Pierre while Marie smiled holding her baby in her arms and gazed at the flowers and the gifts. Her baby had become the most important news event at Essence and in Pierre.

Day after day, Marie cared for him with a growing hope that their prayers had not been in vain, and she would nurture him to become the deliverer. Of course, the little baby had a long way to grow before he could deliver anyone.

At first Marie fed him with formula as the doctor recommended, but the little fellow wanted more. One morning, he repositioned himself on Marie's chest. She thought she knew what this little being was after. She opened her blouse, exposed her breasts, and he attached to her nipple as if he knew just where to find it. Marie felt so connected and so much love for her baby as he tried to suckle. After several days of dry sucking, she began to produce milk. It was the best feeling in the world. She loved nursing and the overwhelming bond that it created between her and her baby. It freed her of her need for brandy, and it made her love this unnamed being even more. Her little baby thrived and grew to near newborn size in just a few weeks.

"**Sergio has finished the** crib," Josephine said, "and Sister Celia and Cecelia have made some beautiful blue and white blankets."

"That is wonderful," said Marie.

"Dr. Frankl said the flu scare is over. Bring me a bottle of breast milk, and I'll watch the baby. Go visit the people in town. They'll be thrilled to see you."

Marie hugged Josephine. After several weeks of caring for the baby night and day, she wanted to share her gratitude for all of the prayers, flowers, cards, and support from the people of Pierre. She hurried downstairs and walked toward the terrace and down the cobblestone road.

Once in town, Marie smiled at the many well-wishers. The miracle baby had already been adopted by the entire community. She was amazed by the welcome she received. The painter, the station attendant, and the store clerk were among a small crowd of well-wishers that surrounded Marie as she walked down the street.

"Sister Marie, how is the little baby boy doing today?" asked the shoemaker.

"Very well," she responded and stopped to give hugs. "Your thoughts and prayers made all the difference."

After sharing embraces, she hurried along and visited the grocer to give an update. She knew that he would spread the latest information through the town. She spent the rest of the day filling her heart with love and support from all the people in Pierre. She walked to Paradise, but Javier was not there. She had wanted to tell him about the miracle baby and left word with Maggie, his bookkeeper. Then she headed for home with a full heart and eager anticipation to see her beloved son and hold him once again.

40

One day well into the baby's recovery, Helen paid a visit to Villa #4. Jubilant to see her, Marie rose from her rocking chair, holding the baby in a blanket, and welcomed Helen with a kiss.

"Please sit," Marie said. "I want you to hold him."

Helen took a seat and received the little guy with open arms. "He smells so nice, a little baby's fresh powdery smell."

Marie smiled. She had just bathed him. His little body wiggled as if he feared he might fall, and his arms stretched out as did his tiny fingers. Helen calmed his tension by holding him against her bosom. She pulled the blanket snugly around him and slowly rocked, the motion mesmerizing the baby. It only took a few moments before Helen looked up at Marie, her soft brown eyes filled with tears. She hummed to the baby as she rocked, his blue eyes fixed on Helen's face.

"Go take a break; I'm going to hold him for a little while," whispered Helen as she smiled at the baby.

"Thank you," Marie said, and tip-toed downstairs with a basketful of clothes. She had so much to do. She folded laundry and cleaned the kitchen. She stood on the screened-in porch after ironing her habit and enjoyed the cool mountain breeze. She looked beyond the evergreens, toward the mountains and the sky, which was a beautiful shade of blue, and found herself humming the tune of the Moldau, a symphonic poem about the magical flowing sounds of the Vltava River.

Her thoughts returned to her baby—his round head, his small face, his eyes, and his tiny mouth. She loved his warm scent and the cozy feeling of his warm body. She was in love with everything about him. No language could explain the way she felt: a love and joy she had never encountered before the baby came into her life.

After the chores, she stretched out on a small sofa to relax and drifted to sleep. An hour later she awoke and called to Helen, but there was no response. She hurried upstairs to check. The rocking had stopped, and Helen held the baby above her head, their eyes locked in a stare.

"Are you okay?" asked Marie, her heart still pounding.

Helen lowered the baby, rubbed his face against her cheek, and resumed a slow rocking motion as if she had not heard Marie's question. She looked up with a big, happy smile as Marie approached.

"He is the one. If there was a doubt, let it be no longer," Helen said. "He is the one."

Marie nodded. She needed no proof because she already knew. He was the one.

After a few more minutes of rocking, the little fellow closed his eyes. Helen whispered, "He's asleep."

Marie took the baby from Helen and laid him down for his nap. She placed a cover over his tiny body, then went and sat in the chair at her desk. Helen's eyes had filled with tears again. Marie reached out and squeezed her hand. Helen wiped her eyes with some tissues and whispered that the little fellow's sensory awareness had overwhelmed her.

Marie gave Helen a moment to collect herself then moved her chair closer. "What name is appropriate for the little Prince of Essence?" she asked softly. She shared some of the names suggested by the sisters: Mason, Bacon, Rene, Pascal, Pierre . . . the list had grown long.

Helen explained that the wrong name could take away the boy's innocence and any essence already accrued. She wanted to consider the options with Poulou and emphasized the importance of his name.

"He must have a great name. One day he will become a great leader and free the slaves of Cogito existence."

Helen finished, got up, walked over to the baby, and gently touched his head one more time. Then she gave Marie a warm embrace and assured her that she would be in contact soon with a special name.

The next day, Marie waited nervously near the phone. She held and rocked the baby saying names out loud all day long to see if he would react to the name he was meant to have. She worried that Helen and Poulou might pick a strange name for him. The long day of waiting passed, and after praying for a great name, Marie fell asleep after nursing the baby.

The next morning the phone call came, and Helen put an end to the speculation.

"Poulou agrees," she announced to Marie. "The Prince of Essence will carry the surname of Dasein. A being in the world always engaged with the world through Sentio, he will be the one who leads the slaves of Cogito existence to freedom."

A long pause followed. "What did you say?" Marie finally asked.

"His name will be Dasein," Helen repeated.

Marie paused again then smiled in realization. She remembered from her reading during the philosophical dig that *Dasein* was the German word Heidegger used to explain the experience of a living, thinking, and feeling being in his book, *Being and Time*, which opposed the idea of Cartesian existence, a being who only thinks—Cogito.

"It's a great name!" Marie agreed.

After thanking Helen for the name, she held the baby

and began to rock. Marie had hoped for the surname Pascal; nevertheless, she accepted the name, which seemed to fit her little baby. As she rocked, she repeated "Dasein, Dasein . . . ," to the smiling baby.

The next day, Josephine came to sit with the baby, and Marie made the announcement.

"His surname is Dasein."

Josephine crinkled her nose. "Strange."

"I know," Marie agreed. "It is strange. Dasein!"

Josephine held the baby as Marie readied to go into town and said, "Dasein, Dasein, Dazaney."

He frowned and passed some gas, making Marie laugh.

At the grocery store, the grocer wanted to visit and call Dasein by his new name. Marie smiled and thanked him for his kindness. She walked to Paradise to visit Javier. She wanted to share her joy with him, but again he was not there. Maggie reported he had gone to Barcelona for business.

41

The day after the announcement to the grocer, the adults of Pierre flocked like children to visit Essence and call the baby's name. Marie allowed the visitors to wait in the foyer of #4 then she watched the baby in her room while Josephine came down and checked each one of the visitors for the sniffles and carefully instructed them on how to wash their hands in the kitchen.

Marie required everyone to wear one of the masks provided by Dr. Frankl before entering her baby-blue-decorated room. Essence had not needed a nursery before Dasein. Marie had redecorated her room with mobiles and stuffed animals, and last week Sister Serelia had painted a flower garden on the lower half of the walls with yellow, red, and white roses bordered with purple heather, and a green field studded with daisies. The room had a feeling of the Garden of Eden, and Marie's bed was adjacent to Dasein's crib

The knocks on the door of Villa #4 continued endlessly as Josephine screened and welcomed the visitors. At one point during the morning, the line extended from Marie's room all the way out the front door.

Marie escorted the visitors into her room two at a time and explained the meaning of Dasein's name as they approached his crib.

"Can we hold him, please?" asked the grocer who had come with his family.

Marie let him hold the baby for a minute, and Dasein cooed and burped for the grocer and his wife. They said his name, and he burped again.

The grocer's children, Jacques and Joan, a cute, blond little boy and red-headed girl, wanted to hold him too, so Marie held him as they looked on. They wanted to pull down their masks and kiss his scalp, but she could not allow that, so they gave the top of his head a little pat.

Two old fellows, tavern dwellers, made their way to the front of the line. Marie was nice and allowed them to call his name from the door but did not allow them inside because they reeked of alcohol and cigarettes.

In the afternoon, when the tavern owner showed up with Ogie, they were well dressed and clean. Marie let them in and led them to the crib, and Dasein gave them a stare, almost a glare, after they called his name. She could see their grins beneath their masks and heard Ogie mumble.

"He's just like his mother."

The tavern owner nodded. "In a good way."

"Thank you," said Marie.

Javier showed up after the crowd left, and Marie was thrilled. He was sober and looked well, handsome as always. She let him hold Dasein, and he rocked him in his arms for more than an hour. The baby stayed calm and stared at Javier the entire time without making a noise. Marie talked about the years gone by since the first Saturday sunset café dinner, the dig, and prayer vigil. Javier listened and acknowledged with sadness how time had passed them by.

When he got up to leave, Marie saw tears in his eyes. She put Dasein in his crib, returned, and gave Javier a long embrace. She thanked him for his love and support, but he said very little, seeming so humble as he walked out of her room. She wanted him to stay but could not say the words.

Mary Elizabeth came by after Javier, and Marie began to cry in the comfort of her embrace. She explained how she loved Javier, and Mary Elizabeth reminded her that she had something far more important to do with her life now. She told Marie that Javier needed time to straighten out his own life that had been ransacked by alcohol.

After they sat for a while Marie agreed with Mary Elizabeth about Javier. But then Mary Elizabeth told her that Javier had settled their financial obligations after he heard about the situation from Poulou. The news caused Marie to cry again and left a warm glow in her chest. It was so comforting to know Essence was safe and that Javier was the reason.

She closed her eyes and saw a vision of her and Javier together at Essence. The vision was interrupted when Mary Elizabeth got up from the rocking chair and said goodnight. Marie rose from her chair to embrace and thank the Mother Superior for her support. After she left, Marie lay on her bed and wondered if she had experienced the compass with her vision of freedom with Javier. After nursing Dasein, she closed her eyes and saw Javier's image as bright as the sun in her reflective consciousness. She opened her eyes and the room was dark. She fell asleep.

The following Sunday Helen baptized Dasein during sunset on the balcony porch with more than three hundred people in attendance including Javier, Sergio, and the builders from Catalan.

Marie gave Dasein his Christian name, Antonio, and announced, "Antonio Dasein is the prince and deliverer; Essence is his mother and Pierre his father."

The crowd applauded loudly. At that moment, Pierre and Essence reunited as one big, happy family, and Marie was so proud.

42

"Helen, this is beautiful. What a gorgeous view of the lake. And I love your terra cotta," said Mary Elizabeth, standing on the veranda of the Spanish castle in Vichy. She looked around and gave compliments, one after the other, on the castle's ornate furnishings: marble tables, velvet-cushioned chairs, crystal chandeliers, and the large, beautiful impressionistic oil paintings of Monet's garden in Giverny.

"I know the children love it here," she added.

"Thank you."

"The children are across the lake playing on the swings," Poulou said. "Come here and sit by me on the sofa, Mary. I'll show you."

"Thank you. I saw the children playing," she smiled. "I need to stretch my legs after the ride from Pierre." Mary Elizabeth continued her leisurely walk through the large open room.

Poulou went on, "Stretch them out, and I will massage your shoulders. They must be tired."

"I'm fine," she said, and turned toward Helen who watched from the bishop's chair—her throne. "You wanted to see me. Is it about Dasein?"

Helen poured herself some brandy and took her time to respond. "Would you like a glass, Mary Elizabeth? We distilled the brandy from our own wine."

"No, thank you."

"Poulou, how about you?" Helen asked.

"Oh, my goblet is still half full. I might take some in a little while." He seemed a bit stung by Mary Elizabeth's rejections.

Helen sat back sipping from her glass and answered her Sister's question. "Yes, I want to discuss our plan for nurturing our little Spartacus."

Mary Elizabeth's eyes widened at her choice of words. "You believe he is the deliverer."

"He is the deliverer; I know this in my Sentio. I have experienced his awareness," Helen said. "But we have to prepare him for the task. I want no more language—written or spoken words—used around him until he is at least four years old," Helen ordered.

"But why?"

"So that his Sentio can fully develop," she said in a calmer tone. Helen believed a baby's brain formed its major connections at a frenzied pace for the first three years, and she wanted Antonio's Intentio dwelling in his sensory consciousness, stimulating Sentio connections until he was at least four.

"How will he learn without language?" asked Mary Elizabeth.

"Einstein did not learn language until he was four."

Helen now believed that the reason the children had not experienced her compass was because of their underdeveloped Sentios as a result of learning language too early, which had enslaved their Intentios to Cogito like an addiction.

"He will need to learn to read," Mary Elizabeth protested.

"He will learn to read when it is time," Helen insisted. "Besides, reading is not so important. Many great artists never learned to read; Spartacus could not read. I know what is best."

Mary Elizabeth nodded as if to concede.

"He will never watch or hear the picture box. TV is a tool used by clever marketers to control a child's mind, robbing the child of free choice—"

"Winston tastes good . . . like a cigarette should," Poulou said, interrupting Helen, and raised his brow at Mary Elizabeth.

"My point exactly," Helen agreed.

"I understand the dangers of TV," said Mary Elizabeth.

"The child is not aware of free choice in our society. It's a shame," Helen said. "Children expose their minds to horror, and the horror remains in their memories forever. It cannot be erased, and the institutional conditioning remains for the rest of their lives—imprisoning their Intentios to revisit the institutional imagery and language of the greedy marketers. I have seen orphans damaged beyond repair. I will not allow the conditioning and institutionalization induced by the smut on TV for Antonio."

With that final decree, Helen downed her shot of brandy.

"I understand, but what you ask is impossible," Mary Elizabeth said. "We cannot stop the children or the visitors from talking around Antonio. Radio and TV are everywhere. They are impossible to defend against."

When Helen said nothing in immediate response, Mary Elizabeth walked toward the lake. The horizon sky had filled with dark clouds. When she turned around, Helen met her doubt-filled eyes.

"We must find a way. The future of humankind depends on our decisions and actions."

"I will do my best," Mary Elizabeth promised.

Poulou stood up from his thinking position, held out his goblet, and pointed at Mary Elizabeth with the index finger of his drinking hand. "I have an idea. We'll continue to make everyone wear masks. Dasein was born prematurely, so let's embrace his infantile immune system. We will confine him to the villa until he is four years old."

"Yes, masks might work," Mary Elizabeth responded. "You cannot talk through a mask. And we can invoke a ban on TV viewing at Essence. Perhaps we will limit the ban to #4. The children love their Saturday morning cartoons in the dormitory."

Poulou grinned at Mary Elizabeth. "As do I."

He listed his glass in a toasting motion. "Mary, we could make a great team, you and me."

Helen interrupted by walking over and putting her hand on Mary Elizabeth's shoulder. "Mary Elizabeth, you will instruct Marie how to nurture Antonio's sensory consciousness," she whispered. "I suggest to use solid geometric objects painted in the primary colors, the toys of Archimedes—"

"You mean like balls, cubes, wheels, and oblong blocks?"

"Yes, and picture books without words." Helen walked back to her chair. "Then I will lead Antonio through his first sunset after his Sentio has fully developed. Marie needs to understand that there must be no human conditioning of Antonio's sensory consciousness."

"But what about Marie?" Mary Elizabeth asked. "She needs to agree to this too. She should hear it from you."

Helen smiled. "Marie understands Sentio. I am relying on your Cogito, Mary Elizabeth, to create the scaffolding for Marie's nurturing of Dasein. Tell her that I will call and give her my support on how to nurture our little Spartacus."

Poulou spoke up from the comfort of the sofa. "What about some companions for Antonio? He needs to grow up with a semblance of family. In order to create connection and purpose for his being, for his mission, he needs companionship beyond transitioning orphans."

Helen nodded. "I have already taken care of this concern. There are two young orphans I have accepted for that reason, who will become like brother and sister to

Antonio. They will arrive next spring when they can toddle. The children, Polly Dubois and Alex Shaw, are living in a temporary home in Northern Ireland. I accepted them last week. Their families were killed in separate explosions last year during the height of the violence."

"Why Irish orphans?" asked Poulou.

"The Irish have strong Sentios. Freud found the Irish resistant to his psychoanalytical nonsense."

"Helen, you would have been a great mother with your odd mothering instincts," Poulou said. "What about a father?"

"Javier has agreed to act as Antonio's father figure when the time is right, and I think that Marie will agree," said Helen.

Poulou arose. "Mary, I think that we are done. Would you like some brandy before you go?"

"No, thank you. I need to get back to Essence and inform Marie." She turned toward Helen and curtsied and then pivoted to find Poulou had snuck up behind her. He gave Mary Elizabeth an awkward embrace. She patted Poulou on the back then hurried off with Pepé, who drove her to catch the bus to Pierre.

43

It was late at night when Mary Elizabeth arrived at Essence to share the news from Vichy. She found Marie half-asleep, nursing Antonio on the bed. Marie reached and turned on a small lamp, and Mary shared salutations from Helen and Poulou then caressed Marie's sleepy head.

Pulling the rocking chair close, Mary Elizabeth took a seat and explained in a soft voice how Antonio's Sentio was to be nurtured. Marie's ears perked as she heard the words *no language*. She sat up on the bed and felt her stomach drop as her vision of the next few years with Antonio were replaced with a strange new plan. Her mind began to race as she placed Antonio in his crib.

"But when can I teach him to talk?" she asked.

"Not until he is four," Mary Elizabeth said calmly. "Helen wants to make sure that his sensory consciousness is developed before he engages his Cogito. And we must be vigilant not to condition Antonio's feeling consciousness, like Pavlov did with his dogs."

"You mean like giving him rewards to control his behavior or nursing him to stop his crying?" Marie asked. "But I can use my judgment?"

"Yes, Helen trusts your judgment. She will call you with her specific concerns. She sends her support and love ahead of her words." Mary Elizabeth smiled and departed.

Marie knew that Helen had reasons for her plan, but she had a plan too. She sat up for several hours stewing. She believed her own plan to use an alphabet language would be better, where a single letter, like K, means kiss. She wanted to be ready to argue with Helen when she called.

But the next day when Helen's words came by phone, Marie was too tired to argue, and Helen explained that she had already set in motion what would be needed to support her in nurturing Antonio's Sentio. Marie listened while biting her tongue, and after hanging up she felt all alone and defeated. Helen's plan was already being implemented.

Mary Elizabeth had placed Villa #4 on quarantine and Marie was relieved of all of her duties at Essence. The other sisters moved out of #4 later that day. Mary Elizabeth moved to #3. Sister Josephine and Jahn Phillips moved to Villa #2.

The following day the visitors stopped coming. Marie found herself all alone with Antonio, with no need for masks. Sister Josephine called and explained that a black flag had been raised above the cupola, and a second black flag had been placed near the front door to keep visitors away. Josephine also explained that Mary Elizabeth had informed the mayor and the Pierre town council of the unusual situation and the need to protect Antonio's immune system. Helen had spoken with Dr. Frankl and gained his support for her plan.

Marie got scared and cried on the phone. She did not want to live under a black flag. She felt so alone. Josephine explained that the flags were symbols to remind others not to disturb the nurturing of Antonio. Even though the flags were symbols, Marie was still all alone under a black flag. After hanging up Marie's chest tightened, and her heart felt empty. She cried until Antonio awoke in his crib. She wiped her tears and faked a happy smile. *What will she do now, all alone with her baby?* She picked up Antonio and rocked while nursing him.

That night the sisters joined together in a quiet show of support. They brought dinner for Marie with a cooking and cleaning roster, so she would know who to expect and when. She still felt alone but grateful for their support. The Catalan sisters would provide the essentials for her and Antonio's existence.

The following day brought more support. The sisters brought groceries and picked up all of Marie and Antonio's dirty laundry. Sisters Celia and Cecelia stayed all day and cleaned #4. They scrubbed and cleaned the kitchen and bathroom floors and Marie's bathtub. The sisters' support overwhelmed her and renewed her faith in Helen's plan.

Two days later Helen called and reiterated that Dasein's Sentio needed protection from outside influences. Helen seemed to be sending a message to batten down the hatches. After her talk Marie pulled closed all of the curtains and drapes. She took Antonio from his crib and began rocking him. In that moment of darkness, Antonio filled her emptiness, and their bond grew tighter. Marie held him in her arms until the next morning.

The big bell startled them at 7:00 a.m., enough that Antonio paused while nursing and waited for the rings to stop. He stared at Marie with his big blue eyes as if he might cry. When the rings ended he resumed nursing. Marie had noticed that he tuned in to all sorts of external sensory. The chirps of birds and the sounds of crickets had turned his head, but the bell had frightened him. She adjusted his nursing schedule to avoid the rings, and then he made it clear by crying that he did not want to be left alone in his crib during the rings. He did not want to be left alone ever again, period.

The sounds of his crying resonated deeply in Marie's Sentio and directed her attention to meet his wants and needs. He wanted to be held. She did not know what else to do other than stay by his side, and so for the next week she held him morning, noon, and night. During her sleep, she lay in the bed with her arm stretched over into the crib so that he was not alone.

On Sunday, when Josephine came over, she looked at Marie with concern. Marie could not hide the stress and exhaustion on her weary face. Josephine shook her head and hugged Marie.

The following day Josephine returned with a note that stated she was to relieve Marie for the day—a mother's day. Marie needed to get organized. Josephine's face and the note were a welcome sight. She thanked Josephine and wrote that there were two bottles of breast milk freshly pumped in the fridge. They shared a quiet embrace, and Marie left her room in silence while Antonio remained asleep.

She took a shower downstairs and went to see Helen and Poulou. The bus ride provided beautiful scenery filled with mountains, streams, heather, and evergreens. The sensory of the trees and the clear blue sky drew her attention, and her language-thinking mind relaxed.

Poulou and Helen greeted her with hugs at the bus station in Vichy then they rode by Jeep to the castle. Marie was happy to be with them but said very little until greeting Jacki, Alice, Louis, and Alberto on the veranda. Her former students were studying to become freedom instructors at the castle, while the school building and orphanage were being erected across the lake. Seeing the grown-up children reminded Marie that what she was doing would someday lead to freedom for all humankind from the slavery of Cogito existence.

Marie had fun swinging on the beach with Jacki and talked about old times with her students. She watched the new orphans playing across the lake, a wonderful view that brought many happy memories of watching the children play at Essence. The kids recharged her Sentio.

When she got back to Essence later that evening, Marie

entered the villa and saw Sister Josephine standing at the top of the stairs. She appeared upset and ready to leave, so Marie hurried for the stairs. Josephine shook her head and whispered that she had gotten Antonio to lay in his crib. She thought he might be asleep.

Josephine stepped softly down the stairs and led Marie to the kitchen. She explained that Antonio did not need to be rocked for his Sentio development. He liked rocking because of the comfort—his little mind was seeking pleasure as babies do.

"Remember you are nurturing little Antonio to be free," said Josephine.

Marie shook her head in agreement. She knew about the three wills, Freud's idea about pleasure, Nietzsche's ideas about power, and Helen's idea about freedom and meaning. Marie understood that too much pleasure was not good for Antonio nor was encouraging his sense of power by giving him what he wanted when he cried.

"Thank you for reminding me," Marie said, and then opened the fridge and gazed at a food tray of sliced meat, cheese, and fruit, enough for a week. Josephine had also cleaned the dishes in the sink. She smiled at Josephine who grinned, and the two shared a warm embrace.

"I need to go," Josephine said, and slipped out the front door as Marie tiptoed upstairs.

Things got easier after that day. As Marie held Antonio day after day, she learned when to put him down. She learned to interpret his needs from his desires. He cried at first, but then he grew more content as she learned to resist giving into his desires for excess pleasure and to avoid power struggles with him.

CHAPTER

44

At first, Marie had a difficult time not speaking around the prince. She'd been prone to talking to herself before Antonio came into her life, and in her first days with him, before Helen's decree, she had told him almost every day that she loved him and that she was going to take care of him. But after the decree, not speaking became easier. Their unique way of communicating transcended spoken words, and her urge to speak to him waned.

Reading his little blue eyes became easy for Marie, and her little baby boy was a master communicator, signaling with his eyes the way he liked to be held, carried, and fed. And for the first time in her life, she began to experience her sense of being in what she believed was her Sentio. She still thought with words, but at times she found herself using primitive grunts and weird sounds to communicate. She wondered: *If she had found the roots for her own private language in Sentio? Wittgenstein, the philosopher whose books she'd read during the dig, must have been wrong.* Then she remembered he did not know about Sentio.

Days and weeks passed, and she and Antonio advanced their communication skills with facial expressions, gestures, whispered sounds, and touch—to near eloquence.

Marie recorded her observations in her journal titled *Learning Nature's Language.* Subtle cues became paramount for understanding and delivering joy. She used soft touches with her lips and blows from her mouth onto his body to tickle, and he tried to mimic by blowing on her cheek when she changed his diapers. His attempts at blowing on her cheek warmed Marie's heart in ways that she had never felt for another human being. Sentio communication was much deeper and more profound, giving her an experience of love which she had never dreamed possible between two human beings.

He crawled as an infant, precocious, Marie wrote in her journal. *As a two-year-old toddler, he played like a five-year-old. Helen's suggested colored geometric figures served as his repertoire for mundane sense communication. When he was upset, he picked up the red cube and grunted. The green ball meant that he was happy and was always displayed with a smile. The yellow, orange, and blue wheels, which were connected together with pegs, represented more complex mood states.*

As his mind developed, Antonio played with tinker toys. He created complicated structures during his most creative times of play—before sleep—and he looked at picture books without words as Marie turned the pages, and she thought that he understood the stories.

One day while cleaning, Marie found some pictures that Antonio must have stored under the bed. His private drawings. They were odd, perfectly drawn circles and spheres with triangles and straight lines. Marie replaced his drawings and wondered how he had traced such images. He must have used her teaching books, but when? How?

The next day, she paid close attention as he played on the floor. He played for hours every day. She gave careful observation trying to find out how and when he drew. For several days, she watched but no clue.

Then one morning while rocking, she looked up. He had climbed onto her trunk and over onto her desk chair and raised his little arm to pull a sheet of paper from the desk, as if he knew the paper would be there. He climbed down and crawled to his toys and then used the tinker toy wheel like a compass and drew a perfect circle. Marie could not believe her eyes. *That little rascal.* After he got the paper from her desk, he drew all afternoon then hid his drawings under the bed. Marie smiled to herself as she peeped. She could not believe how well he could draw.

She realized Antonio had the vision and ability to draw like an artist, and yet he had never been instructed on how to draw. She wondered about John Locke's *tabula rasa* idea, which she had read about during the dig. Antonio had abilities naturally through his Sentio that she had never thought possible.

Several days passed. She forgot about the blank tablet of Locke, had stopped worrying, and appreciated Antonio's ability to draw. They settled into a routine. Their days started at 6:00 a.m. and they went to bed at 8:00 or 9:00 p.m. Antonio would free-draw for hours every day, creating weird things with his vivid imagination.

At night before sleep, he loved to flip the light switch on and off and tried to get Marie to play hide and seek in the dark. She had taught him the game one night when the power generator failed, and he picked the game up quickly. He won every time they played. He had another sense or something, and Marie was no match for his Sentio in the darkness.

Marie weaned Antonio when he turned three, and he grew to love oat cereal, milk, and fruit. Apricots were his favorite. Then he went through a growth spurt and required more sleep, and some days he would take a two-hour nap. Marie could tell when he needed a nap because his eyes got tired, but sometimes he signaled his need for a nap by flipping the light switch on and off. He had mastered communicating his needs.

When lying with her on the bed, Antonio appeared to

study her. One day after play Marie took a nap. When she awoke, she found him sitting quietly alongside her, watching her breathe, and using his hand to feel the air rush in and out of her nose. He stared at her mouth as if he could see the breath escape and return.

Soon after, Marie discovered that Antonio could discern her Sentio state long before her own Cogito had time to understand. If something made her sad, Antonio would smile before he would look sad—perhaps to affect Marie before she herself realized that she was feeling sad.

If she awoke in the morning with cramps or upset from a bad dream, Antonio's face would reflect how she was feeling as she opened her eyes. He could probe so quickly with his Sentio, and he reached out to everything in his environment, understanding objects and non-objects through sensory, and much faster than Marie. Helen had talked about how she experienced Sentio twice as quickly as Cogito, and Marie believed Antonio's little mind processed sensory twice as fast as her own.

One day they visited Mary Elizabeth's room downstairs. Antonio used his mouth for pleasure and also to discover how hard or soft the furniture was. His facial expression looked like a little genius, furrowing his brow with serious eyes as he crawled through Mary's room testing things by touch and using his mouth to determine hardness. He left no marks, finished his work, and gave a wide-eyed look of a conqueror. Marie looked him in the eyes and could not hold back her laugh. She thought about some of the philosophers that she had read about. He was like Aristotle. He needed to understand everything.

Marie wrote in her diary: *It is interesting to watch him; my words can't do justice to what I have observed during these years with Antonio. I believe that he has another sensory beyond what I have, and I know he has the most curious mind I've ever witnessed.*

Antonio seemed to use deductive reasoning in his play

with Marie. He knew in advance the effects of her actions. She watched him anticipate where the ball might end up when she wound up to throw. As she shifted her weight to leverage the throw, he moved in anticipation to where the ball might go.

Fascinated, Marie spent hours watching him learn and investigate. The library dig—and particularly Aristotle's treatise—had provided her with great insight. Each time she introduced him to a new item, he tested and investigated it with Aristotle's four questions of nature: *What is it made of? What form is it? Who made it? What is it used for?*

Marie gave Antonio her hairbrushes; she had three. He played with and tested the objects with his mouth. *What is it made of?* Next he compared the shapes of her hairbrushes. *What form is it?* He did this all without language. Marie understood his natural questions through his actions of trial and error and his effort to compare her brushes to other things. Then he appealed by pointing at Marie as if she had made her hairbrushes. *Who made it?* He tried to brush his soft curly brown hair. *What is it used for?* He knew this from watching Marie brush her hair.

Nothing escaped his Sentio, and he had a memory of everything in their villa. It was eerie how he returned things, which Marie had forgotten to replace, like her stockings and hairbands, to their proper place in the dresser. He was neat as could be—almost too neat for Marie.

Antonio seemed able to read Marie's face when she was sneaking something from one room to the other or something new into their room. She suspected that he could see the glimmer or excitement in her eyes, and she could not hide or disguise any feeling or intention from him. Sometimes he did not even have to look at her to respond to her feelings.

How?

Marie was amazed, but at her core she had some understanding of what allowed Antonio to sense these things;

her own Sentio had grown more sensitive. She knew her Intentio still dwelled in Cogito, but she had experienced brief moments of awareness through Sentio, through her experiences with her son.

One morning Marie slept late and awoke to a banging sound. She ran to find Antonio beating his hand against the French window in the sitting room. He had pulled back the curtains and was pulling on his lip while he continued to bang with his other hand. He stared at two little children through the window. Marie saw Josephine and remembered that Helen had sent a letter to her stating that Josephine planned on bringing Alex and Polly to the window to see Antonio so the children could experience each other in their Sentios. Marie had forgotten about the planned meeting on the first day of summer. Time was flying by.

Polly and Alex looked to be about three years old and scared, their eyes wide open. Alex had brown eyes and brown hair, and Polly had red hair and blue eyes. Josephine stood between them holding their hands. Once Antonio's banging stopped, Polly and Alex put their fingers in their mouths. When Josephine ushered the children away, Antonio began to cry and banged on the window, harder and harder. When Polly turned and looked over her shoulder at him, he stopped.

After closing the curtains, Marie held him. His little body twisted and squirmed. He wanted to go outside and be with them, and she wanted to tell him who they were. She got an idea and sat down and drew a picture story of Josephine, Alex, Polly, and Antonio. He watched her draw and calmed down. She was uncertain if he understood her story, but when she stopped drawing, Antonio began to draw. He finished the story with the three little children playing together and two adults, Marie and Josephine, watching them play. He understood.

The next morning, Marie heard soft knocks on the window and sensed that they might be from Polly and Alex. Antonio heard them too. He ran to the window, and all three children froze and stared at each other. Antonio leaned forward and put his tongue on the window, and Polly reached up and placed her hand against the window pane trying to feel his tongue through the glass. Alex's eyes had locked on Antonio's. He did not move. Josephine rounded the corner and pulled the children away, and Antonio began to cry. He seemed to know that Polly and Alex had a special connection to him. Marie gave him a hug as her eyes filled with tears. She wanted to tell him that it would not be long before he would be playing with his companions, like siblings.

* * *

The day before his fourth birthday arrived, Marie had a feeling that it was time for him to learn language. She invited Helen to come over and assess his Sentio. Early the next day Helen made a visit to #4. She slipped upstairs and sat with Marie while Antonio played. After an hour, Helen gestured she needed to be alone with Antonio. Marie slipped out of the room while Antonio was busy drawing.

She waited anxiously downstairs for the verdict. Was he ready for language? It would all depend on his Sentio development. Only Helen could decide.

Two hours passed. Marie prepared potato soup for dinner and gently knocked on her bedroom door, signaling to Helen. After eating, Helen took Antonio to the balcony porch and held him in her lap as they watched the winter sunset. She rocked him during twilight, and Marie watched from inside the school building, wondering what her decision would be. Was he ready for language?

Marie waited and waited until darkness fell. Helen gave no sign, so she returned to #4 and waited some more. In pitch darkness, Helen returned with Antonio by her side, and her twinkling brown eyes met Marie's anxious ones. They stood in the foyer speechless, and Marie knew immediately.

"He's ready," Helen whispered as a tear ran down her cheek.

Marie embraced her, holding back her own tears after four long years of silence. How many times had she wanted to say that she loved him? Too many to count. Antonio reached to embrace his mother's leg. Helen maintained silence, waved good-bye, and started down the steps. Marie remembered that she had forgotten to tell Helen happy birthday, but the words froze on the tip of Marie's tongue. It was too late. Helen had disappeared into the night.

She looked down into Antonio's beautiful blue eyes, took his hand, and led him up the stairs to the bedroom. Marie lifted his heavy little body into an embrace, joy beaming from her face. She held him in the rocking chair in silence for several minutes, contemplating her first words to him. She turned him around, and he knew that something was up. He looked so serious. His wide eyes widened more as Marie tried to speak. He could sense her words about to come out, and she began to cry and choked on her words.

Antonio frowned and squinted, his expression sad. Marie hurried to get out her words. "I love you. . . . Oh, I love you so much. . . . I love you. . . . I love you, darling."

Antonio pushed back from her embrace with a look of concern and began to cry. Marie shook her head and smiled until Antonio finally smiled. She could see his little mouth trying to mimic her own facial expression, and she let out joyous humming sounds that she knew he understood. She waited a moment and then tried language again.

"Happy birthday!" exclaimed Marie, hoping he would understand the association. "Happy Birthday!"

But the words seemed to scare him; his face turned serious, and he again frowned. Marie sat back and held him in silence after that. After a few minutes Antonio relaxed, smiled, and then returned facing forward. They rocked in silence as Marie pondered how inadequate language was for expressing love. The Sentio experience of her being with him and holding him seemed to mean more to him than any language thought. Antonio drifted off to sleep with Marie's arms wrapped in love around his tiny waist.

It did not take Marie long to figure out Antonio processed language through his Sentio. He learned like a natural sensualist and used the alphabet as if he had invented it himself. With Marie's help he spoke in syllables and proper phonetics. He learned most words after experiencing them. In the kitchen after breakfast he would walk around and review. Red apples tasted sweet; lemons tasted sour; grapes tasted bitter and sweet. Pepper burned—he learned that fact the hard way after biting on a green jalapeno. The juice squirted into his eye, causing him to cry. Marie had helped him wash his eye under the sink. Antonio now gave Marie a cute little smile whenever he saw a green pepper.

When given a taste of language and the freedom to learn more, he wanted to know everything. He drank it in as quickly as Marie could offer it up. She could keep nothing from him. He would point his finger at something for which he didn't yet know the word and wait for her to reply. After her reply, he would test his pronunciation, repeating the word aloud. He would say the name and point again at the object to clarify. He produced the cutest smile when he knew he was right. He sensed Marie's pride and acknowledgment before she could say the words to praise him.

His curiosity grew as he learned more language and surpassed Marie's own understanding of the cause and effect of common things. He asked about the most important things. *What is Earth? Fire? Water? What is air? How about the heavens? And why do things fall?* Marie recognized Aristotle's five elements in his questions, and she believed he also had sensed gravity.

Antonio wanted to know everything and had no understanding of boundaries. Soon Marie discovered that she had no privacy. She tried to explain to him that certain things were private; there were some things she did not want to talk to him about. But he did not seem to understand.

After his fifth birthday, Marie spent time teaching him about personal privacy. She modeled the matter for him when he made it clear he did not want her messing with the geometric drawings he kept hidden under the bed.

Marie pointed to his drawings and said, "Your drawings, me not touch or bother." Then she put her hand on her trunk and said, "My things you not touch or bother."

Slowly but surely, Antonio began to develop appropriate boundaries and tact.

He had grown into a handsome young lad with the largest Mediterranean blue eyes. Marie loved to dress him in his little brown suit for their Sunday visits with Aunt Helen and Poulou. On occasion Josephine, Alex, and Polly would join their Sunday trips to Vichy where Poulou would play with the three children on the swings and on the beach while Helen, Josephine, and Marie would sit on the veranda and talk about the children.

On weekday afternoons Antonio got to play, and he easily fell into playing with Alex and Polly. He loved them, and Marie did too.

During the spring of his sixth year, it was nearing time for Antonio to go to school. Marie and Helen talked and made preparations for a smooth transition. On his first day of summer preschool, Marie and Antonio had a nice breakfast in the villa and sat on the screened-in porch together. She could tell he was anxious.

"You are going to preschool this morning. You know we have prepared for this day."

Antonio nodded and looked sad. Marie knew the reason he looked sad was because he could sense her own sadness.

He asked a million questions. "What will I do? What are you going to do?"

Holding back her tears, she shook her head unable to answer, gave him a big embrace, and washed the jelly from his little fingers in the kitchen. She dried his hands, got down on her knees, and hugged him again for the longest time.

She gathered strength and walked with him to the door of #4 where she felt another wave of sadness. When she opened the door, Antonio ran from the villa and stopped to watch the other children playing on the terrace for a moment. He turned back toward her with a sad expression on his face, his little mouth puckered as if he might cry, which squeezed Marie's heart.

"Go play and have fun," she managed to get out.

Antonio said, "I love you, Mother," and smiled at her with a twinkle in his large blue eyes.

Marie felt a warm tingle inside her chest and was comforted for the moment. Polly and Alex walked up to Antonio as Josephine watched from the playground. Without a word and with gentle kindness in their eyes, they each grabbed a hand and pulled him onto the playground, and all three ran toward the swings.

Marie was able to gather herself, slowed her tears, and waved to Josephine, but as soon as she went back to her room and saw the little drawings under the bed, tears rolled down her cheeks. She ran out of the villa and into Pierre and caught the first bus to Vichy. She needed love from Helen and Poulou.

She cried when Poulou met her on the veranda at the castle. He consoled her with his gentle, sensitive embrace and manner, no words said. Helen came down and embraced

Marie and then listened patiently as she explained her morning farewell to Antonio on his first day of preschool.

Marie decided to spend the day with Helen and Poulou. They sat on the beach and talked. Helen told her that it would be best for her to start teaching again in the fall.

That is the answer. I need to stay busy. Marie felt relieved and stretched her legs, relaxing on the beach blanket. Talking with them was so reassuring and comforting, and Helen was so right. It was getting late. She got up, hugged Helen and Poulou good-bye, and thanked them. She hurried to the castle as Pepé was waiting on the veranda to drive her back to Pierre.

Upon returning to Essence and after putting Antonio to bed, she began preparing her lesson plan for the new school year. When classes started in the autumn, she wanted to be ready to teach first grade. At 2:00 a.m. she got tired, stared at the clock on her desk, and remembered that horrible morning when her baby had stopped breathing. She remembered then, *she had so many reasons to be grateful.* Antonio's life alone in the villa with her had ended, and though sad, she knew Helen's plan had set him on the path to greatness. She closed her books and looked over at Antonio who was sound asleep on her bed. She turned out the lights and cuddled up next to him.

After school began, Antonio and Marie shared Villa #4 with Josephine and Mary Elizabeth. Mary had suggested Antonio move into Sister Phillips' old room, but he did not want to. He continued living with Marie in their baby-blue room that looked like the Garden of Eden, of which he knew every inch.

Two years passed and Antonio had formed special relationships with Alex and Polly as Helen had wanted. Marie treated them like her own, and the three children played together after school, during the week, and on weekends. On Friday night they would sleep together in a makeshift tent in Marie's room, and Josephine would read them stories by flashlight, reminding them of Cogito, Sentio, and Intentio, Helen's paradigm for the enterprise of being.

Alex and Polly were a joy for Marie and had brought purpose to Antonio's life. He included them in everything that he and Marie did. Josephine was such a positive influence on Polly and Alex, who were beautiful, well-behaved children, and Marie appreciated Josephine's insight on how to parent Antonio. Josephine had become like a real sister to her. They shared coffee every morning and watched the sunrise from the screened-in porch of #4.

Antonio wanted to be a big brother to all the orphans. He had empathy for the other children; he had a mother, and they did not. Most of the older children seemed to like his attention, but some didn't.

During a sunset experience on the porch after school began, Marie explained to Antonio that the children had to find their own solutions.

"They have to experience the solution through Sentio and not just Cogito," Antonio said.

Marie nodded to agree; her little boy was so wise.

Antonio knew so much more than the other children, even the older ones, as Marie found out when she taught him in first grade. She spent much of her time teaching him humility. She gave him instructions to give the other children the chance to answer questions in class. He told her that he tried to keep the answers to himself, but sometimes they just popped out of his mouth. And his answers had proved superior to Marie's understanding on many occasions. And he had always waited to correct her until they were alone, which amazed Marie.

When he began second grade, his teacher reminded Marie daily how surprised she was by Antonio's quick mind. *A pleasure to teach, he is—and so smart. I wish that I had twenty just like him,* raved Sister Pauli, in a report to Marie.

Another section of the report upset Marie.

Antonio has a strange vision of the world. He talks about seeing lines, little grids in the clouds, which no one else can see. In class, Antonio solves simple arithmetic with advanced methods. I believe that he has figured out the Pythagorean theorem on his own.

Her reminders began to scare Marie. She feared what might happen if Antonio was declared a genius. She might lose him, so she downplayed his special abilities to her sisters and even to Helen. Marie tried to dismiss the concerns by telling Sister Pauli that Antonio had a great imagination, but Sister Pauli would not let her observations be dismissed. So Marie agreed to observe Antonio for visual hallucinations as suggested by the mysterious grid lines, which he had claimed to see in the clouds. She wanted to satisfy Sister's concerns and divert attention away from Antonio.

For the next week she paid special attention to Antonio's visual descriptions. She noticed that his little eyes saw and reported things when she could see nothing, like the movement of air. But he did not report seeing lines in the clouds, so Marie felt satisfied. She did not look at his secret drawings because they were private, and she was afraid of what she might find. She concluded the lines Antonio had reported seeing were indeed just a healthy imagination. She gave the good news to Sister Pauli on the following Monday during breakfast.

Two days later, Sister Pauli came forth with another concern and met Marie in her first-grade classroom during recess. "The children were playing with their geometric figures, and I made an unusual discovery while quizzing Antonio during the exercise."

"How fun," Marie smiled, hoping to soften Sister Pauli's stiff upper lip. "He loves to be quizzed."

Sister Pauli's forehead wrinkled. "I know that Archimedes demonstrated that the volume of a sphere is two-thirds the volume of a cylinder of the same diameter and height. Antonio seemed to know this quite naturally. When it was his turn for show-and-tell, Antonio demonstrated the calculation in front of my class.

"I watched with my second-graders and looked on with confusion, unable to follow his presentation. I took my seat in silence and waited for him to finish. I knew that his conclusion was correct, but I did not understand his method."

"Antonio loves attention, Sister Pauli," Marie said. "I think that he was just showing off."

Sister Pauli left in a huff, and Marie felt a heavy pressure on her chest as if she could not take a full breath. She knew Sister Pauli would not let this go.

The afternoon bell rang, and Sister Pauli returned to

Marie's classroom with Antonio in tow, leading him by the arm. She held Antonio by his shoulders after parading his scared face in front of her desk. Sister looked as if she had something to prove. Marie was taken by surprise and rose up from her desk to join Antonio. His hands were shaking.

"Antonio, how did you know the volume relationship of a sphere inside a cylinder?" asked Sister Pauli.

Antonio said nothing and turned his scared eyes toward Marie, who had crouched beside him and rubbed his curly brown hair. Marie smiled at Antonio and then furrowed her brow at Sister Pauli. Marie knew only a little about Sister Pauli. She had been a community algebra teacher who had gotten fed up with Xs and Ys and the whole Descartes thing, before answering her calling to their freedom order. Marie was unfamiliar with her method of inquisition, and she certainly did not like the harsh tone she was taking with Antonio.

Antonio relaxed in Marie's embrace and explained his thought process. "I could see the relationship of the surround distance to the in-between distance of the two structures. I could see the cross-areas stacked into a cylinder and tapered into the sphere from the center to the top and bottom. I imagined the ratio of these objects with their similar area equations. It's obvious that the sphere is four-thirds divided by two. The ratio of the volume of the sphere to the cylinder, two-thirds, is quite easy to see."

Sister Pauli thanked Antonio and dismissed him to go play. Antonio ran away as quick as he could. "Sister Antoinette, I think that Antonio is a prodigy. He knows fractions and even pi, as he has surmised."

Marie did not think of Antonio as a prodigy, but she struggled with how to respond. The pressure to breathe returned as she was unsettled by Pauli's attitude, which seemed to be a mix of fear and awe. Marie wanted to discourage this line of thought.

"Antonio is just like you or me. He is no prodigy. Antonio has a strong Sentio. He was conscious of everything before the world could confine him. Don't you see?"

Sister Pauli continued to peer at Marie sternly, communicating that she was not deterred.

"Please, just let this be." Marie's eyes began to tear up.

Sister Pauli seemed moved by the tears so Marie began to cry as hard as she could. Sister Pauli embraced Marie and assured her, "I will not say a word."

Marie thanked her. "You have comforted me," she said and breathed an internal sigh of relief.

Sister Pauli smiled, turned, and walked away. Marie relaxed her sad countenance, but despite the assurance, she was concerned by Sister Pauli's reaction. She knew others would be curious about Antonio's special vision and insight. She did not want him labeled a freak. His mark on the world would be greater than anything mathematical. His destiny was not that of a prodigy.

That night after his bath and brushing his teeth, Antonio came to bed, and Marie gave him a tight embrace. "I love you so much, Antonio. Would you tell me if there are any other things you see that might be different?"

"Of course, Mommy. I just didn't think I was different than Polly or Alex or any of my classmates. Sister Pauli surprised me."

"What else do you see, Antonio?" Marie asked with concern, wanting to understand. She could tell that Antonio was smiling to release the tension in her face.

"I see what you see when we run, like when you ran with me on the playground yesterday," he answered. "I see curves and the points that emerge on the curves, forming lines and ripples in midair as your body surface, your arms and legs, stream through the air. The lines represent the changes in velocity as you accelerate, creating ripples. I know this now from my experiments with Alex when we were swimming in the water with Javier. Our movement in the air is just like what it looks like moving through water."

Marie answered with another loving hug. She whispered, "Antonio, I want you to promise me something, a very special promise. Can you do that?"

"Yes, Mommy," he said.

"I want you to promise me that you will never tell anyone else what you see."

Antonio looked sad for a moment then he looked into her worried eyes, and his expression grew solemn. "I promise that I will never tell."

"Antonio, all of these visual things will be our little secret for eternity."

"But why mother? Why are you upset?"

"I'm not upset. I'm here to protect you from the fault-finders of the world. The fault-finders will try to separate you from me and your true essence."

Marie paused with tears in her eyes, and Antonio nodded as if he understood. He embraced her, and she felt his cheeks on her bosom, warming her heart. They made a sacred bond with his promise to keep his vision secret forever.

CHAPTER

48

Antonio grew into a handsome lad and a natural leader among the orphan children. He knew everyone and everything about Essence.

Shakespeare's plays, *The Charterhouse of Parma,* and *Anna Karenina,* remained out of reach on the top shelves for the older kids in the school library. The curious Antonio had read them all by the age of ten. He read the encyclopedias too. He confessed it all one night as he and Marie lay together in bed. Marie did not get upset because she understood that he had an insatiable appetite to know and understand everything.

The next morning after waking Antonio she handed him her Bible. "I want you to read Matthew 5, 6, and 7 every day."

He flipped to the section and smiled. "Tolstoy's favorite, the Sermon on the Mount. I will do as you say, every day."

One month later on Marie's birthday, Antonio told his mother he had a big surprise. She smiled at his cute grin and walked with him to the balcony porch. Josephine had made a cake, and Polly and Alex joined to sing and wish her a happy birthday.

After eating a piece of the delicious lemon cake, they enjoyed a glorious sunset, the sky filled with blues, pinks, and violet—Marie's favorite colors. During twilight Marie shared embraces, thanking everyone for remembering her special day. Josephine led Polly and Alex back to the dormitory while

Marie and Antonio continued rocking on the porch until darkness fell.

Marie spent the rest of her birthday awake in bed talking to Antonio. He told Marie he had committed the Sermon on the Mount to memory and changed some of the words. He sat up and gave a recitation as his surprise birthday gift. Marie hugged him for her best birthday gift ever. Antonio pulled away and smiled, and then his face grew serious as he shared his final words.

"Seek ye first the Sentio of Eden, and all will be made available to you."

Marie's mind filled with wonder. Without so much as a suggestion from her or anyone else, Antonio had used Helen's exact words for how to restore humankind's vision of freedom. She tried to disguise her reaction to the mind-blowing revelation: *He is the deliverer. He will free the mind of humankind by restoring Sentio.*

"That is so true, Antonio. I love your version," Marie told him calmly. She wanted to confide with Helen before making a big deal about her observation.

Antonio's eyes grew wide because as always Marie knew he could sense her feelings, whether she wanted him to or not, and he felt her internal excitement. After she kissed him good night, she lay in bed awake the entire night, too excited for sleep.

The next day after school Marie went to Vichy and told Helen what Antonio had said, and the two embraced; they both knew. Antonio would see the world through the consciousness of Eden one day, and he would free man from Cogito existence. Marie thought back to those lonely years during the dig and then the years of prayers, and Helen expressed how proud she was of her and the digging dozen. Marie thanked Helen for allowing her and the sisters to pray. Helen smiled and nodded, saying the prayers had worked and were part of her vision for freedom.

49

Another two years passed. Antonio developed some independence from his mother and became preoccupied with trying to figure everything out: the plumbing and how light bulbs worked. Marie encouraged him. When the children or Sister Phillips had questions or doubts about anything, they came to Marie, and she would find Antonio, who was usually playing in the woods with Alex. But sometimes Marie found him playing with the girls in the chapel.

Marie knew Antonio had a natural attraction for girls, but she did not know that he had become a willing co-conspirator with several of the orphan girls, who enjoyed trying to alter their Sentios. She found out from Josephine one morning while sharing coffee on the screened-in porch. Antonio had assisted several girls in experiments designed to heighten their sensitivity for a true essence life. Marie smiled at Josephine's description until she heard the details.

"Antonio has been exploring sensuality and erotica out of curiosity and for a good reason. He knows that there is something special about intimate touch given or received from another human being that makes his brain feel funny . . . as he described a warm tickling sensation between his eyes. He wants to harness the energy of intimacy," Josephine explained.

Marie did not know how to respond. "Did Antonio tell you that?"

"Yes."

"I'll look into it."

But Marie found the subject awkward and put off addressing it with Antonio. A few weeks later when she was finishing up her lesson plan at the end of the day, Sister Pauli marched Antonio and Polly into the first-grade classroom.

Marie looked up and thought, *Not again.*

Polly looked scared, and Antonio was looking down at his shoes. Marie took a deep breath to calm herself.

Sister Pauli nudged Antonio toward his mother. "Go ahead and tell your mother what you told me."

Polly looked horrified. Antonio would not look into Marie's eyes. She was taken aback by the look on his face and jumped in, "Sister Pauli, what on earth could they have done?"

Letting his words out in a rush of breath, Antonio said, "I was trying to make Polly's head spin by sucking on her budding bosoms." After speaking Antonio darted his eyes at Sister Pauli.

Polly appeared to relax after Antonio's confession. She smiled and acknowledged that her head was indeed spinning when Sister Pauli found them naked in the changing room of the chapel.

"I asked Antonio to do it. I did not mean to hurt anyone," said Polly. She looked at Antonio with sorrow.

Marie was relieved. While this was certainly unsettling news, it was innocent. She wanted to handle the situation on her own and dismissed Sister Pauli.

"Thank you, Sister Pauli. I will take care of Polly and Antonio."

"Well, I should hope so," Sister Pauli huffed. She twirled and marched out of the classroom in a display of authority and disgust.

Once Sister Pauli was out of hearing range, Marie embraced them both. The erotic nature of humans was natural, and she did not want them conditioned to fear intimacy. Marie believed that the male and female forms of the Sentio of Eden should be encouraged and not conditioned.

She had taught Antonio about erotic play. Marie had told him that it was a natural, sensual pleasure of excitement. She knelt down in front of them and explained, "It's okay for you to play erotically, but you need to make sure that it is in private."

Marie rubbed them both on the head and smiled. Polly was as cute as she could be with her red hair and blue eyes.

"Antonio is my Prince of Essence," said Polly as she squinted and wrinkled her freckled-covered face. "He is my Fabrizio and Count Voronsky too," she went on as she took Antonio's hand, waiting to be dismissed.

"You are so cute, Polly," said Marie. "You remind me of myself when I was a girl. Have fun. Go play."

Marie watched the two angels run free, but she wondered why Antonio was quiet. Perhaps he was still upset by Sister Pauli's behavior.

The following day after school, Antonio walked with Marie. He held her hand and confessed that he was no angel. He told her about his erotic self-play and his many different fantasies. He had created sexual fantasies with all of the sisters at Essence including the Reverend Mother. Marie could not help but stiffen when she heard of his desire for her sisters. She tried to hide it. She thanked Antonio for his honesty and assured him she would help him understand his fantasies. She dismissed him to go play, and then she wanted to cry.

Too embarrassed to tell her sisters, she went to the library after dinner where she ran into the four-eyed librarian, Lucy. They had become friends after Antonio's arrival, when Lucy brought her flowers and kept Marie posted about the library reconstruction. Marie felt the weight of something that she did not understand on her shoulders.

"Is something wrong Marie?" asked Lucy.

Marie's resolve crumbled as she embraced Lucy and broke down in tears. She choked out the reason for her distress. Lucy listened with understanding and explained that Antonio's problem was common and that she had helped many mothers find answers in the child's psychology section. She recommended several books for Marie to read, from Freud to Rogers. Marie took the books and gave Lucy a warm embrace. She hurried back to Essence to read and find an explanation and solution for Antonio.

After reading on the subject for several days, Marie took a moment before sleep to suggest to Antonio that he refrain from using the sisters for erotic fantasies and instead think about nature while doing his play for his own excitement. Antonio arched his brow and then turned over to sleep.

In the morning Antonio admitted that he did not understand what Marie meant, so she gave him the books from the library. He read the three books, and after a few days of reflection, he explained that his own concerns and shame had been produced by institutionalization. He disagreed with the books that promoted more institutional thinking. He told Marie that his fantasies were natural and not an evil force driving him toward evil. Marie got upset at first, but then she calmed and decided to take the matter to Helen in Vichy.

Another week passed, and one morning before school Antonio asked his mother what his aunt Helen thought about the matter.

"I have not had a chance to get her opinion."

"How about on Sunday? You can go to Vichy, and I will stay here with Josephine."

"Maybe, we'll see," said Marie. She had been putting off her trip to discuss the embarrassing matter with Helen.

Finally, she gathered courage and went to Vichy on Sunday. She shared the bare minimum needed to gain Helen's opinion without explaining any of the specifics of

Antonio's fantasies. Poulou smiled at her with a twinkle in his eye as if he knew what she was holding back. But he said nothing until Marie finished talking about fantasies and erotic play.

Marie was taken back when both Poulou and Helen agreed with Antonio's perspective. Helen explained that Antonio simply had very sensitive Sentio tracks for a young man, and he needed to keep his tracks from becoming a passion or an addiction that would take away his freedom by imprisoning his Intentio. Variety seemed to be a healthy solution.

"Variety?" asked Marie.

"Yes," said Helen, and Poulou concurred with her recommendation.

She embraced them both and left.

Odd, that they recommended variety, Marie contemplated on the bus ride back to Essence. When she walked into the Villa, Antonio was waiting for her in the foyer. She explained to him what Helen and Poulou had said. Antonio smiled and shared a warm embrace.

"I knew they would agree with me, Mother. They understand the experience of being in the world," said Antonio.

The matter was the first time Antonio had argued with Marie. He hugged her again and thanked her for helping him. She was proud he had held fast to his position. Antonio said he did not understand why someone who wrote a book with such scant evidence should have the power to dictate how others should feel, act, and think. Antonio was becoming his own man, and Marie sensed he was ready to lead others.

Later that night after sunset, she and Antonio shared their most profound thoughts about existence and essence. Antonio's bed was next to Marie's. He could roll over and hug her at any time, and she could do the same. But this night, they lay awake on their separate beds and talked after enjoying a glorious sunset.

The twelve-year-old Antonio spoke up with his concerns about others dictating to him. "Life is a gift to you and me. What right does anyone have over another? My compass and yours are as good as anyone's. We are all made to be free."

"Yes, Antonio, I agree," replied Marie. "But there is this concept called the greater good. We must learn to live together. Some older institutionalized guys created ethics and laws for the greater good without any idea of greater freedom or the compass. Instead they prepared a social contract so that everyone would feel secure after giving up their liberty, but greedy, self-centered leaders figured a way around the contract and used the contract to make others conform to their beliefs and desires."

"You mean like the existentialists? I am an intentialist like Aunt Helen," Antonio replied.

"I know that you are, darling. The existentialists over-looked the compass that Helen found. I think that the existentialists were fed up with institutionalized man, and they just wanted freedom. Even if in their haste they did not find freedom, they tried. Many of them were victims of World War II. I do not blame them per se."

"What is the greater good anyway?" Antonio asked.

"The greater good has to start with the *one* before the *we*," Marie answered.

"I agree, Mother, about the one being priority. Otherwise we become slaves of our own we existence, we of yesterday, today, and tomorrow. Someone in power can use we against the one who disagrees to win the argument, but it may not be the truth. Only the one can see the vision for freedom through Sentio. Freedom cannot be seen through individual or collective cogito, only through an individual's Sentio."

"You will find that some people believe they know what the greater good is for you, me, and everyone. I believe that one needs the Sentio of Eden to find greater freedom for all.

Whatever I can do for others to help them achieve the Sentio of Eden is for the greater good."

After Marie stopped speaking, Antonio looked at her and confessed, "I know that I will be the deliverer and free humankind from Cogito existence."

He was still. His eyes were clear and bright and his face set, his strength and promise impossible to ignore. Marie felt a warmth in her chest and smiled; it was the same warm, committed feeling she'd experienced the night she became Antonio's mother. Her Sentio understanding transcended her Cogito. Antonio knew his destiny and was ready to embrace it.

Marie encouraged Antonio to become a leader of freedom after that fateful discussion. Each night before bedtime, she accompanied him to visit the dormitory. He told stories to the little children, which he had learned from Sister Josephine. He gave them hope for love on their journey to greater freedom. Sometimes as many as ten children would gather and listen to his every word. Then he would visit the older children, explaining to them one at a time what they would need for a life of freedom. He always emphasized that they would need to allow their attention to dwell in Sentio when not attending to the demands of school or work.

"Always return your attention to your essence. Stay Sentio!" he said with confidence and authority as he finished.

The children nodded in agreement.

He gave them hope and love. It was his version of doing something for the greater good. Marie smiled and nodded at his words. She was extremely proud of him.

Most early evenings after dinner, Antonio would sit and rock on the porch with Marie, Polly, and Alex while they waited for the sunset, a thunderstorm, or just rain. But the sunset was the most important experience for Antonio. Marie knew that he wanted to experience Aunt Helen's compass experience.

One cloudy summer night, Antonio and Marie were all alone after twilight. He commented, "I love to watch the mountaintops disappear at night because I know they are still there. I can still sense them in my Sentio even though I can't see them."

Marie nodded. "Someday the mountains will disappear completely."

"But they will remain forever in my Sentio reflections."

"You are right, my love."

Antonio smiled at her and asked about the compass. He said he wanted to create his own compass for keep, but Marie reassured him that it was not for keeping. Even though Marie had not experienced the compass herself, she knew what the experience entailed from her years of studying Helen's philosophy.

"Your Sentio will become dull at times. You will have to renew your sensitivity to maintain a vision for freedom," said Marie.

"Let me see if I understand. Your consciousness of nature allows you to have a vision for freedom when life is confusing and without meaning?" asked Antonio.

"Yes, it does," said Marie.

Antonio smiled and asked another question.

"What is on top of the mountain, mother?" he asked. "I mean the mountain of freedom."

"Well . . . more freedom. Someday, you will jump through the portal on top into eternity," Marie explained, "and you will experience the ecstasy of infinity."

"You mean my finitude day?"

Marie did not want to consider such a sad thought. She knew that it would disturb him as well, so she reminded Antonio of Helen's Compass of Freedom experience to redirect his attention.

"Remember the Sentio and Cogito blend for your sunset experience as given to you by Aunt Helen. If your consciousness is of Eden, then Helen's guided experience might reveal the compass."

"But Mother, how can I be sure that my Sentio is capable of experiencing Eden?"

"You will know by your sensitivity and the powerful Intentio that emerges and runs through your mind when you close your eyes. You will know."

Antonio was quick to identify the most important matter of her discussion. "How can I renew my sensitivity?" he asked.

The cute, thirteen-year-old, blue-eyed, curly-head was so very sensitive. Marie could not imagine Antonio needing to worry about renewing his sensitivity. It was everything she could do to keep a straight face with her answer.

"Love is the only way. But the love that I speak of is not easy to find. There are many kinds of love. The Greek philosophers described four types of love: *agape*, *philia*, *storge*, and *eros*. But these alone will not be enough to renew your sensitivity. Many experiences will appear to be the right love. But when love increases your sensitivity to experience the Sentio of Eden, then you will know that it is the right love."

"That sounds like a strange type of love, Mother," said Antonio.

"Yes, Antonio, it is strange love," Marie agreed. "It is what Helen and the Sisters of Freedom have dedicated their lives to give freely to the orphaned children of the world."

"Well, your love is strange, Mother. Alex, Polly, and I are proof."

"Yes, you are proof. And I am proof of your strange love," Marie said, then she thought of when Helen first discovered the special love. Helen had observed the orphans hugging the fishermen from Pierre and noted that the fishermen experienced a heightened sensitivity during the Saturday night sunset celebrations at Essence.

"Aunt Helen discovered strange love," said Marie.

"There will be times when mundane existence will take you away from your essence. Everyone in life needs strange love to renew their sensitivity."

Antonio nodded. "So will I need to find and experience strange love for the rest of my life."

"Yes. When you leave Essence, finding strange love will be essential for maintaining your consciousness of nature and a vision of freedom." Marie stretched. It was getting late and beginning to sprinkle. "We need to get to bed. You and Alex have to gather the fish at Paradise for the sunset dinner tomorrow. Come along."

Marie pulled Antonio up from his rocking chair into a big embrace. She experienced the most freeing love from his embraces. They walked down the steps and ran to the villa holding hands as it began to rain.

51

"**Wow, the water is** swift today," Alex commented.

"It rained late last night," Antonio reminded him, as they patrolled for fly fishermen. They were collecting fish for the Saturday night café dinner at Essence.

"Hey, there is a fisherman on the ground between those rocks!" Alex exclaimed. "He looks hurt."

Antonio followed close behind Alex, walking cautiously over the rocks and through the shallow rapids. When they reached the fisherman, he appeared to be unconscious and was face down close to the water.

"He must have slipped and struck his head," said Antonio as he and Alex dragged the man away from the water. They rolled the man over. "It's Javier!"

"Oh no!" cried Alex. He splashed cold water on Javier's face in an attempt to revive him.

"Wake up, Javier! Wake up! Please wake up!" Desperation crept into Antonio's voice. Javier mumbled groggily, but his eyes remained closed. "We need to get him to my mother at Essence."

Antonio and Alex struggled to help Javier stand by grabbing him around the waist.

"He has muscles all over," Alex grunted.

"He's like a rock," murmured Antonio.

Then Javier's brain cleared momentarily, and he muttered, "What happened?"

"Javier! Javier!" Alex shouted. Javier closed his eyes without reacting to his shouts but kept staggering forward. "I don't think that he knows his name. He is as lost as a baby lamb."

Antonio was holding Javier's back as best he could to keep him from falling. Alex quickly gathered Javier's tackle and stood underneath his arms while he and Antonio walked him to a shady place on a ledge jutting over the stream.

"Alex, go get Marcel," Antonio said. "We'll need him to carry Javier back to Essence."

Alex hurried off, and Antonio moved Javier closer to the ledge and then looked for some logs, thinking perhaps he could roll Javier onto Marcel from the ledge. He found two knotted logs and dragged them next to Javier and waited for Alex to return.

Javier remained on his back with his arms and legs spread out on the ground. Antonio rubbed his chest to see if he would wake up, but it was no use. After about twenty minutes, Antonio heard Alex's voice in the distance, stood up, and saw Alex leading Marcel with an apple in his hand.

Antonio yelled, "Over here."

Alex guided Marcel through the shallow rapids, nudging the mule closer to where Javier lay. Alex tied Marcel to a rock and went to help Antonio. They tried to roll Javier, but the logs would not turn. "Damn these knots," said Antonio. "This is not going to work."

He and Alex each grabbed a leg and dragged Javier to the edge. Alex got Marcel and walked the mule into the pool of water beneath. While Alex steadied Marcel, Antonio rolled Javier's limp body onto the mule. Marcel gave a couple of kicks and tried to buck as Javier's body straddled its back.

"It's okay . . . it's okay, boy." Alex calmed the mule, patting his face and holding the reins tight. Then he walked

Marcel and Javier out through the shallow water. Antonio jumped down and used his hands as a stirrup and lifted Alex up onto Marcel behind Javier to keep him from sliding off. Antonio pulled on Javier's leg so that he was balanced on Marcel's back.

Antonio took the reins and began the long journey up the steep mountain. It was slow going for Marcel. Antonio led him around the steep incline through the loose rocks and then changed course to a flatter, more solid but longer way. Antonio knew that with Javier's current state they couldn't risk Marcel stumbling.

By the time they made it to Essence, Javier was more responsive. Antonio rubbed Marcel's face, praising him for his hard work and tied him on the porch steps. Then the boys slid Javier down, and he landed on his feet. While he was somewhat awake, he still couldn't walk on his own. Antonio and Alex acted like human crutches as they marched him one foot in front of the other into the school building and to the infirmary.

Once inside, Javier flopped onto the bed. Antonio smiled at Alex. "Good work."

Alex looked at Javier. "He is a lot longer than I thought."

"Stay here, Alex, I'm going to get my mother." Antonio ran through the hall and out the door.

Over in the chapel, Marie was busy preparing for the fish dinner celebration with Sister Celia when Antonio interrupted.

"Mom, please come quick. Javier's hurt. He needs you. He is in the infirmary."

Marie dropped what she was doing and ran behind Antonio to the school building and down the long hallway, tracked with mud. Inside the infirmary she found Alex holding Javier's arm to keep it from hitting the floor. Javier had almost rolled off the bed. Marie and Antonio pulled him back squarely onto the mattress.

Marie established that Javier showed some signs of con-sciousness. Periodically he would open his eyes and mumble some nonsense then flail his arms and legs in confusion. But his breathing was regular.

She turned toward Antonio. "What happened to Javier?"

Antonio began to explain the ordeal, and Alex con-firmed with excited nods. Marie listened to enough of the story to understand.

She instructed Antonio, "I need you and Alex to go get Dr. Frankl. Bring him here as quickly as you can."

"Sorry we did not get the fish for the dinner," said Alex.

"That's okay, darling."

The boys departed, running down the hallway. Marie took a wet washcloth and covered the bump on Javier's head. She cleaned up the room and took off Javier's boots. She suspected that his drinking problem still had a hold of his Intentio. She wanted him whole again and free.

It only took twenty minutes for Dr. Frankl to arrive with Antonio and Alex in tow. He lifted the wet cloth on Javier's forehead, and Marie could see from the increased swelling that Javier had suffered a severe blow to his head. His condition was serious. Dr. Frankl asked Marie to take the boys outside. She grabbed Alex and Antonio's hands and led them out into the hallway, where they waited with mount-ing tension.

Dr. Frankl emerged wiping his hands on a towel, looking concerned. "He will need to rest without any stimulation. We can't move him now. It is too dangerous. Any fluctuation of his blood pressure could be catastrophic. I will be around tomorrow." He wrote down his instructions and handed them to Marie.

Please keep his head at thirty degrees. Bed rest, no exertion, no stimulation, lights, or sound until he regains consciousness. Keep the room cool. Feed him soup and broth when he regains consciousness.

Marie read the instructions. "Thank you, Dr. Frankl. Antonio can hook up Marcel and take you back into town."

"Thanks, but the walk will do me good. Alex and Antonio are two fine young men. Sister Marie, you and your outfit are to be commended. Every time I see Antonio I think about you and that bitter cold, December night."

Marie smiled, and the two boys beamed under Dr. Frankl's praise. But they remained concerned because he had not said Javier would be okay.

"Call me for any concerns," Dr. Frankl said.

"Thank you. We'll see you tomorrow." Marie bowed her head politely.

She left Antonio in charge at the infirmary. She went to explain the situation to the Reverend Mother. Mary Elizabeth was upset to hear of Javier's accident and uncertain condition. She gave Marie permission to cancel the fish dinner and to shut down the big bell for the next three days. Marie spread the news to Josephine and Sister Phillips.

She hurried back to the infirmary and found Antonio and Alex sitting silently by Javier's bed in the dark. They were like two angels watching over him.

Marie whispered, "You did a great thing. I love you both."

They sat together listening to Javier's regular breathing. After a couple of hours, Marie suggested the boys should get dinner and some rest. She would take the first night's watch. She told Antonio that he, Alex, and Polly could split up shifts to watch Javier starting the next day. The excited boys ran to tell Polly.

52

The next morning Polly arrived early for her shift. She opened the door and awoke Marie, who had slept stretched out on two chairs. Marie rubbed the sleep from her eyes. She stood and pulled back the curtains and lifted the shades briefly to look at Javier in the sunlight then she pulled them closed so he wouldn't be overstimulated.

"He needs a shave and a bath," Marie commented.

"Can I help, please?" asked Polly.

"Of course. Fill the basin with some warm water in the sink across the hall."

Marie pulled off Javier's socks, shirt, pants, and shorts, keeping him covered with a sheet. Polly returned with the basin filled with warm water, a lamb's cloth, and a bar of soap. Marie used the lamb's cloth and began washing his chest and his arms with minimal stimulation. She carefully washed and dried him from head to toe. Then Marie rolled Javier toward Polly to wash his back. The sheet fell onto the floor, exposing Javier.

"Oh my, is that what a full-grown man looks like?" asked Polly with incredulity. She was smiling with the white visible in her eyes.

Marie tried not to make it a big deal. "Yes, man is made to complement a woman for creation and pleasure. His essence is for her essence and vice versa as designed by nature," Marie explained, unsure of herself. She was more nervous about how Polly would receive her words than her seeing Javier's anatomy.

"Well, I believe that Javier could be a lot of pleasure for someone," Polly commented with a twinkle in her eye.

Marie managed to gather herself without laughing. "Let's cover Javier with the sheet. Polly, could you hand me his pillows so that we can prop up his head?"

The sheet secured, Polly fetched the pillows. Marie repositioned Javier to thirty degrees and left to empty the basin, leaving Polly to stand guard. On Marie's return, Javier awoke with a start and mumbled something to Polly.

"It's okay, Mister Javier. Sister Marie is saving you for pleasure. I mean she is going to shave you later."

"Where am I?" Javier asked in his baritone voice. He pulled the sheet up, covering his bare chest.

Marie approached and put her hands on his to reassure him. She showed him with a hand mirror the large swelling on his forehead. Javier struggled to see, sighed, and fell back asleep.

"I'll shave him later," Marie decided.

"I guess he's getting better."

Now that Javier was sleeping, Marie left to get some rest, leaving Polly to keep watch for the day shift. "Come and get me if you have any questions. Sister Phillips will check on you later."

Marie reported to Mary Elizabeth and then stretched out and fell asleep on her own bed. She dreamed of Javier. Later that night when she returned for her shift Javier's eyes were open. Polly had been joined by Sister Phillips, who had given Javier a shave. No more stubble. He seemed calm and somewhat aware of his surroundings. He did indeed seem to be getting better.

With Marie's arrival, Sister Phillips took Polly to the dormitory. Then Antonio and Alex came by to check on

Javier. They were happy to see him awake; their excitement overflowed through their voices while telling Javier what had happened. Javier talked for a moment then grabbed his head. Marie realized that it was too much stimulation for him. She sent the boys to check on Marcel and to get some rest.

An hour passed and Javier fell asleep. He turned and tossed and seemed restless. Marie poured soup from her thermos and whispered for him to awake. The smell of soup seemed to stir him. He opened his eyes, and she began spoon-feeding him. He smiled and fixed his gaze on her. He reached and touched her cheek. Marie paused, holding the broth-filled spoon still, frozen in time. It was as if Javier had touched her mind and heart at the same time that he stroked her cheek with his fingertips. Marie felt the tingling sensation of his warm caress between her eyes and her heart pounded. She forgot to breathe for what felt like forever then returned the spoon to the cup and stared into his big blue eyes.

"I just wanted to make sure that you were real," he said. "Your veil reminded me of my dream. I thought that you were an angel."

Marie smiled and said his guardian angels were Antonio and Alex. She told him the whole story from the boys finding him on the rocks up to that moment. They talked all night long.

The next morning, Marie excitedly chirped about Javier's progress to Polly when she came to relieve her. Polly smiled, and Marie could see that Polly knew that she was smitten with Javier.

There was a knock on the door. Dr. Frankl stepped in so Marie and Polly stepped out. When Dr. Frankl finished his examination, he came out of the infirmary and was happy to report that Javier was no longer in crisis. But he still needed to stay quiet for two more days.

53

Antonio acted differently toward Marie as he, Polly, and Alex rocked with her on the balcony porch the following night. Marie figured that Polly had suggested to him that she and Javier were lovebirds.

"Mother, why can you not marry or have children like me?" he asked.

"Well, Antonio, I have chosen to marry God."

"Yes, Mother, but God is not the marrying kind. You need strange love too."

"My darling. You give me strange love every day."

"But someday I will have to leave Essence."

"Sister Marie, Antonio is right," Polly jumped in, "You and Javier are meant to be. This accident was no accident." She then added, "The Sisters of Freedom do not take a vow of celibacy. Sister Josephine told me."

Marie's face blushed after Polly's comments, and then Alex pointed at the beautiful violet hues above the purple clouds. Marie smiled at Alex and focused on the horizon sky. Polly was right about the vow of celibacy, but Marie had never intended to marry. The children's brazen insight into her connection with Javier was both unsettling and exciting. She let the conversation die as they watched the sunlight fade into twilight.

Javier improved over the next two days and then went

back to his place at Paradise. The following Saturday he returned to Essence with gifts and flowers for the children. He shared his gratitude with the Reverend Mother and all of the sisters and stayed for dinner.

During dinner Javier asked Marie to join him for a walk. He said that he had something very important that he wanted to tell her. She agreed and then smiled at how Antonio and Alex's faces lit up. As she and Javier left for a walk, she saw the boys run into the woods. They followed her and Javier, hiding and watching from a distance. They thought they were hidden, but Marie could see them. After Javier took her hand, she and Javier walked farther up the mountain. She quickly forgot all about the boys spying on them.

She enjoyed Javier's warmth as they held hands and shared childlike grins. She could tell that he wanted more than Paradise had to offer. He wanted her, but she needed to know more about his intentions. The most important things in her life right now were Antonio and the children at Essence.

"Marie, I want—" He was interrupted by the sound of a stick breaking.

Marie smiled and enjoyed his nervous blue eyes. "We are not alone."

"I kind of figured that," Javier said, and looked over at a moving tree branch.

"Why don't you spend the week here at Essence? The children love you," Marie suggested. "I'll fix up the infirmary."

"Well, if it means I'll get to see more of you, then I'll do it," he said, and looked again toward the swaying branches.

Marie grinned and lifted her voice to the trees. "We are leaving if anyone wants to know." They heard footsteps running through the bushes.

Javier and Marie walked down the mountain holding hands. When they got back to Essence, Marie fixed up the infirmary, changed the sheets, and put a fan in the window. All alone, she shared a tender exchange with her fingertips on Javier's lips. He embraced her with a strength that she had never felt before. And she enjoyed being held by him as they shared a kiss. She knew that he wanted more. When he released her from his embrace, Marie said goodnight. But at the door she looked over her shoulder. He looked so handsome with his boyish grin, approaching her. She turned and they embraced once more. She hesitated for a moment, smiled, and left.

From the balcony porch Antonio, Polly, and Alex watched Marie skip back to her villa.

Polly whispered, "Lovebirds."

"*Shh!*" said Antonio.

Alex shook his head. "This looks bad Antonio."

Antonio smiled. "No, this is good if Javier has the right intention."

"I agree," said Polly.

"My mother looks happy. Let's go see if Javier looks happy."

Alex and Antonio snuck down the stairs of the school building like spies, crawling their way down the hallway toward the infirmary. Meanwhile, Polly went to get some water and walked past them. Holding a pitcher full of water, she knocked on the door to the infirmary.

The door opened. "Hey, Mr. Javier. Would you like some ice-cold water?"

"Thank you sweetheart." He smiled and took the water. "What are you doing here?"

"I saw you and Sister Marie, and I wanted to say hello. I have to go. Good to see you."

"Thanks," Javier said.

Polly smiled again as he shut the door, then she turned, and walked toward Antonio and Alex, lying on the floor. "Javier looks happy too."

"Thanks Polly. Good work," Alex said, getting up from the floor.

Antonio furrowed his brow. "Polly, keep an eye on Javier."

"I will," she grinned.

Antonio wanted to discuss some private matters about Javier with Alex, so they left Polly to play on the swings while he discussed Javier's alcohol history. He was concerned because he understood that alcoholics often relapsed.

"The self-created passion for alcohol imprisons your Intentio," Antonio said. "Aunt Helen and Uncle Poulou explained the disorder to me. It's hard to free your Intentio once you are addicted."

"I know," Alex said. "Let's give Javier a chance. Maybe we can help set him free."

"Maybe," Antonio smiled. "I am pulling for him."

"Me too," said Alex.

The following night, Polly ran up the stairs and found Antonio rocking on the porch in early darkness. The extra-large full moon overhead shone directly over Andorra.

"Antonio, they are sitting near the bluff," exclaimed Polly.

"Who is?"

"Marie and Javier. Come on, hurry! They're smooching near the bluff."

Antonio raced down the steps and ran ahead of Polly to see. He had a weird feeling that was both happy and embarrassed that his mother would do such a thing. Running through the woods in the moonlight, he stopped just in time to go unnoticed. He dove behind a bush and rolled. He raised his head and saw Marie and Javier sitting on the big rock by the bluff, kissing in the moonlight. Polly eased up behind him, and she was breathing loud.

"*Shh!*" Antonio put his finger to his lips.

"They have been there since sunset," Polly whispered. "It's so romantic."

Polly and Antonio were huddled close together, watching from behind two fir trees. Antonio admonished Polly as her face almost touched his.

"Be still, Polly. They've stopped kissing."

Marie and Javier remained locked in a tight embrace. Antonio tried to keep Polly quiet. A hooting owl landed just above them on a branch and startled Polly. He had to lie on top of her and place his hand on her mouth to prevent her from screaming. Javier looked in the direction of their noise, but he didn't see them.

Then Javier spoke softly in Marie's ear, and Antonio and Polly could just barely make out his words.

"Marie, you know before my fall that I was headed for an alcohol relapse. Alcohol and drugs are imposters for true essence. When I was drinking, I knew everything. I was connected to all the wrong things. It was the wrong connectivity. I feel so free here with you tonight." His eyes beamed as he stared down at Marie's angelic face.

"I know what you're feeling," she said. "I too was headed toward oblivion. Before Antonio came into my life, I was hitting the brandy four times per day. When I started nursing him something happened, and I no longer needed my Napoleon brandy."

Hearing how Antonio had helped Marie stop drinking, Polly gave Antonio a sweet smile, making him blush.

Javier caressed Marie's arms with his large, gentle hands. He professed that she was the reason for his newfound sensitivity and made his intentions clear. "I would like to have a relationship with you and build a gymnasium for ball play at Essence and serve as a coach for the children. I have a plan for a grand improvement, and I want to be with you, Marie, to share our sensitivity."

Marie felt her entire body fill with a tingling sensation she had never known before. She knew that she was meant to say yes to Javier and move forward in life with him. She wanted to take the risk. She looked into his eyes, and they reminded her of Antonio's beautiful blue eyes. She expressed her feelings.

"I love you, Javier. You are just what our family needs: someone with newfound sensitivity. You see, it is difficult to renew sensitivity living in mundane existence. Even at Essence existence can become mundane. I . . . we need someone like you to push us to greater heights of sensitivity."

They embraced and kissed once more. They rolled and laughed then Marie helped Javier stand. She gave him another kiss then skipped away toward #4.

Antonio and Polly waited until Javier walked toward the infirmary before speaking.

"Sensitivity? Hmm . . . ," Polly mused. "He wants to share sensitivity."

"Yes, I think I understand," Antonio said, pursing his lips.

The next day, Marie told Antonio and Polly about the gym. They reacted to the news as if it was a surprise and began spreading the word about Javier's plan to the other children. Antonio realized Javier's intentions brought new life, a rejuvenated feeling to the beings at Essence, and his physical presence had generated excitement; his masculine charm mesmerized the sisters and children.

Javier got the royal treatment during dinner in the chapel the night after Marie had made the announcement about the gymnasium. Alex and Antonio kept a close eye on Javier, making sure he did not drink any brandy. Antonio whispered to Alex that they needed to remain skeptical of Javier because of his alcohol history, just in case. Alex agreed.

Antonio and Alex noticed no one else seemed concerned about Javier's history. The little girls rubbed his afternoon stubble and begged to hear his baritone voice. After dinner Javier sat on the terrace and listened to the children sing and then joined their songs with his deep and powerful voice.

Even Marie sat in Javier's lap and bounced on his knee before sunset, completely carefree.

The next night Marie, Antonio, Polly, and Alex stood on the terrace watching Javier sing with the children. Polly commented, "He has charm."

"I agree. He has muscles too," murmured Sister Phillips, who had walked up next to Marie.

They watched the children climb on Javier who enjoyed the children with laughter as he rolled them over his back and shoulders in play.

"I think I love him," Marie said and looked at Polly. "I have always loved him."

Polly nodded and smiled, agreeing with Marie.

Antonio looked surprised but didn't say a word. He glanced slyly at Alex, who nodded. Antonio and Alex had devised a plan to explore Javier's intentions.

The following day Javier watched with interest from the balcony porch as Antonio and Alex prepared for a fishing trip. They dug up some worms and gathered their long bamboo canes with fish line, hooks, soft lead, and corks. Javier met Marie after breakfast in the chapel and asked her to fix them a picnic lunch. The boys had invited him to go fishing with them. Marie gave Javier a curious look and pulled him into the kitchen and talked while she made sandwiches.

"I would love to hear the questions they are going to ask you."

Javier smiled. "I'm honored and proud to be their guest. They're taking me to their secret pond."

Marie looked Javier in the eyes. "You are special. I've never been to their secret pond."

"Let's go, Javier," yelled Antonio.

"Hurry up," said Alex.

Polly came rushing into the kitchen with some fresh grapes from the garden, washed them under the faucet, and packed them in the basket. Javier grabbed the basket and escorted Marie and Polly out of the chapel. All three men got hugs from Marie and Polly.

Antonio turned and motioned with his arm. "Follow me." He led the way into the thick pine forest behind the playground. Javier followed behind Alex as they walked toward the famous secret pond on the other side of the mountain. They hiked for about thirty minutes in near silence before coming to a clearing. The hidden mountain pond arose beneath a natural rock wall, and the still green water was well camouflaged by ferns, moss, and willow trees. On their right, a twenty-foot waterfall fed a nearby stream. Javier found some shade and a nice rock for their basket while the boys loaded their hooks with worms. Antonio handed Javier his cane pole, and they dropped their lines for fishing.

The boys grinned at Javier's smile.

"Thanks fellows; this is a beautiful place," he said.

"It's our secret," said Alex.

"Don't worry. I'll never tell. Besides, I'm not sure I could find this place by myself," said Javier.

Antonio jumped right in once Javier settled into his spot. "What do you mean about sensitivity and my mother?"

Javier was taken aback by the direct question. At first he didn't understand where Antonio had heard him speak of sensitivity. Then it dawned on him. *Ah, the boys overheard my talk with Marie.* He leaned back after creating a stand for his pole. He was about to answer when Alex interjected.

"Here's what I understand: if you grow old and numb to things like the death of a little baby bird who falls from his nest, then you might not think of baby birds the same way."

Javier nodded and exhaled deeply. "Well, Antonio, you and Alex have experienced heightened sensitivity. So you have experienced the right sensitivity. And you know that it's a fleeting thing. No one can hold on to it for very long. So you must renew sensitivity to continue experiencing it."

"How about my mother? Does she help your sensitivity?" asked Antonio.

"Men and women are built to stimulate each other's sensitivity in some respects. But in other respects, a man and woman can also destroy one another's sensitivity," Javier explained.

"Why is that?" asked Alex.

"I do not know. I just know by experience."

"So does that mean you don't want to marry Sister Marie?" asked Alex.

"It is not like that, Alex." Javier knew the reason for the trip. The boys wanted to know if he intended to marry Marie. Javier was not used to being questioned about such delicate matters, but he knew this conversation was important, so he searched for the right words.

"I just don't want us to grow numb in married life. Life is a challenge to overcome the repetition of mundane things. The only way to overcome feeling angry or numb is to rejuvenate your Sentio sensitivity. We all need sensitivity to experience our consciousness of nature and our vision for freedom. My alcohol abuse numbed me to the experience. I lost my way earlier in my life and then again when I fell and struck my head. You two saved me."

The boy's faces beamed with joy. Alex placed his pole in a forked branch that he had stuck into the ground, stood tall, and looked out over the pond. "I know. It's like when new orphans are brought to Essence. It's always the same. But I always gain from being around them when they discover that we care and understand. We give the same love and intimate hugs that we were given. Like perfect strangers, we find sensitivity in knowing and loving each other."

"Sometimes when little orphan girls are brought to Essence, I can see in their eyes a desire for human sensitivity and recognition, and they seem special to me for that reason," Antonio said quietly. "Sometimes it feels as if there is a little man in my brain who wants to hug them and tell them that everything will be okay."

Javier sat up tall between the two thirteen-year-olds. He looked from one to the other, struck by their insight into subjects that were beyond their years. He pulled them into a group hug and then reached to catch a tear rolling down his cheek.

"Antonio, you and Alex are growing into special men who will be great Sentio leaders."

"Why do you say that Javier?" asked Alex.

Before Javier could answer, Alex grabbed his fishing pole with excitement, tugged as the tip of the pole curled, and lifted his cork out of the water. A large bream was hooked through the gill. He had caught the first fish.

"Here, let me unhook him," offered Javier. He grabbed the fish with his large hands and pulled the hook out. "He is about a half pound. Nice catch, Alex!" He threw the fish back into the pond.

Alex was proud and modest. "I got lucky."

"Good one," Antonio congratulated Alex.

When the excitement died down, Alex repeated his question to Javier. "Why do you say that we will be great Sentio leaders?"

"I say that because you boys already know how to find strange love," Javier answered. "Marie told me all about it. It is the most important thing for survival in the world. Believe me. You will need to be able to find strange love to maintain your sensitivity and stay on the true essence highway. I failed in that venture. I thought that I was well prepared, but I did not know about the love shared for freedom."

Alex threaded a big worm on his hook and lifted his line back into the water. As soon as his cork hit the water, he yelled, "I got another one!"

Javier jumped up to help Alex secure his second catch. He grabbed the wiggling fish in midair. "This one is a little bigger than your first," Javier smiled and rubbed Alex's head.

Alex held up his fish for Antonio to see before throwing it back into the water. Antonio gave little attention to the second catch. He seemed preoccupied.

"I know what you are saying, Javier," Antonio began, "but to find strange love you must stay genuine, truthful, and honest. Any little orphan girl can tell if you're trying to take advantage. She will become numb to you quicker than a fly fisherman setting his hook. You must be vulnerable and expose your willingness and desire to share sensitivity. The orphan girls must see the innocence in your heart, or they will not give you strange love."

"Antonio, you are too wise," Javier responded with awe and respect towards the young boy. "You understand strange love better than anyone. Alex, listen to what your brother is saying. And remember fellows, after you become acquainted with a strange lover, you must be aware that over time she will likewise need to renew her sensitivity. Otherwise, she will blame you for her troubles. It is why divorce is epidemic. When you lose your sensitivity you want to blame someone. Your strange love partner is the easiest person to blame."

"I see," Alex said. "We all must keep finding strange love to maintain sensitivity."

"But what about marriage?" Antonio asked.

Javier shook his head. "I do not have an answer."

Antonio lamented, "Aunt Helen doesn't either."

Javier added, "But if there was a way to measure sensitivity, then I think that a married couple would do well to keep their levels as high as possible for the keeping of Sentio and the vision for freedom. You see, over time most of us become numb to one another. The phenomenon of loss of strangeness sets in as repetition destroys our sensitivity." Javier looked around for the lunch basket.

"When I study at the university, I am going to discover a way to save your marriage, Javier," promised Antonio. "Do not worry."

Javier laughed, patting him on the head. "I'm not even married yet."

"I know, but it can happen so fast. I'll tell my mother too."

Javier gathered some food out of the basket. He passed a meat sandwich to both boys and pulled one out for himself. "Marie makes great sandwiches." He took a bite and talked with his mouth half full.

"Fellows, what we talk about has to remain here. The women may not understand our talk about their role in maintaining our sensitivity. What we say must remain our secret. Can everyone agree?"

Antonio and Alex both nodded as they continued chewing in delight.

CHAPTER

55

A year passed, and Javier continued living in the infirmary while he oversaw the builders from Catalan erect the gymnasium. By midsummer the framing neared completion, but the structure still lacked a permanent roof. Marie and Antonio paid a visit to Javier near the construction site behind the play area. It was a beautiful morning, and Javier and Sergio were talking and pointing. Marie could tell that Javier was excited.

Antonio threw a soccer ball at Sergio, and the two began playing while Javier walked over and embraced Marie. She told him how proud she was and what a wonderful thing he had done for Essence. They gazed at the closed-in structure with its roof of tar paper over plywood.

Marie followed Javier inside the gym, and he showed her the smooth, shiny pine boards for the gym floor.

"Beautiful," Marie said, and found Javier's smiling eyes.

"Just wait until you see what I have in mind for the roof," he said.

Javier went on to explain he would be gone for a couple of days. He was going to Barcelona to see about some refurbished tile for the roof.

"Hey Javier, this is going to be amazing, an indoor ball court," said Antonio, stepping inside the gym.

Javier reached over and embraced Antonio. "Thank you."

Antonio wrestled him in play and pulled up on Javier's shoulders and whispered in his ear. Marie overheard him say that he, Alex, and Polly were planning a surprise for her twentieth anniversary as a Sister of Freedom. Marie walked over and pulled Antonio down from Javier's back.

"Stop that! Someone is going to get hurt," she said. Antonio shook his head to differ and ran outside to get his soccer ball.

Javier gave a smile and then a kiss to Marie. He pulled back and whispered sensually, into Marie's ear, "Happy anniversary."

His words tickled and created a warm feeling in her chest. She wanted Javier to hold her and gave him a look of yearning. He gave her the embrace she wanted but not as long as she wanted. It was getting late, and she knew he needed to get on the road. Javier gave Marie a little kiss.

"See you in a couple of days," he said in a soft voice, turned, and waved at Antonio and Sergio.

"Goodbye, I love you," Marie cried.

Later that day on the playground, Antonio and Alex were freeing June bugs that someone had tied to the swings with sewing thread. Marie approached holding Polly's hand and overheard Antonio.

"Remember what I told you. Act surprised when my mother mentions her anniversary."

Alex nodded.

"Let's all go sit on the porch and watch the sunset," Marie called out.

"Just a minute, Mother," Antonio yelled back.

They succeeded in releasing the bugs then ran around Marie and Polly and up the steps, jumping into the rocking chairs.

"That was kind of you boys, to free God's anxious little creatures," Marie praised them and followed Polly to a chair.

"Perhaps that will be our theme tonight, our talking points, after sunset."

"Polly, be still." Antonio moved closer and smacked Polly's arm.

"Ouch!"

"I missed him!" lamented Antonio as the green fly flew away.

Marie reconsidered her talking points as all four rocking chairs moved to-and-fro in asynchrony.

"Never look down into the abyss. Use denial appropriately." Marie smiled, looking forward to the discussion.

"How odd our topics will be," Alex said. "But interesting."

The rocking slowed as the horizon began to glow on the evening's sunset stage. The to-and-fro of the chairs gradually achieved harmony, a single fused beat as the wood slats grooved the cedar floor. A slight breeze blew, and white, wispy clouds—fine brush strokes—appeared high above on the canvas sky. Then the master painted with broad strokes on the purple canvas above the mountaintops, brilliant shades of orange, yellow, and pink.

"I will always remember this sunset," said Polly. "The scent of the fresh cut pine trees near the gymnasium will serve as my reminder."

"I just want to enjoy the experience through my pre-reflective Sentio," commented Antonio.

Marie sat up tall before speaking. "Tonight is an anniversary of sorts for me. Twenty years ago I fell into the abyss of despair."

Antonio reached into his pocket and pulled out a small piece of paper, unfolded it, and held it out for his mother to see. He grinned. It was an old photo of Marie from her previous life.

After Marie peered at the photo, she asked, "Where did you get that?"

"From Aunt Helen."

"Let me see," Polly demanded, pushing in closer.

"Mother, your eyes are brighter now and full of joy," Antonio remarked with reverence.

Marie smiled because the picture was a black and white photo from a newspaper.

"Sister Marie, you could be a star on any stage. You are the most beautiful woman I have ever seen. You are much more beautiful now than your picture when you were called Anna Simmons," added Polly.

"Thank you," Marie smiled.

Alex seemed anxious. He had said nothing and fidgeted as Antonio looked at him. His crush on Polly had become more and more obvious in recent weeks, and he always seemed to be trying to impress her. He spoke up as he looked down toward town.

"The town of Pierre looks so tiny from Essence. The parked cars look like toys from here. If I were still a little orphan boy, I might choose to reach down and pick one up for play."

Marie ignored his comments about Pierre and asked, "Alex, how do you think I look now compared to my old self as Anna Simmons?"

Alex looked at her with a serious expression, then his answer rushed out in a flood of nerves. "Well, you look swell to me. For one thing you smile a lot. Compared to the Reverend Mother and the others you are my favorite. You call me darling, and that makes me feel special. I love you as much as I do Sister Josephine."

"Thank you, Alex. I love you too."

56

After they rocked in peacefulness for several minutes, Alex sat up a little straighter and cleared his throat, breaking the silence. In a mature voice he asked, "Sister Anna Marie Simmons Antoinette, how long have you been here at Essence?" his voice squeaked at the end of his question. His eyes darted back and forth between Polly and Marie.

Marie knew Antonio had encouraged Alex to be more mature around the worldly Polly Dubois, and was sure that was why Alex used her full name to ask his question.

"Thank you, Alex, for asking. I've been here close to twenty years, and thank you for being here. I wanted us to be together tonight. It's nights like these that define us and give us hope for eternity."

Polly congratulated Marie on her twentieth anniversary and smiled directly at Marie before turning to look into Antonio's eyes. While Alex pursued Polly, her attention was on Antonio. Alex was a late bloomer, but Marie knew he would blossom into a beautiful young man. At fourteen, he was still a premature-looking lad with glasses framing his inquisitive countenance. Marie knew Polly thought Alex was cute—another tidbit Antonio had shared.

"Come and sit in my lap, Polly," Marie beckoned the girl.

Antonio seemed preoccupied thinking. "What did you mean? How does one use denial appropriately?"

"I mean we should not live in fear of falling down in life nor should we focus on our finitude," Marie explained as she cuddled Polly. "Freedom requires taking risks. You, Polly, and Alex will understand as you get older. Right now you are invincible, and your minds can only see infinity. I was like that once. Adults do well to reclaim some of their dreams of infinity and denial so as not to live in fear."

Sister Marie breathed a sigh of relief, content with her answer. Sometimes Antonio, with his young wisdom and insight, challenged her in ways that created doubt about her own views.

The evening's sunset played glorious, and the pink and violet colors dominated the sunless, twilight sky. Antonio grew very quiet and closed his eyes. He said nothing for the longest time. Marie looked at him several times. The twilight and moonlight merged and produced enough light to appreciate a beautiful purple rain cloud. Antonio opened his eyes. Marie pointed to the cloud.

"It is raining over there," said Polly.

"Yes, it's raining somewhere almost every minute of the day," said Marie.

"Rain is vital for life," Alex added.

Antonio's face lit with joy. "I know, Mother, that you were talking about the end of existence. My life, yours, Polly's, and Alex's too. But it does not scare me anymore because I know that my Intentio will live on through eternity, as will yours."

Marie looked at Antonio and felt so much joy in that moment. Antonio's face beamed.

Then Polly chimed in. "Me too. Existence does not scare me. I believe that I was once Cleopatra. Antonio was my Marc Antony."

"Polly, you have such a beautiful imagination. You are full of wonderful ideas," said Marie.

"Yes, Polly, I agree. You have a spectacular imagination,"

Alex said, acting mature and worldly as he complimented her with his chin held high. He seemed unfazed by Polly's attention to Antonio, oblivious as young boys often are.

The conversation continued as Marie tried to explain absurdity.

"The rain falls and the sun shines on both the good and the bad, and sometimes lightning strikes. Absurd things happen."

She explained facticity. Helen disagrees with the existentialists who believed facticity, unchangeable facts from your past, must become the limits for authentic living. We believe in the true-essence-self achieved through Sentio, and the existentialists believe in false true-essence-self created through Cogito. You will not have to worry about facticity. You will always live as authentic human beings searching for greater freedom through Sentio. What could be more authentic than a human being searching for greater freedom for all?"

Antonio and Alex nodded to agree as Marie continued. "The existentialists advanced our perspective on free choice and institutional effects and such. But they tried to institutionalize our consciousness to their version of true essence. At Essence we try to lead you back to your Sentio by experiencing the consciousness of nature. We want to create a vision for freedom to guide you to live true, true essence lives toward greater freedom for all."

Marie finished with tears in her eyes. For a moment while speaking, she had visited memories of her life before joining the Sisters of Freedom—her facticity.

"Why are you crying?" asked Antonio as he stood and wiped away his mother's tears. Marie leaned all the way back in her chair. Polly got up from her lap, and Marie was silent for a long moment. Then she smiled, and Antonio went back to his chair. She did not answer the question and simply encouraged everyone to resume rocking during the early nightfall.

In the moment of quiet just before the darkness of night, Marie reflected some more on her life as Anna Simmons. Antonio teased her with his own serious look—a furrowed brow and a squint—and asked, "What are you thinking about, Mother? Where is your Intentio?"

"I guess that I'm thinking about eternity. I hope my Intentio finds this memory someday, and I awaken in eternity, enjoying this moment with you forever."

Marie's rocking slowed. Antonio moved over to sit in his mother's lap. She held him and hugged his long muscular body; he had grown larger than her.

Polly nodded to Antonio.

Marie noticed. "It is getting late. We need to go to bed soon." She tried to rally her three little angels. They seemed mesmerized by the sounds of owls and crickets. Marie sat back in her rocker and Antonio rubbed his face against her cheek.

"I am not sleepy," said Alex.

"Me either," agreed Polly.

"We can't go to bed yet, mother," said Antonio. "I have prepared something for your anniversary."

"Oh, my little sweetheart. You did not have to prepare me anything. We should hurry. Polly and Alex need to get to their rooms before Sister Phillips comes looking."

Antonio popped up from his mother's lap with a theatrical snap. He turned on the lights and began parading in front of her. He tucked in his shirt and pulled up on his trousers. He explained to his audience that he was on stage in a London theater. He was about to perform for the Queen of Andorra.

"I am going to deliver my whistled sounds of love. My love is for the greatest lady ever born: Anna Marie Simmons Antoinette."

Polly and Alex smiled and crept forward in their chairs. Marie looked on, holding back tears of joy. Antonio whistled the sounds of the river as it was intended. He made sounds like a flute in a rendition of Smetana's "Moldau." Polly whistled, and Alex chimed in with humming sounds. Then Marie joined in.

When the tune finished, Marie hugged Polly and Alex, thanking them for her best anniversary ever. Antonio stepped down from his stage, and they all shared a final, big hug. Then Marie led them quietly off the porch and through the chapel to the dormitory.

Polly and Alex went to their separate rooms and Antonio requested his mother stay with him in the hallway for a moment. They waited in silence. Antonio loved to watch others fall asleep because he knew that they were still there. It was like watching darkness fall on the mountaintops. He peeked in as Polly drifted off to sleep and then Alex.

Antonio smiled at his mother. "I hope that Alex can visit Polly in his Sentio when they are asleep," he whispered.

"Antonio, you are my little Spartacus. You delivered some special Sentio tonight for keep."

As they walked back to #4, he said, "I am going to be like Spartacus and lead the slaves of language-thinking exis-tence to freedom. I will lead them through the consciousness of Eden. I had the compass experience tonight. I know where I'm supposed to go."

Marie stopped in her tracks at Antonio's revelation. He had experienced the compass!

Antonio turned towards her. "Mother, I am going to Harvard, and I will wear a long white coat. I'm going to con-tinue Emerson and Thoreau's revolution. Aunt Helen told me what happened to them. I'm going to lead a revolution of consciousness. You will see."

Marie said nothing. She shared her overwhelming joy with a warm and happy embrace, tears streaming down her cheeks. She wiped her tears and affirmed his experience, and in silence they hugged again. Marie released him and walked holding his hand. As they entered the villa, she realized this night was Antonio's graduation to young adulthood as much as her twentieth anniversary from climbing out of the abyss. Antonio had experienced the compass and his vision of freedom. She could not wait to share the news with Helen and Poulou.

57

Marie called Helen early the next morning and explained she and Antonio were coming with a big surprise, an announcement. During the cab ride to Vichy, Marie's heart pounded with excitement as she squeezed Antonio's hand. She could not wait to tell Helen of his compass experience and vision. Antonio smiled and reminded her that it was just a vision; he had not done anything yet. She shook her head and smiled at his modesty because she knew how much his compass experience would mean to Helen.

The yellow cab pulled up in front of the castle, and Marie and Antonio got out. Antonio paid the driver, and Marie hurried around to the back and entered the veranda from the side. Poulou spotted her, got up from his chair, and shared an embrace. Helen joined in the welcome, sharing a hug with Antonio and then Marie.

Marie whispered in Helen's ear, "Antonio had the Compass of Freedom experience."

Helen's eyes widened, and she turned and gestured to Poulou, who put his arm around Antonio's shoulder and led him on a walk toward the lake.

"Please sit down Marie, and tell me," said Helen.

Marie could not sit down. She bubbled with enthusiasm. "He did it! Antonio had the compass experience! He did it." The corners of Helen's crimson lips lifted, but she remained silent and calm. "His freedom vision was of himself in a white coat at the Harvard School of Medicine."

Helen looked thoughtful. "Two weeks ago I told him about a breakthrough at Harvard in the consciousness research laboratory. I wonder . . . I will find out if this was a genuine compass vision."

Marie hugged Helen and sat with her in the swing. Helen waved and got Poulou's attention; he and Antonio came running toward them. Helen got up, embraced Antonio, and winked at Marie, who pulled Poulou onto the swing as Helen led Antonio toward her office.

"I guess Helen wants me to stay with you," said Poulou.

Marie smiled and shared the exciting news about Antonio's compass experience.

"Oh my God! Helen has done it! The compass is not a hallucination. The experience is real." Poulou enveloped Marie in a celebratory hug, kissing her on the cheek.

"We will find out soon if Antonio's vision was genuine," said Marie as she pulled back from Poulou.

"Helen will know," Poulou agreed. "She has heard so many false claims. Only she knows what the powerful Intentio of Providence from the consciousness of Eden feels like."

Marie waited anxiously as Poulou started to swing. He called for Pepé, who brought them tea and milk, but Marie's stomach felt like a knot; she was too nervous to drink.

Twenty minutes later Helen emerged from her office with Antonio in tow. Marie could see the excitement in her eyes and the confidence on her face. She ran and embraced Antonio who was grinning from ear to ear. After their hug, Marie put her arm around his waist and pulled him close.

Poulou got up from the swing, walked slowly toward Helen, and then pulled her into an embrace. Tears streamed down Helen's cheeks as she spoke softly to Poulou about Harvard.

After their long embrace, Poulou wiped his face and Helen's with his handkerchief and turned toward Antonio and Marie. "Harvard?"

"Yes, Harvard," Antonio said. "I know that's where I'm supposed to free the slaves of Cogito existence." Antonio spoke with a new air of maturity and reverence. His compass experience had provided the bearings for his mission to find greater freedom for all.

"Well, you could not have picked a more difficult place to launch your revolution. I will help you. We will do it," said Poulou.

Helen smiled at Marie, who threw her arms in the air and embraced Poulou. She knew that if anyone could help pull this off it would be him.

"I know what we can do," Poulou said. "Antonio, I have a friend who is the Dean at Max Planck University. Let me talk with him, and we will come up with a plan of how to get you accepted at Harvard."

"I want to go to Harvard Medical School; that is different from Harvard undergraduate," Antonio said. "That is where I will set the world free."

Helen smiled. "Let us work on this, Antonio."

They enjoyed each other's company after the big announcement, and Poulou took Antonio out on his sailboat while Helen and Marie sat on the veranda in lawn chairs, enjoying the summer breeze.

"Do you think it will be possible for Antonio to go to Harvard?" asked Marie.

"Honestly, I think Poulou will find a way."

Marie relaxed and watched the sailboat on the lake and enjoyed the beautiful sensory of the summer day. After a few moments of silence, Helen got up, pulled Marie out of her chair, and gave her a warm hug.

"I am so proud of you and Antonio," she said.

Marie stood almost eye to eye with Helen. She smiled at

her and noticed that Helen looked younger than her. Helen's skin was smooth with the most beautiful eyebrows framing her soft brown eyes, with not a wrinkle to be found on her face or neck. Marie wore her veil all of the time because it hid her gray hair and wrinkled neck. Helen's hair was long and honey colored.

"How about some brandy?" Helen asked.

"No, thank you." Marie sat back down and leaned forward to ask Helen a personal question. "Do you think that your body has followed your Sentio back to Eden?"

"There is no other explanation. The doctors who have examined me say that I am an anomaly, a work of natural selection—perhaps nature's test for the potential survival advantage of rejuvenation," Helen said. "But of course I know better, as does Poulou."

"I think I would like a rejuvenation," Marie smiled ruefully.

Helen grinned and changed the subject. "Our orphanage across the lake is doing really well."

"It is beautiful," Marie said. "I've heard from Alice and Eva, and they love working with the children. I'll come back and visit, soon." Marie hesitated, then said with resolve, "I want to make the trip back to Eden like you and Poulou."

Helen met Marie's eyes and reached to hold her hands. "I am helping Poulou rejuvenate his Sentio. He went through the rejuvenation a while ago and recently began to lose sensitivity. Why don't you come down next Saturday? I will show you what we are doing."

Marie's face lit up. "I would love to."

Antonio and Poulou returned dripping water on the veranda from their swim after sailing.

"The water is cold," Antonio said. "I love the feeling of water on my body."

"Come on," Poulou said. "Let's go get some dry clothes."

Antonio followed on Poulou's heels.

"Hurry, Antonio. We better get going back to Essence before it gets too late," said Marie.

Poulou turned. "You can't leave. Please stay the night."

Antonio looked at his mother.

"Okay," Marie agreed.

"Mrs. Ophelia, two more for dinner," Poulou yelled to the kitchen. "Pepé, bring us some champagne. I want to give a toast."

Poulou and Antonio ran upstairs to change.

After a few minutes, they returned clean and sparkling. Antonio wore his uncle's shorts and shirt. They gathered around the dinner table and took their seats. Pepé placed two trays of salmon and pheasant then fruit and drinks on the dining table. After Poulou said grace Marie got up to serve the food.

"Please, Marie, sit down," said Helen.

Poulou grabbed the salmon plate and gave it to Antonio. "We'll pass it around."

Marie enjoyed some sliced oranges and apples. Antonio drank a liter of milk and then a large glass of water. He looked at Marie who was taken aback by his guzzling noise.

"I was thirsty," he said.

Poulou looked over at Marie and added, "He's a growing young man."

Antonio finished the last of the pheasant, and Poulou finished off the bottle of champagne. They gathered around the swing on the veranda, and Poulou told stories of his travels in South Africa. After the story about him finding a lion cub and a chimp that behaved like brother and sister, Helen turned up the music, and they listened to old songs on the BBC.

When "Moon River" started playing, Marie danced at Poulou's request. Antonio lifted his elbow, and Helen grasped his arm as they danced under the starry sky to romantic tunes until long after midnight.

The next morning Marie awoke in the guest room under the canopy of her bed. Antonio lay beside her, sound asleep. He had crawled beside her after getting up from his cot. Marie began thinking about Harvard. She did not want Antonio going to America. She believed America was dangerous. She decided not to say anything because deep down she did not think Antonio would get accepted to Harvard Medical School. But perhaps he could become a doctor at another school and still free humankind. She got up and left Antonio sound asleep in a fetal position on the bed.

She joined Helen on the veranda to work on a plan to help Antonio follow his vision of freedom. While they were talking, Poulou's friend from the Planck returned his call and explained what it would require for Antonio to get into Harvard. Marie listened and could see Poulou's mind churning as he processed the information. He hung up and continued processing.

After Antonio awoke, all four sat down at the picnic table for coffee and muffins. Poulou went over what his friend had told him, about getting into Harvard.

"There is a guy, Kaplan, who has a strategy for getting good students into American medical schools. My friend at the Planck recommended him. I think that he is our best chance," said Poulou. "Here is what we'll do . . ."

After Antonio's compass experience, everything changed. Poulou's friend the dean, the head of administration at the Planck, helped Antonio enroll at the University of Maryland University College at Heidelberg where he began taking basic science courses required by American medical schools via the mail. Antonio also registered and started taking correspondence courses in mathematics from the Planck. Sister Serelia served as his advisor, monitoring his progress. Then he got his study guides from Kaplan and commenced studying the critical areas of physics, biology, and chemistry he would need to know for his medical school entrance exam, the exam for freedom.

Sergio had created a passageway from Antonio's mother's room through a closet to Sister Phillips' old room to give him a private place for study. He had his own desk and chair, a sofa, and his own bathroom. He still slept with his mother in their room, but he enjoyed the extra space. He had more time to study without interruption, and study he did.

His mother was spending more time with Javier, and she also visited his aunt Helen on the weekends, taking Aunt Helen's journey back to Eden course. She taught his mother about the mystics and a variety of techniques to help her surrender her Cogito mind. Aunt Helen also exposed her to the work of a mystic, Evelyn Underhill, who had found Sentio via another route. But his mother struggled with mysticism. After focusing on nature through Sentio, her Intentio would find something that she had been thinking about in Cogito— and suddenly—her attention would go right back to language thinking, finding language thoughts laced with worry and fear. Antonio tried to help her, but it seemed impossible for her Intentio to escape Cogito for more than a few seconds. His mother could not keep her attention dwelling in the inner sanctum of Sentio. Antonio had the opposite problem with his studies. He had to keep redirecting his attention to Cogito, but his Intentio could dwell in Cogito for hours if he wanted. His Intentio was free, and it dwelled in his Sentio.

After two years and countless hours of studying, Antonio completed his undergraduate exams at Heidelberg and correspondence courses at the Planck. He'd developed a routine, and he continued studying six hours per day for several more weeks until he read through Kaplan's study guides twice. Then he used study cards and reduced his studying time to four hours per day, giving him more free time to enjoy his family at Essence, especially Alex and Polly.

Alex flipped through a handful of study cards and read out the questions to Antonio, one after another—Charles's law? Boyle's law? Avogadro's law? The Krebs cycle? The force equation? Kinetic energy equation? Antonio sat with his feet propped on his desk in Sister Phillips' old room. He fiddled and drew geometric figures while he listened to the questions and then waited for his Intentio to find the answers.

"Give me something hard?" asked Antonio. He knew all of those cards.

"Bernoulli's equation?" Alex asked.

"He is one of my favorites. Bernoulli described the velocity and pressure relationships of fluids, which I have observed—"

Antonio stopped himself and asked Alex to quiz him

from the other stack of cards on the windowsill. He did not want to talk about his vision of the world that he had promised his mother never to disclose or talk about: the motion of air moving around objects, or the grid lines caused by the Brownian motion of water vapor in the clouds. He would never tell a soul even though he could explain why he saw these things. And he knew others had seen his vision of the world too. His promise to his mother was sacred, and he would never tell.

He got up from his desk and walked around the room and recited the laws of thermodynamics then lowered his eyes for a moment. Out of the corner of his eye, he saw Alex looking out the window at a bluebird chirping on the cupola.

Alex had grown into a handsome young man more than six feet tall. Almost as tall as him. He and Alex worked out every day, doing push-ups, chin-ups, and jumping jacks in the new gymnasium. Antonio enjoyed the fact that Alex had grown big and strong like him. They wrestled and played rough, and it was exhilarating.

Antonio snuck up and grabbed Alex as he looked out the window. He put him in a firm but teasing hold around his shoulders and neck. Alex dropped down in near escape, and Antonio bumped against the desk maintaining his grasp.

"*Shh!*" Alex said. "You know Josephine and Marie will get upset if they hear us wrestling inside the villa. Let's take a break and get Polly. I want to practice for our play."

Antonio released him and gave a playful shove. "I had you."

"No you didn't. I could have escaped if I didn't have these cards in my hand," Alex replied, and pushed against Antonio's arm.

Antonio walked away and called. "Polly! Alex wants to practice before the play."

Polly was next door sewing with Marie and Josephine, finishing the costumes for their musical play, *Esselot*, their own rendition of Camelot. "Just a minute, I'm almost finished with my gown."

Through Sister Josephine's encouragement, Alex and Polly had decided to pursue a life centered on Sentio through acting. Antonio supported them and agreed to be King Arthur in their play. Marie and Josephine were directing the musical, and Antonio enjoyed learning to act and encouraging his little brothers and sisters. His noble knights, the children of Essence.

Tonight, Alex would debut as the gallant Lancelot and Polly as the beautiful and genteel Guinevere. Alex and Polly had become lovebirds during the long weeks of practice. Antonio was happy for Alex and gave him a little push as a reminder when he saw Polly coming down the hall.

"Here she comes . . . Guinevere."

CHAPTER

59

They watched as Polly made a dramatic entrance. Sliding her outstretched arms along the wall of the joining hallway and taking large slow steps as if she were breaking free from the surly bonds of Cogito existence.

"Never let it be forgot . . . ," she raised her hand to her forehead, took another step, dropped her hand, and continued, "that there once was a spot, and for a brief shining moment, it was known as Esselot."

When Polly finished, she ran to embrace Antonio and then Alex, who lifted and twirled her. Polly landed on her feet and said, "O Lancelot, I am going to the chapel to get ready. Meet me there in a few minutes, and we can practice our lines in the changing room."

"I will," Alex said dramatically then looked at Antonio and shook his head. They followed after Polly who hurried out of the villa.

The Essence campus came to life as the play grew near. People congregated outside of the chapel. While Polly changed, Antonio and Alex ran to the balcony porch hoping to catch the sunset, but dark clouds had gathered and blocked their view.

The people from Pierre were making their way up the cobblestone road.

"We better get going," said Alex.

But Antonio wanted to keep rocking. "I want to remember this moment before you and Polly become superstars," he said with a grin.

Alex gave him a friendly punch on the shoulder and pulled him from the chair. They hurried to the chapel and found Polly singing her lines in the changing room. She looked so excited gazing at her face in the mirror, creating a purple haze around her beaming blue eyes with a tiny brush. She had covered her freckles with powder and painted her lips bright red.

Josephine knocked on the door, came in, and handed Polly a dozen red roses. Polly started crying and purple makeup streamed down her cheeks. Josephine smiled with tear-filled eyes and wiped Polly's face with a tissue. Then Marie came in and put her arms around Josephine and Polly. Alex hugged Josephine, and Antonio walked over and hugged his mother and Polly. After sharing embraces and encouraging Polly, Marie and Josephine left to prepare the children for the opening scene. Antonio left Polly and Alex in the changing room and went to check out the crowd.

The chapel grew noisy as people took their seats. Antonio pulled back the curtain and peeked at the audience. Poulou was wearing a black tuxedo, and Aunt Helen was wearing a beautiful, green evening dress. They took seats in the front row near the stage. Sergio walked toward the back of the chapel; he had built the platform stage and the round table for the show. He set up the sound equipment and the spotlight. Josephine walked up and hugged him. Antonio knew that Sergio loved Josephine, and she loved him. They had shared love in simple ways during the practices for the play—hand touching and eye touching. It was interesting to watch them.

Javier made his entrance with a loud hello to the Catalan twins. He was wearing a shiny, brown suit and blue shirt with white roses in his hand. He walked up front after buying his ticket and sat next to Poulou.

Sister Celia and Sergio raised the big spotlight into position, and Sister Serelia stepped up onto the stage in front of the green curtain. The chapel grew dark. The spotlight came on: yellow, then red, then blue, then back to yellow. Sister Serelia raised her arm to deflect the bright light, moved forward, and spoke into the microphone.

"Welcome to Esselot," she said, and the crowd cheered. "Written, directed, and produced by our very own Sisters Marie Antoinette and Josephine Joseph. Starring Polly, Alex, and Antonio. Co-starring . . ."

"Antonio, come on," Alex said in a forced whisper. "You're in the first scene."

Antonio tied his robe tight and grabbed his crown from Alex. As Sister Serelia finished the intro there was more applause. Antonio found his place on stage, and an eerie silence filled the room as the curtain lifted. A magical moment followed, and Antonio had everyone's attention. He turned toward the children, and his noble knights' faces froze—stage fright. His mother had warned him about the phenomenon.

Antonio exuded confidence and walked to the front of the stage as King Arthur and began the play with a dialogue with Merlin, who was in the form of a wooden Raven and the voice of Sister Serelia.

"Caw, caw, caw," said the Raven.

"Merlin, I need your help," King Arthur said. "You brought me the round table so that all of my knights would have an equal seat. But now I must help them develop mutual respect for one another."

"It is impossible to have mutual respect unless one can transcend circumstance and chance affinity and find what is identical in each knight," Merlin said. "Caw, caw."

"What is identical in each knight?" King Arthur pondered Merlin's suggestion. He turned to the audience, pulled out his sword, and raised Excalibur above his head. "Intentio! Intentio!" He swirled his sword. "And our will for freedom."

"Caw, Caw."

The lights dimmed.

Polly's voice rang clear and melodic from behind the stage as she made her grand entrance with two first-grade girls supporting the train of her white and green dress. Antonio could not believe it as he listened to her voice. Polly had blossomed into a leading lady. He raised up from his kneeling position as King Arthur and made his plea for Guinevere's love, holding her hand and then kneeling at her feet. The lights dimmed.

The lights raised and Guinevere sat by herself, and Alex entered the stage and sang loud and deep as Lancelot. The chapel roared with applause.

King Arthur gave his final monologue. Then Guinevere and Lancelot sang once more, and walked away into the sunset. The crowd of more than two hundred gave a standing ovation.

Josephine and his mother joined the cast upfront at Alex and Polly's urging and received white roses and a loving embrace from Javier. Josephine pulled Sergio out of his seat and onto the stage, and the crowd roared once more in appreciation.

Antonio went to find Aunt Helen and Poulou. The tavern owner greeted him and said the show was ready for Piccadilly Circus and Times Square. Antonio smiled and wheeled toward his Uncle Poulou, who gave rave reviews. Aunt Helen hugged him and told him how proud she was. And she could not believe how well Alex and Polly had performed.

Antonio explained that Josephine had taught Polly and Alex method acting—an effective style of acting. Their repetition exercises appeared to free Intentio from Cogito, producing realness. He believed the founder of the method must have known about Sentio, and Aunt Helen thought so too.

They all gathered on the terrace afterward for a

reception on the balcony porch. They played music and danced until late into the night.

As they left the party for #4, Antonio told his mother he needed to break up the monotony of studying. His acting practices had helped his studying in a strange and unexpected way by strengthening his Intentio.

During the last year before the exam, Antonio played basketball in the gymnasium to break up the monotony of studying. Javier had taught him, Alex, and Polly how to play the fun game. Competitive basketball helped Antonio focus his attention wave even more. He needed less time to study and spent more time pursuing the sunshine for Sentio: nature, human love, warmth, food, sleep, exercise, rest, and health. Aunt Helen had taught him about the sunshine of sensory consciousness and of course avoiding passions and addictions.

Javier moved into the attic of #4, so he could teach poetry and coach at Essence, but Antonio knew he really wanted to be close to his mother. He made a loft apartment out of the large open space, and it was a really neat crow's-nest. Antonio knew that his mother enjoyed having Javier near. He did too. Javier had developed a sensitive Sentio after giving up alcohol, and he had become a great strange lover and coach.

With only two months to go, Antonio studied every day and did practice tests on the weekends. Kaplan knew how to prepare for a test, and Antonio figured out his method; he aced his practice tests.

During the last week before the exam, Marie, Alex, and Polly sat with him all through the day. They stayed up late and fell asleep on the sofa past midnight every night. When Antonio tired of studying, he would look at his mother, Alex, and Polly cuddled on the sofa and feel encouraged. He experienced a strange warm glow in his chest as if the goodness from somewhere beyond this world was flowing through him. He experienced joy as he worked to fulfill his vision for freedom, which made him work even harder.

The exam date had been on the calendar in the kitchen for three years when his mother announced only three days to go. It seemed impossible that it was so close. Antonio had conveyed to his mother that he would find a way to fulfill his mission even if he flunked the exam. But deep down he knew he was going to do well. Conquering the entrance exam had become his priority mission. It was the key to setting humankind free, and he had left no stone unturned in his preparation.

Two days before the exam Aunt Helen came over and met with him alone in his study. He believed that he was ready, and she had come to test his readiness. She laid Marcel's old saddle on his desk and asked him to calculate the volume in cubic centimeters. He nodded and got up, looking for his ruler to take measurements, then stopped, turned around, and smiled.

"I will submerge the saddle in my tub and measure the displaced volume," he said.

His aunt nodded in approval.

Antonio knew that he could also derive the volume by weighing the saddle or using an integration method he learned from studying calculus.

"I'm glad to see your Sentio is still alive and well after three years of Cogito preparation," said Aunt Helen.

She asked him to explain pi, the ratio of the circumference of a circle to the diameter; she asked about the imaginary number i; she asked about e, the natural log and the basis for calculating compounded interest and population doubling times; she asked about the four forces of the universe: the weak and strong nuclear forces, electromagnetism, and gravity.

Antonio gave correct answers to all of her questions. Aunt Helen patted his back, and he smiled at his mother who appeared in the doorway of his study.

"His Sentio and Cogito are a perfect blend, and his Intentio is as strong as mine," Aunt Helen said.

Her encouragement gave him confidence. He was ready.

CHAPTER

61

The day before the exam for freedom, Uncle Poulou drove Antonio to Paris to stay with a friend, who had been his uncle's roommate at the Munch years ago.

"Louie's apartment is only a few blocks from the testing site," said Poulou.

"Convenient," Antonio said, staring at the education building. "Could you stop? I want to check out the site."

After Poulou pulled over, Antonio got out of his uncle's car and walked a few paces down the sidewalk to the entrance of the testing site for his examination, and saw signs already in place directing students to the testing classroom. He felt his chest tighten and swallowed several times to relax. He turned and looked up at the twelve-story, green brick building then felt a gentle hand on his shoulder.

Poulou had caught up with him after parking the car on the street. He grabbed Antonio's hand, leading him down the sidewalk toward Louie's place. His uncle remained silent, and Antonio was able to relax by redirecting his attention to the charming buildings, built centuries ago.

Poulou's friend Louie lived alone in the tall, brown building on the corner of Bourbon and Charcot Street. They climbed three flights of narrow stairs, and Antonio knocked several times on the door. No answer. Poulou stepped up and knocked several more times. The blinds went up, and his friend came to the window. The door opened, and Poulou shouted Louie's name and embraced his friend. They were the same size.

"Poulou, my dear mate," Louie said. "It is so great to see you. You look wonderful."

Poulou grinned, turned, and put his hand on Antonio's shoulder. "This is Antonio."

"The genius." Louie reached to embrace Antonio, patting his back. Antonio reached down to hug Louie's shoulders and shot a grin at his uncle. Louie seemed like a fun-loving man like Poulou.

"Come in, come in," Louie said, pulling back from the embrace with Antonio. He led them through his clean kitchen to the den where an old TV buzzed with a fuzzy picture screen. "My window to the world has lost its signal."

Poulou walked over and asked, "Do you mind?"

Louie shook his head, and Poulou turned the TV off.

Louie looked old and walked with a limp, but his eyes had a twinkle. When Poulou asked about his limp, Louie called it foot drop. "Not too bad," he said. "A complication of my diabetes."

Poulou patted Louie on the back again and thanked him for opening up his apartment. Antonio turned and looked around the room; there were books spread everywhere and two floor-to-ceiling bookcases filled with more books.

Poulou caught Antonio's gaze. "Louie is an avid reader. He knows something about everything."

"But not as much as your uncle knows about nothing," Louie smiled.

Antonio laughed. He had heard his uncle's story about *Me and Nothingness* many times.

"You must be hungry," said Louie.

Both Poulou and Antonio nodded.

"Sit down," he said. "I've got some soup ready on the stove."

Louie had made French onion soup for their dinner and served it with wheat rolls, molasses, and hot tea. After dinner they had wine, and Poulou and Louie laughed and talked about old times together.

"Louie, your soup gave rise to an Intentio that dug up a lot of old memories from the Munch." Poulou explained to Antonio, "That was all that they fed us, soup and bread."

Louie nodded. "I'm reminded almost every day."

Poulou talked about the art of scrounging, and it was interesting for Antonio to hear a different side of his uncle. He enjoyed the conversation and jocularity for several hours. Then he requested to be excused. He ran to the car to get his suitcase and upon his return explained he needed to rest for his exam.

Louie directed him to the guest bedroom, which Antonio found to be a stuffy room with a small cot. After hanging his change of clothes up, he raised the window, enjoyed the cool breeze, and rocked in a creaky chair near the window.

Looking out from the room toward the horizon, Antonio listened to the sounds from the Paris street: motors, horns, and an accordion from the café below. It was different, the urban sound, a stirring noise, which kept his attention on edge. After several minutes he was able to relax by directing his attention toward the faded, pale yellow paint on the walls of his room. He could hear Poulou and Louie through the wall telling stories while playing cards.

Antonio felt too excited for sleep and continued rocking. After sunset, he found his Intentio and tried to center on its nothingness and serenity within, not engaging Sentio or Cogito. His meditation relaxed him. He rocked, centered on nothingness, and lost track of time.

CHAPTER

At 7:00 a.m. the alarm clock rang, and Antonio got up from the rocker, feeling refreshed after several hours of meditation, dressed, and snuck out without making a sound. He grabbed a bagel and a cup of juice at the street café. He walked to the exam site filled with enthusiasm and confidence but also anxious because he had never taken such an intense examination. He hoped Mr. Kaplan knew what he was doing when he made his study course.

He climbed the stairs and walked down the hall to the vacant classroom where he was greeted by a serious looking man in a black suit who verified his admission card and identity.

"I'm the proctor," he said and told him to take a seat at the end of a long table.

Antonio nodded to acknowledge him and moved toward his seat, noticing the sunlit, pale walls, and detecting a chalky smell from the blackboard. He sat at the table and pulled out a pencil from his shirt pocket. Soon more than forty students had paraded into the room, most giving anxious smiles to one another, while a few brimmed with confidence. The majority were French, but a few were British. This was the only site in Paris that offered the exam in English.

Antonio's chest tingled and his hands began to shake. He lowered his eyes, took a deep breath, and readied for the exam that might determine the future of freedom for the human race, a future which seemed to be heading for the clouds with the loss of individual freedom.

The proctor came over, looked him in the eyes, and handed him the test booklet, which was thick and held closed by a red seal. "Do not break the seal!"

Antonio's palms began sweating when the proctor reminded everyone to make sure that they used a number 2 pencil; otherwise, the test results would not be accurate. He felt queasy as a tight knot grew in the pit of his stomach. He had never heard the term a number 2 pencil. Looking around in panic, he found a friendly student who looked at his pencil.

"*Oui.*" The young male student nodded with a smile, and Antonio breathed a sigh of relief. His pencil from Essence met the standard.

The proctor said, "You may begin."

Antonio broke the seal and hurried through the test booklet as fast as he could. He finished the four-hour morning session in two hours. It also only took him two hours during the afternoon session. His Sentio would project the entire page, like a photograph while his Intentio searched for the answers in his memory files, then he filled in the answer with his pencil. He took Sentio photographs and stored every question and answer in his memory so that he could verify his responses later.

After the exam, Poulou met him in the hallway with a grin. "You did it. Forget about it for now, and let's go have some fun." His uncle grabbed his hand and pulled him down the stairs. Poulou's words were like music to his ears.

63

"It's time to party," Poulou said as they stepped outside onto Bourbon Street.

Antonio hugged his uncle and then walked alongside him until they arrived at his car, parked in a crowded lot.

"What about Louie?" Antonio asked. "I wanted to thank him and say good-bye."

"He went to visit his ill sister. I gave him some money and invited him to visit the castle in Andorra next month."

Antonio thanked his uncle then jumped into the car, and off they went to a grand hotel near the Eiffel Tower. The beautiful, sprawling, seventeenth-century structure rose up in grandeur among three other tall modern buildings on the horizon. They parked, got out, and made their way across the brick pavers into the lobby where a large red, white, and blue French flag hung on the wall above a marble statue of a dolphin with water flowing from its mouth, filling a wishing well.

At first glance the hotel looked empty, but the clerk at the front desk said all the rooms were taken. Poulou reached for his wallet and handed him some money. The nicely dressed clerk, wearing a green beret like Poulou, looked again and found a special room, vacated earlier in the day by a German diplomat.

Antonio followed his uncle back outside where Poulou

grabbed their suitcases from the car and paid the valet. They took the lift to the seventh floor and found their room, #700, at the end of a long hallway. When Poulou opened the door, Antonio gazed in awe at the Louis XIV suite, which reminded him of the Spanish castle in Vichy with a fireplace, velvet chairs, and a canopy over the bed.

After laying the suitcase in the chair, Poulou joined Antonio by the fireplace. Antonio turned, gave his uncle a hug, and thanked him for coming with him. Without Poulou he would never have had a chance to fulfill his vision for freedom.

Poulou smiled and congratulated him on a job well done. He said he admired him for his years of hard work and then patted Antonio's belly and suggested they check out the Owl bar for some food, drink, and festivities. Antonio nodded, and Poulou led him back to the lift. On the tenth floor the elevator doors opened into the entrance of the bar where stools were occupied by nicely dressed young men and women. To the left, windows decorated the walls of a larger room filled wall-to-wall with happy people.

They found a booth. Antonio ordered a turkey sandwich with beans, and Poulou got up and danced with some friendly women. Antonio watched his uncle while enjoying his meal, and took the last bite as his uncle approached. Poulou hurried to drink some wine and then introduced Antonio to his three beautiful young women friends: Saro, Maro, and Sonya, who knew his uncle from before. Poulou wanted to get away from the loud music, so everyone retreated to their hotel suite for conversation and wine.

Soon their conversation turned into tickling play with ostrich feathers, taken from a large ceramic vase near the fireplace. The women requested Antonio and his uncle put blindfolds on while they disrobed.

Odd they have blindfolds in their purses, Antonio thought as he fastened his blindfold. Soon he and his uncle played a game where they chased the naked women's giggling sounds, trying to catch one with the feather for a tickle in hopes of creating laughter. Laughter meant the woman being tickled would share a kiss with the blindfolded tickler. His uncle had invented the parlor tickling game, named tiggles.

Antonio had never played such a game, but he was a natural at finding the women and making them laugh with ease. He enjoyed their kisses and listening to his uncle's excitement when he got kissed.

After several rounds, he and his uncle changed roles with the women. The women dressed and put on blindfolds, while Antonio and Poulou stripped down to their undies. The goal was not to laugh when being tickled, or you had to share a kiss, but it was impossible not to laugh because of the ladies' contagious giggles and their tickles. After the women cornered Antonio, they pushed him on the bed, rubbing their hands all over him and tickling him in a frenzy. He opened his eyes and saw Poulou approach, appearing upset because the women were cheating by using their hands.

"That's enough!" Poulou yelled. "The party is over."

While putting on their clothes he whispered to Antonio that the Sisters of Freedom would not enjoy the game. Antonio smiled to himself thinking that Sister Pauli would not like it, but Polly and his mother probably would.

The women shared embraces, gathered their things, and departed with happy faces after Poulou gave them some money to go dancing.

"Bye, Saro, Maro, and Sonya," said Poulou.

Antonio waved good-bye and looked out the window at the Eiffel Tower, which was lit up, drawing his attention as it flashed red, white, and blue.

"Could we go there?" he asked.

Poulou waved his hand. "Come on."

They took the stairs and caught a cab out front. When they got out of the cab, Poulou met some more beautiful young ladies on the sidewalk who wanted to sell sensitivity. Antonio noticed his uncle seemed to attract young women for some reason, and Poulou could not resist. The tickling game had created an insatiable appetite for a happy slap, as he called it. So Poulou bought one at a good price, but then the lady told him she would have to deliver the slap in private.

"Wait for me in the nightclub across the street," Poulou told Antonio.

The club had a strong musky odor. Antonio took a seat at the bar, ordered a lemon twist, and watched some flexible women dance on a stage behind the bar while Poulou was collecting his "slap" in the hotel down the street.

64

Finally his uncle came back with flushed cheeks. It looked as if he had received two slaps. But he was smiling.

Poulou responded to the question on the tip of Antonio's tongue, "I turned the other cheek," he said.

"I thought so."

Poulou wanted to walk, so Antonio followed his uncle outside looking up at the Eiffel Tower as they passed underneath. The gas street lamps and the seventeenth-century architecture of Paris reminded him of Pierre. They crossed over several blocks, passed by an old café, and found their hotel. The sounds of music and dancing filtered through the elevator shaft as they rode to the seventh floor. Antonio hurried to their room, afraid that his uncle might want to revisit the tenth floor. Waiting by the door he waved for Poulou, slipped in behind his uncle, and jumped on the sofa.

"Uncle Poulou, I love this sofa. You can have the bed."

"Are you sure?"

Antonio nodded. Poulou smiled and pulled a pillow and blanket from the bed and handed them to him.

"Thank you, young man. Louie's cot took a toll on my back last night."

The second night they visited Versailles and entered a grand casino that his uncle said was like Monte Carlo. Poulou explained to Antonio about gambling as they sat at a table and sipped on wine in the lounge, and then he took him to the craps table. After throwing the die a few times, Antonio figured out how to hold and toss the die to produce the tumbles that allowed him to roll a seven anytime he wanted. And he wanted to make his uncle happy. Gambling produced a thrill, an inner tingle, and Antonio enjoyed the feeling. He understood how it could become an addiction after his uncle suggested at one time he had been addicted to gambling.

Poulou placed the bets, and Antonio rolled the die. They won a lot of chips in a short time, and many people gathered around the table and gave yells and screams every time he tossed the die—it was exciting. They called him a natural.

He got nervous when his uncle and the smiling faces started cheering his name, "Antonio! Antonio! *Le naturel.*"

Then Poulou got nervous and nudged him. He whispered to roll another number, anything but seven, so Antonio rolled an eleven. The casino guard came over and stood behind them. Poulou gathered their chips, and they hurried to the cashier where they traded their chips for seven thousand pounds.

"Wow!" Antonio said as his uncle turned and embraced him.

They slipped away to another room, took a table, and enjoyed a glass of red wine, listening to a guy who played old tunes on a piano. After a few songs they got up, and Poulou placed their winnings in the man's top hat, an act of generosity that Antonio agreed with. Poulou was a kind and generous man; Antonio was proud of his uncle for helping the piano player. They left and rode a horse-drawn carriage all the way back to their hotel.

The next morning, Poulou loaded the car, and they began the five-hour drive back to Pierre. About an hour into the drive, Poulou interrupted Antonio's silent stare.

"How did you do?" He gave a chuckle. "I mean, on your exam."

Antonio grinned. "I knew all of the answers. I checked my study books this morning."

"You knew all the answers," Poulou said and began laughing hysterically. He settled down after a few minutes and patted Antonio on his knee. "You knew all of the answers," Poulou repeated and began whistling an old tune.

Antonio liked the tune his uncle whistled and enjoyed the ride. He loved to watch Poulou drive. He was mesmerizing behind the wheel, waving and smiling at people. He seemed to know everyone in every little town they drove through.

"Why do I have so many thoughts when we drive?" asked Antonio.

"Well, your Sentio gets bombarded by sensory packets, and they drive the Intentios that search through your memory files."

Antonio smiled and closed his eyes. "How about Intentios during dreams?"

"When you dream your eyes move rapidly back and forth, and your body senses the environment in which you are sleeping. The movement of your eyes and your body's own sensory give rise to Intentios that open Sentio and Cogito files—and in some cases, recent files—which you may have prepared to dream about. Imagine the Sentio and Cogito files, the source of dreams, of primitive man."

"Huh . . . I'm glad I have my files from Essence."

"I have some bad memory files, but I have learned to keep my Intentio away from them," Poulou said. "You are a lucky young man, Antonio," he grinned. "Keep your files as happy and healthy as possible."

"What do symbols tell us about our dreams?" Antonio asked. He had read one of his uncle's books on the symbols of dreams.

Poulou chuckled. "Don't worry; dreaming about a pin cushion doesn't mean that you are dreaming about a woman's breast. Throw that Freud stuff in the trash bin."

Antonio raised his eyebrows. *Pin cushions and a woman's breast—how odd.*

"Symbols are symbols within the context of consciousness. Forget about the psychopathological junk and sub-consciousness."

Antonio nodded. He knew what Poulou was trying to say. Aunt Helen had told him the same thing about dreams and symbols. Poulou shot him a quick smile. Antonio nodded and closed his eyes for a nap.

When he awoke, the car was stopped on a mountain plateau. He could see other nearby mountains peaks, and the sun was setting. Antonio got out and found his uncle sitting on the hood of the car. He put his arm around Poulou's shoulders, and they watched a heavenly structure form out of the purest white clouds in the sky above. It looked like a beautiful, majestic building with little square-windows. Poulou said that the clouds were in the form of a pueblo and that it was a sign of something to come. A sign of something good for humankind, a conscious symbol of a gentle time in human history.

"A sign of something good," Antonio repeated.

The silhouette of the Pueblo persisted into darkness; the sign of something good endured. Antonio believed his uncle was right. He knew something good was about to happen; he had done well on his examination for freedom.

They got back in the car and continued driving. The stretch of road widened, and Antonio turned on the radio. As the signal grew stronger, he found a station that played romantic songs from the past.

"Leave it there," said Poulou, and they enjoyed the songs on the station.

"Uncle Poulou, how do you and Aunt Helen stay young?" asked Antonio.

"I believe it's because of what your aunt says: somehow strange love affects our Sentio and our bodies, turning back the genetic clock. I have never felt younger in my life."

Antonio looked out his window. "I wonder why my mother has not experienced the rejuvenation."

When he turned back to look at his uncle, Poulou said, "It could be for a number of reasons. Don't worry. Just give her a lot of love."

Antonio nodded with confidence. "I will flood her with love."

"I know you will," Poulou laughed and turned left at the sign: *Thirty kilometers to Pierre.*

Six weeks later, the results came back. A perfect score. Antonio was the youngest student from Europe to make a perfect score on the admission test and was awarded the Louis Pasteur scholarship for graduate studies in medicine.

Congratulations! headed the letter Antonio received. He showed Marie, and she noted it was the same word that had started Helen's journey to freedom at Essence. Marie took the letter to Helen and Poulou in Vichy, and they shared a small celebration on the veranda.

"Now he has to get accepted to medical school," Helen said. "He has a scholarship and a perfect score on his entrance exam."

Marie understood and reassured Helen that he would get accepted somewhere.

"He must get in Harvard," Helen insisted.

Marie pretended to agree, but really she didn't believe Antonio needed to go to America. He could achieve the same anywhere in Europe. She did not want him to go so far away from home, and America was dangerous.

Marie walked over and hugged Poulou on the swing and hoped that he would agree with her about Antonio not needing to go to America. But he didn't. He told her to listen to Helen because she believed in Antonio's vision. Marie pursed her lips at his response and returned to say good-bye to Helen.

Before leaving she remembered what she had wanted to ask Helen. "What is a happy slap? Antonio said that Poulou bought a couple while they were in Paris."

Helen shook her head and looked over at Poulou on the swing, "That Poulou! He lets women slap him on the face to invigorate his sensibility."

"Oh. Antonio told me it looked like Poulou had been slapped." Marie looked at Poulou. "Tiggles?"

His face turned pale as he stood up from the swing. "Let me explain," he said.

Grinning, Marie shook her head and departed as Helen asked him, "What are Tiggles?"

* * *

After his eighteenth birthday, Marie and Antonio went on several interviews to prospective schools in Europe, but Antonio had his sights set on Harvard as he had envisioned in his compass experience. Marie tried to change his mind because she wanted him closer to home. When she shared with Antonio during sunset, he explained that he needed to follow his vision of freedom without Cogito interference.

Marie remained silent as they sat holding hands, rocking on the balcony porch. Antonio flashed his Mediterranean blue eyes at her with a hint of tears and adjusted the red bandanna he used to keep his long hair in place. He had vowed a year earlier to let his hair grow until he could set the Americans free. After adjusting his hair, he reached and squeezed Marie's hand. She felt her heart sink.

"You can learn medicine anywhere."

"It is not what I must know, Mother. I have seen; I know what I must do," Antonio said. "Then I will find what I need to know to lead the Americans and then all humans to freedom."

A part of her continued to resist Antonio's explanation, and she had created an argument in her Cogito as to why he should not go. But after a long moment, Marie squeezed his hand to convey her understanding. She knew in her Sentio that it was the right decision, but that did not make it easier.

Another week passed and Poulou's friend, the dean at Max Planck, called. He had sent some application materials for Antonio's submission to Harvard, the school of William James. Marie had received the materials and hid them in a drawer. She knew she was delaying the inevitable, but she was not ready to face it. She told the dean the materials had gotten lost in the mail.

Later in the day Helen called Marie and told her that a team of researchers at Harvard had discovered Sentio and Cogito; she reiterated that Antonio was supposed to be at Harvard. Marie had nothing to say. She did not like Harvard. She gave a brief thank you to Helen and hung up the phone.

The next day, Marie felt bad about hiding the application materials in her drawer. When Antonio asked if she had received them in the mail, she pulled the materials out and showed him. He jumped and screamed for joy. He was so happy.

"From the cradle of Sentio, I will launch my revolution to restore humankind's consciousness of nature and their vision for freedom," he said and hugged his mother.

At that moment, Marie found herself wanting him to get accepted because he wanted it, but she still felt a deep ache in her chest, an emptiness, when she thought about Antonio going to America. Then something happened to her. Everything slowed down, and she began to see and hear things with greater acuity. She felt dizzy and lay on her bed, thinking she had caught an inner ear infection. She heard Antonio take his application materials into his room and place them on the desk, and then he returned to lay next to her and hummed sounds as she used to hum to him when he had colic as a baby. She fell asleep in his arms.

The following Friday Antonio heard more good news: Poulou's friend at the Planck had arranged for Antonio's studies at Essence and the University of Maryland University College to transfer as credits for a degree in mathematics at Max Planck. All of his basic science courses, his correspondence work at the Planck, and his papers on the theory of calculus and the Laplace transform, verified by Sister Serelia, had earned him a special degree.

Two weeks later, on Thursday after sunset, Poulou made a surprise visit. He wanted to follow up in person because he had more good news.

Poulou explained that Antonio's special degree in mathematics from Max Planck, one of the best schools in the world, was as good as a degree from Princeton since the two schools had recently entered into an agreement to encourage the exchange of faculty and students in math and computer science. When Antonio asked if his degree would be accepted by Harvard, Marie's heart pounded, fearful they'd already accepted him.

"The Harvard admission committee has given special consideration and accepted your application. They want to interview you," Poulou said happily, smiling at Antonio, who was jubilant about the news. "They need you to resubmit your letter about why you want to attend medical school," Poulou added. "They've misplaced it and need it for your interview."

Poulou handed him a large envelope from Harvard. Antonio embraced his uncle, who in turn gave Marie a long hug and whispered, "Helen sends her love."

Marie managed a slight smile then bid Poulou good-bye. At least Antonio had not been accepted to their school. Their brochure clearly stated that students rarely get accepted without a degree from the U.S. or Canada. Then she thought, *Harvard, they don't know what they're doing*, and almost broke down in tears. Antonio approached, put down the envelope, lifted her into an embrace, and twirled, telling her how happy he was and how much he loved her.

After Antonio resubmitted his letter explaining why he had to attend Harvard Medical School, it took several more weeks before they heard from Poulou's friend about the interview. Antonio asked Marie to go with him, so she accompanied him to Munich for his interview with the Harvard admission committee via satellite. One week later, Antonio received the news by mail. He would be starting at Harvard Medical School in the summer. The letter he received gave him just two weeks to accept or decline the offered position.

At first Marie was excited and hugged Antonio because he was so excited, but then she felt sad and wanted to cry. When she went to call Helen about the good news, the truth—that she would be losing Antonio—flashed in her mind and felt like a stab to her heart.

"Hello, Helen. Antonio . . . he got into Harvard." When she said the words, again a searing pain shot through her chest into her heart.

"That is wonderful!"

"No, it's not. It seems too easy," Marie cried into the phone. "I know that Antonio worked hard. But I do not want to lose him." she sobbed. "I hope he declines."

"It is meant to be; he has to follow his compass vision to freedom," proclaimed Helen. "We need to have a grand celebration."

"I don't believe in the compass."

"Marie stay calm, I almost made the same mistake," Helen admitted. "Remember when I was ready to sell Essence? I ordered the end of the praying, which was part of my vision for freedom. Right now it is hard for you to see or to know. But trust me. What you are doing is for greater freedom for all, and your sacrifice will lead to greater freedom for you too."

"What if his compass experience was a mistake? A misinterpretation."

"I know that Antonio experienced the grand Intentio of Providence," Helen said. "Give him a hug and kiss from me and Poulou. I will see you soon."

Marie hung up and left #4 to find Antonio. She did not want to lose him. He had seemed distant and oblivious to her sadness after the celebration over his acceptance letter.

She found him on the porch and rocked next to him, holding his hand. She listened to his soft-spoken words. He understood about her sadness and felt the same way that she did. He squeezed her hand and promised her that he would return to Essence as soon as he freed the Americans. After his mission, he also wanted to join Polly and Alex in Paris.

Marie smiled and gave a squeeze to his hand. "I will join you in Paris."

Antonio smiled and nodded. "We will be together again," he said as they rocked during a glorious sunset.

* * *

Two days later, Helen held a dinner celebration in Vichy in honor of Antonio, Polly, and Alex. As the dinner came to a close, Helen comforted Marie with an embrace. Marie knew that Antonio must leave, but she still did not want to let go of him even though she had known it was his purpose from the beginning, when she had cupped him in her hands on that fateful night under a gas streetlight. For a few seconds while embracing Helen, the feeling of that beautiful moment on that bitter cold night returned, when she had connected with his tiny eyes and knew that she was his mother, bringing happy tears to her eyes. Now she must let him fly and test his wings, for greater freedom for all. He would no longer be by her side at Essence. She leaned into Helen's embrace as sad tears streamed down her cheeks.

"It's what is necessary," Helen murmured in Marie's ear

as she wiped tears from the side of her face with a napkin. "The three orphans—Antonio, Alex, and Polly—have grown up. It is their time to shine. Antonio will free the Americans from their addiction to Cogito. Remember the Americans set us free, and without them there would be no Essence." Marie cried harder, and Helen finished, "And Polly and Alex will change lives through their drama school in London."

"They are so young," Marie said through her tears. "I want to go with them and protect them. The world is so harsh. My three beautiful Sentio beings are not ready to leave."

Josephine came over after hugging Polly at the other table and leaned in to join Helen and Marie. Josephine was losing Alex and Polly, and Marie had never seen her blue eyes look so sad.

Poulou got up and gave Josephine an embrace and spoke softly, "Oh, Sentio, Sentio! I'm here said Sentio with Intentio."

Josephine smiled through her tears, and Marie smiled seeing her smile.

"They will find strange love, and they will find greater freedom for all. They will be fine," Helen assured Marie and Josephine. "Antonio has a great mission. He has to deliver the slaves of Cogito existence. We must show him support."

"All three will do very well," Poulou added. "Marie, you have done an outstanding job, and you too Josephine Joseph. And Javier, what would we have done without him?"

"Javier has been a giver of strange love for me and all three children," said Marie.

Josephine nodded. "Me too."

The four fell into silence, and Marie kept thinking how their lives would seem less vibrant. The three essential members of their family were leaving to start their own lives away from Essence.

Time flew after Antonio received his acceptance to Harvard. Polly and Alex would be leaving soon as well. Marie spent as much time as she could with all three, wanting to soak up every minute before they left Essence. The weeks disappeared and now just days remained before their departure. Marie's chest ached from sadness as the end drew near, and she hid her feelings as best she could.

This is the last Friday that we will all be together, thought Marie.

She and Javier rocked and held hands. Antonio, Alex, Polly, and Josephine rocked alongside enjoying perhaps the last sunset that all six would share together. The three orphans had grown tall and handsome in eighteen years. They were dressed in nice clothes for the farewell party at Paradise.

After sunset they walked together into Pierre under a twilight sky. They met the mayor, Ogie, the butcher, and many others from town and walked with them to Paradise. Time had been kind to the people of Pierre. The grocer and even the tavern owner looked young and healthy. Javier slowed and walked with the grocer, his wife, and their grandchildren. They had contributed the food and drink for the party, and all of Essence and Pierre had been invited.

Antonio and Alex held the doors open as the large group

filed into the lodge at Paradise. Inside the crowd grew noisy until Josephine blew her whistle and got everyone's attention. After an introduction by Javier, the mayor took the stage near the front of the large room. He stood near the fireplace and directed his voice toward the visitors, standing on the tile floor in the restaurant area, cleared of the tables and chairs.

The mayor called Polly, Alex, and Antonio to the front. The three young adults produced beautiful smiles as they stood together on the hearth of the fireplace and were given loud applause. Antonio spoke then Alex and Polly. They all shared their gratitude and affection for their wonderful experiences growing up at Essence and in Pierre. More loud applause followed. Marie embraced Josephine and peered into her moist blue eyes, giving her a loving smile. They were both so proud of their three children, now young adults.

The party began as a celebration of memories, and Marie enjoyed hearing the mayor's old stories about Essence. He mentioned the big bell and the quarrels between Essence and the tavern owner, all long forgotten and forgiven. Helen and Poulou could not attend the party because they were busy making preparations for the final farewell tomorrow night, but Marie planned on telling Helen what the mayor had said about her big bell: that it served as a compass for freedom for the people of Pierre and Essence.

Marie walked up front, stood on the hearth, and shared in detail the story of the night Antonio was born. Dr. Frankl chimed in with a few significant facts about the night Antonio stopped breathing that underpinned that he was a miracle. Then Javier stood up beside Marie and talked about the sunset café fish dinners and the fishing stories shared, the sunset experiences for eternity.

After the memories, music played on the stereo. The children danced, sang, and played music games with Sister Serelia. Marie went around with Antonio and personally thanked the people of Pierre for all of their love and support.

After seeing all of their friends and loved ones and wishing them well, Alex, Antonio, and Polly said goodnight. They wanted to spend some time together near the bluff at Essence. Marie gave them hugs, and Josephine went with them.

At 11:00 p.m., the children left for Essence with the sisters. Marie and Javier spent the last part of the night on the dock where Javier shared his love for her. They danced under the moonlight to nature's sounds: crickets, frogs, and water rushing over rocks. Marie could sense Javier's concern about how the three young adults leaving would affect her.

After they danced, Marie thanked Javier for his concern. He smiled and led her to the lodge where they turned out the lights and closed the doors of Paradise. They walked toward Essence long after midnight and passed by the tavern. The dwellers were winding down.

Javier stopped on the way up the road and found her eyes. "Marie, I know how hard this is for you. I will help you and love you through this."

Marie lifted her cheeks and embraced Javier. "I love you so much."

They released and continued hand in hand, walking slowly toward the terrace.

Antonio, Alex, and Polly were rocking on the balcony porch, so Marie and Javier joined them. The boys shared old memories about fishing at their secret pond and then Marie and Antonio hummed the "Moldau." Polly's eyelids started drooping, so Marie suggested they move the all-night party and spend the early hours of the morning on the screened-in porch of #4. The lazy group got up and walked together holding hands, as Alex supported Polly, and Antonio leaned on Marie.

Javier made coffee as the kids got comfortable on the porch. They stretched out on the sofa and on pallets laid on the floor, waiting for sunrise. Marie watched her little angels fall asleep as she sat holding Javier's hand. She wanted the night to last forever and dreaded the first light of dawn breaking on the horizon, a sign of the inexorable march of time. She thought of all the sunsets that they had enjoyed, the happy times. She fell asleep after daybreak and slept until Josephine came and awoke them around noon to get ready for the party at the castle.

By late afternoon, the buses had arrived to carry them to Vichy for the final farewell party. Poulou had chartered them from Barcelona. Marie and Javier followed as the sisters marched the children into Pierre where they broke formation, running to get on the beautiful buses, which provided unusual comfort, reclining seats, and more than enough room for the sisters and children.

Marie and Javier sat opposite the three celebrities in the second bus. The thought that they would soon be leaving Essence, perhaps forever, played in Marie's mind. Polly and Alex had tickets to leave for London on Monday. Antonio would be leaving for America on Tuesday.

Marie squeezed Javier's hand, looking melancholy about her thoughts as the bus pulled out, revving its engine. They began the ride out of Pierre and through the mountains to Vichy where Poulou and Helen were preparing a grand, final sendoff.

Polly considered the party a graduation and prom night rolled into one weekend. She had made a beautiful dress, and Alex and Antonio wore fancy suits imported from Lisbon— gifts from Javier. Marie looked at the boys and then smiled at Javier conveying her gratitude for more than their clothes . . . for his fatherly love.

Javier had been wonderful in a quiet, loving way and so

307

generous in every way. He took Marie's hand and placed it against his heart and smiled. Marie took his other hand and placed it over her heart. She had fallen deeper and deeper in love with him every day since the first day they had met.

Marie and Javier listened in quiet as the kids talked. Polly and Alex were going to London to study at the Barbican School of Theater and Dance. Antonio predicted that they would all be together in Paris in three or four years. The trio had been planning the rendezvous since they were kids, to live together someday, and Poulou had given them the idea of living together in Paris. Polly was going to be an actress like Anna Simmons and parade around with Antonio and Alex as her entourage. Marie listened to their dreams, which she wanted to come true. She turned and smiled at Javier, who grinned and nodded in silence.

They arrived at the castle, and the children were screaming and laughing as they exited the buses. The sisters could barely control their excitement. Dinner was waiting on picnic tables by the lake under a pavilion, and the children raced to the beach.

On Saturday night, all of Essence and all from the orphanage in Vichy gathered at the castle as many danced on the veranda under the moonlit sky. The cute little boys and girls danced under the watchful eyes of the Catalan sisters. Alice, Jacki, Eva, and Heidi were present and wore beautiful dresses in pastel blues, greens, and yellows. The handsome young adults represented the first class of international orphans to graduate from Essence. Marie and Javier embraced them as they made their way through the greeting line.

Poulou seemed so happy. He was playing Russian tunes on the piano, a concerto by Tchaikovsky and then Rachmaninoff. He loved the Romantics. Antonio gave special attention to his uncle and sat next to him while he played. Marie walked over and rubbed Antonio's shoulders and patted Poulou on the back.

Helen approached and asked Poulou to play Frank Sinatra, and he chose the recording "You My Love" and played it on the stereo, creating a romantic atmosphere.

Antonio had a big smile on his face as he watched Polly and Alex waltz to the song, and he looked so proud of them. Marie sent a smile to him from across the room as she remembered the night of her twentieth anniversary on the balcony porch at Essence. Polly and Alex were so cute on that night of Antonio's compass experience.

When the music stopped, Sister Josephine began to sing one of Edith Piaf's songs about having no regrets. Her beautiful voice needed no help from any instrument and made the night magical as her words, her echoes were filled with such emotion.

Javier and Marie waltzed and twirled around the dance floor, and she noticed Antonio appeared to want to dance with every single orphan girl from Vichy and Essence. Marie watched as Antonio approached. He wanted his last dance to be with her. He gave her a kiss and reminded her that this night would live on in their Sentio memories forever. Marie hugged her little boy, holding back tears as "Auld Lang Syne" signaled the finale. They continued to waltz long after the music stopped.

After gaining everyone's attention, Helen announced they had purchased a new property near Evian on Lake Geneva to build their final orphanage, Essence III. A big cheer erupted. Antonio and Marie walked toward Helen in the center of the dance floor and were joined by Javier, Alex, and Polly.

Poulou stressed, "The French side of Lake Geneva. We hope to finish building the facility by the time Antonio completes medical school. Helen wants him to deliver the christening ceremony. And I will be there, for sure." He smiled at Helen.

Antonio looked at his mother and nodded as if to say he would deliver the christening. He smiled at Javier who had returned to Marie's side. Helen snuck up, said: *Smile!* and snapped a picture after Alex and Polly jumped in.

Javier turned and smiled at Marie. He was like a Sentio anchor for the entire family and had renewed their sensitivity with his strange love. Marie knew that Antonio looked up to him and all three loved and trusted Javier like a father. Marie knew he loved all three of them like his own children. She was glad that he would be busy building a new gymnasium in Vichy after they left. She felt tears welling up just thinking about how he would miss them.

Then Helen announced that Marie would be the new Reverend Mother at Essence, and Sister Josephine would be her assistant. Mary Elizabeth would be the new Reverend Mother in Vichy, and Sister Phillips would be her assistant.

"It's the best possible outcome," Antonio told Marie after the announcement, and she agreed.

When it was time for goodnight, Helen hugged Antonio for a long time. She spoke softly, something about a café dweller. Marie could barely hear, but she understood when Helen asked Antonio to deliver the world from existentialism.

Antonio promised Helen somberly, "I will free humankind from language-thinking existence."

Poulou hugged Antonio and assured him he would keep in close contact, always ready to help if he needed him. Helen and Poulou retired for the night while Marie and Javier sat on the veranda wide awake surrounded by sleepy children, many already asleep on cots under the pavilion.

Marie enjoyed the presence of each one of the celebrities as long as she could, until dawn broke over the castle. Later in the morning, Javier hugged and tickled Marie—Antonio must have told Javier where he could find her funny bone under her last rib on the right.

While in Javier's embrace, Marie looked up toward the sky above the lake and noticed some strange, tiny, grid lines in the clouds. *Strange*, she thought. Marie rubbed her eyes and put on sunglasses, wondering if her sleep-deprived state had altered her vision. She saw Sister Pauli and remembered when Antonio had disclosed that he had seen lines in the clouds when he was in second grade. Marie felt disoriented for a moment, and everything appeared to be moving in slow motion like when she had the viral inner ear thing . . . or so she had thought.

"Is everything alright?" asked Javier.

"Yes," Marie said, and stood up for a moment. But feeling dizzy, she sat down and closed her eyes for a minute, then joined everyone for breakfast at the picnic tables on the beach.

After Mrs. Ophelia's oatmeal breakfast and final fare-wells, the children struggled to board the buses and fell asleep as soon as they hit their seats. The two buses began the journey back to Essence.

Marie still experienced the perception of slow motion and the warm sensations from the party lingered; her sensory experiences seemed more vivid and immediate now . . . and long lasting. Once the bus started moving, she relaxed and fell asleep leaning against Javier.

CHAPTER

After arriving at Essence, Marie awoke feeling exhausted. She made herself walk with Polly to the dormitory. Polly was so excited she wanted to begin packing for London, so Marie helped her and then helped with Alex's things. Polly hugged her and told her how much she loved her. Marie bit the inside of her lower lip to keep from crying and released her sadness with a sigh after Polly left.

Marie headed back to #4 to begin the heartbreaking job of packing Antonio's clothes, which she knew he would put off until the last minute. Time would not stop, but oh, how she wanted it to. About an hour later Polly showed up and offered to help her pack Antonio's clothes, but Marie had already finished. Josephine interrupted and shared embraces with them. Marie could tell that Josephine wanted some private time with Polly, so she went looking for Javier.

She found him at Paradise cleaning the tackle shop and began hugging and loving him, thanking him for his support and then walked alongside him as he swept out the restaurant. He could not hide his sadness even though he tried with a smile.

"I'm going to find Alex and Antonio," Marie said. "I love you."

Javier turned with a tear on his cheek and said, "I'll be home soon."

312

Marie hurried back to Essence and stayed in her room, rocking in darkness, trying to gather strength for Polly and Alex's last night. She avoided joining the children on the porch for sunset because she knew that she would cry and upset their last night together.

Polly and the boys returned to #4 for a moment, and Josephine asked Polly to join her on the screened-in porch. Marie heard the boys say they were going back to the balcony porch.

Antonio and Alex rocked in darkness side by side as Marie slipped down by the school building beneath the porch without the boys noticing. She heard Alex remind Antonio, "Essence will always be my home and you my brother." After a moment the boys got up, and she watched as they came down the steps.

Antonio stopped and gave Alex a long embrace. "Let's go get Polly," he said.

Marie stayed in the shadows, her heart aching. It took her several minutes to compose herself, and after she did, she caught up with all three in the sitting room of #4. Alex, Antonio, and Polly went upstairs to stay together in Marie and Antonio's room the last night while Marie, Javier, and Josephine sat awake downstairs. At midnight, Marie and Josephine interrupted them for good night hugs. They might be young adults, but they were still Marie and Josephine's children. Long after midnight, Marie and Josephine finally fell asleep on the sofa in the sitting room with Javier.

The next morning Antonio, Marie, Josephine, and Javier prepared to walk Alex and Polly to the bus station in Pierre. They were destined for Paris and then London. But first Alex and Polly wanted to say good-bye to the sisters and children and then to Marcel in his stable.

After their good-byes Alex, Polly, and Antonio started running toward Pierre but stopped when Polly realized she could not run in her heels. Marie followed holding Josephine's hand, squeezing gently. Marie observed Polly and Alex would have each other to share strange love and noticed that her words gave a little lift to Josephine's step.

When they reached the depot, the bus was readying for departure. Javier took care of the luggage, loading their suitcases into the storage space on the side of the bus.

Polly said good-bye to Josephine with a warm hug and lots of tears. "I will keep you fresh in my Sentio memories forever."

Polly then shared hugs with Javier and then Marie who whispered, "You are going to be great onstage. Take care of Alex."

"I will."

Polly had waited to say good-bye to Antonio last. She looked into his eyes then embraced him. "You will always be my King Arthur."

Antonio held her for a long moment before pulling back. With tears in his eyes he kissed her on the cheek. "Polly, I love you. Take care of Alex."

Alex hugged Josephine for a long time, and Josephine could not hold back her tears. Marie approached and put her hand on Josephine's shoulder. Alex then hugged Marie and Javier, unable to get out any words.

Marie told him, "Alex, you are a precious Sentio being. You and Polly take care of one another."

Alex struggled to speak and nodded at Marie.

"We will," Polly said softly and put her arm on Alex's shoulder.

Finally, it was time for Antonio to say good-bye to Alex. He reached out and embraced Alex for a long time, both crying uncontrollably. Eventually they let go and Antonio calmed himself. "Brother, take care of Polly. She gets so crazy with her imagination."

Alex met Antonio's gaze. "I know she does, and I will take care of her. Don't forget . . . you need strange love too."

Their show of love for each other brought a fresh round of tears to the adults' eyes.

"I will see you and Polly at Christmas," Antonio promised, wiping tears away. "Stay Sentio!"

The bus engine revved. They needed to board. Josephine got another quick embrace from Alex and Polly, who stopped on the top step and turned for a final look at Josephine, Marie, Javier, and Antonio before following Alex onto the bus.

Alex and Polly waved out the back window as the bus drove off. Antonio stood next to Josephine hugging her. They watched until the bus disappeared. Josephine, Marie, and Javier headed back to Essence, but Antonio stood there longer, as if he could still feel Polly and Alex's waves even after they were out of view. Marie slowed, watching him, and he finally turned and ran to catch up with her.

69

Marie waited at the top of the cobblestone road, and when Antonio caught up she took his hand as they walked toward the terrace. She was trying to use denial appropriately, trying not to think about the fact that Polly and Alex had departed Essence, perhaps forever. She led Antonio up the steps to their favorite spot on the balcony porch. They rocked in silence through sunset, holding hands, exchanging glances, communicating with smiles for love as they had done when Antonio was a toddler.

After dinner they sat up until very late with Josephine and Javier in #4. Exhausted, Josephine shared hugs then excused herself to go to bed.

Javier rocked as Antonio and Marie lay on the bed in their room. Antonio got up and walked around, talking about America. He seemed nervous. Marie watched her two favorite men talking about everything from fishing to strange love and the loss of strangeness. Javier's eyes got heavy, and he lay on the sofa and tried to listen to Antonio but drifted off to sleep.

Marie smiled at Antonio as he took a seat at her desk chair. She stayed awake watching him in silence, hoping he might lay with her. When Antonio finally got tired, he laid himself down on the bed and rolled over into Marie's arms. Her prayer was answered, and she enjoyed every moment—the warmth of his skin; his long, curly hair; and his spring scent filled her Sentio. For several hours, she visited the happy memories of when she held him and nursed him as a baby. They warmed her heart and mended the aching she had felt for the last two weeks. She found strength to face her loss: she was giving her beautiful baby to the world for freedom.

When the sunlight came through her window, she whispered softly into Antonio's ear, "It's time."

He awoke with a smile and gave her a warm embrace. They needed to get ready to catch the bus to Paris. After breakfast, Antonio rang the big bell for the last time. He said good-bye to all of the sisters and cooks in the chapel. He gave a big hug to Sister Phillips, a special sweet hug to Reverend Mother Mary Elizabeth, and a long embrace to Josephine and whispered something funny in her ear. He hugged his little brothers and sisters . . . his friends. Marie could barely swallow after watching him say his good-byes. He meant so much to the beings at Essence.

The walk to the bus station in Pierre with Antonio was much harder for Marie even though she was riding with him to Paris. Javier had to support her most of the way. Once on the bus, they all three sat together in silence. As the bus pulled away, Marie could only think its destination was for their final farewell.

Antonio talked about flying. He had never flown in a plane, and now he would be flying to the United States of America. As Marie felt a wave of sadness wash over her, Antonio reminded her of his purpose. He held her close, Marie's head on his chest, and whispered sounds she had taught him before he learned language. She smiled and repeated the cooing sounds they had shared, and fell asleep in his arms.

Once they arrived at the airport, Javier carried Antonio's backpack, duffel bag, and suitcase to the check-in.

Antonio had his arm around Marie, who walked slowly to prolong the inevitable. On their way to the departure gate, Antonio tickled Marie and reminded her of their tickling wars. Then nothing more was said until the last moment at the gate.

They embraced until the final passengers were called. Marie held Antonio's hand as he moved towards the plane, not letting go until their hands pulled apart. Their eyes continued to meet as he walked, and Marie spoke before Antonio turned away.

"Pardon me, for any way that my institutional self may have harmed you."

Antonio ran back to embrace his mother. "You loved me so much, Mother," he said through his tears. "I feel your love in my Sentio always."

Marie's tears came from deep within, and she could not suppress her sobs. Antonio held her until they both calmed then looked at Javier.

"Come here, Javier. You are part of this too." He pulled Javier into the embrace.

"I love you both very much," said Javier.

"Take care, Mother. I want you and Javier to share strange love tonight in Paris and all the way back to Pierre tomorrow."

Marie and Javier smiled at each other, and her sadness was lifted for the moment.

Antonio walked over and handed his ticket to the flight attendant, wiping away new tears. Marie followed and touched his shoulder to assuage his new wave of sadness. He explained that his tears flowed out of respect and in love for her Sentio nurturing, for her sacrifice. At that moment, his words created a special Intentio for Marie like the sounds from the big bell at Essence.

"Do you know who you're supposed to meet at Harvard?" she asked, and Antonio nodded. "And you have

Uncle Poulou, Aunt Helen's, and my phone number. I will see you at Christmas. I love you."

Antonio turned from his mother and boarded the plane.

Javier led Marie to the window to watch the plane take off and put his arm around her. Antonio found his window seat and fastened his seat belt. He looked out of his window and found Marie, their eyes meeting. She waved and forced a smile.

Antonio waved with his beautiful smile. Marie knew how comforting it was for Antonio to know his mother was receiving love. She was warmed by the thought as his plane soared into the atmosphere.

After a quiet and pleasant night in Paris, Marie and Javier took the bus back to Pierre, arriving after sunset. During the long, sad walk to the villa, Marie dreaded the moment when she would have to walk into #4 without Antonio. Javier helped her up the steps and opened the front door. Marie stepped inside using denial as her shield and flipped on the light. The memory of standing in the foyer with Antonio on the night that language instruction began, on his fourth birthday, flashed in her mind.

Wanting to be strong for Javier, she took a deep breath and turned toward him as he closed the door. On the wall beside the door she saw one of Antonio's geometric drawings from when he was toddler, one of his private drawings that he kept hidden under her bed. The green circles, squares, cubes, and spheres were perfectly drawn and the drawing was signed: *I luv you, Antonio.*

She looked at Javier and bit her lip trying to hold back her tears.

"Antonio must have put it there before we left," he said.

Marie could not hold off her emotion any longer, and Javier approached to embrace her—

"Surprise! Surprise!" The lights came on in the sitting room, the stairwell, and the kitchen.

Startled, her tears stopped when she saw Poulou jump

out from the sitting room with a big grin. He walked toward her with a note and flowers in his hand, a single large tear rolling down his cheek.

"The tavern owner sent white roses for you," Poulou said, setting them down on the table.

Behind him were a roomful of smiling faces—the grocer, the mayor, the butcher, and many others directed their loving and caring eyes at her. Marie was overwhelmed.

Helen rushed to embrace her and explained that Josephine had invited her and the others for a surprise show of support. Mary Elizabeth, Sister Phillips, Alice, Jacki, Louis, Eva, Alberto, and Sister Pauli came into view from the kitchen, and the Catalan gals made their way down the stairs with glowing smiles.

Marie forced a smile and rested her head on Helen's shoulder. "He's gone," she said in a low voice. "My baby."

Helen embraced her then pulled a picture from her pocket, taken at the final party Saturday night in Vichy. Marie looked at the picture of Polly, Alex, Antonio, and Javier, who looked so handsome. She stared at the young woman in between Antonio and Alex in a blue and white habit . . .

She looked up at Helen who was smiling at her. The beautiful young woman in the picture was Marie as she looked twenty years ago.

"Antonio has set you free," Helen whispered, "as you set him free. Your Intentio has been set free to dwell in Sentio, and you have rejuvenated."

Marie wanted to cry, but she couldn't produce any more tears. She'd used them all up. Antonio had given her more love than she had ever received in her life in those final weeks.

He set me free.

Javier stepped forward and looked at the picture in Helen's hand. "Antonio and I told you. Polly and Alex did too. You've looked so young this last week," he said, joy beaming from his face.

"But my hair and my eyebrows are still gray."

"Your hair will take time to rejuvenate," Helen explained. "My hair took nine months to change. Your body has changed so slowly over the last few months that you were unaware of your rejuvenation."

Marie leaned into Javier's embrace and fixed on his beautiful blue eyes. She indeed felt like a twenty-year-old woman again.

Javier's eyes filled with emotion. "I feel free and I love you, Marie. You, the sisters, the children, Antonio, Alex, and Polly have freed me." He lifted Marie off her feet and twirled.

Helen looked over at Poulou and moved to the center of the room.

"Quack! Quack!" Helen said and gained everyone's attention. She waited for the sounds of laughter to subside. "Antonio will be back after he frees the Americans—Polly and Alex, too. We will all live together at Essence III, soon. I've had another compass experience. It won't be long now."

After Helen's announcement, Josephine lifted the corners of her mouth into a beautiful smile. Marie looked closely at Josephine's face; it was smooth and without wrinkles. And her eyes had a youthful twinkle. Marie felt a warm glow from Josephine; her Intentio dwelled in Sentio now. Sergio walked over and embraced Josephine.

Marie looked over at Mary Elizabeth and then Sister Phillips. They too looked so young.

The cheers rang out, and the happy group shared jubilant embraces. Poulou broke out the Napoleon brandy and raised his goblet, and Helen gave a toast to Marie, Sister Phillips, Josephine, Mary Elizabeth, the sisters new and old, and to all the others from Pierre who had gathered for love and freedom.

"Without you none of this would have been possible,"

Helen said. "To anyone who consents to direct their attention to give love to others for true freedom, they will experience the power of a special love that is doubly blessed. It will free them emotionally and provide a new vision of nature and freedom. And one day they will find themselves back home in Eden."

JC HOWELL is a new author who writes with a postmodern style exploring the nature of being, love, and freedom.

Born in America January 15, 1958, he received his undergraduate education at the University of Tennessee in Chattanooga, completed medical school in Baltimore at the University of Maryland in 1984, and finished his medical residency at the University Hospital in 1987. For most of his life, he has studied, taught, and practiced medicine. Five years ago, he began a writing career.

Sentio is his debut novel. His thread about love and its connection to greater freedom for all continues in his sequels *Strange Love in America* and *Beyond Hedonism*.

Sentio

JC Howell

Author website: authorjchowell.com

Publisher: SDP Publishing

Also available in ebook format

Available at all major bookstores

 **SDP Publishing**

www.SDPPublishing.com
Contact us at: info@SDPPublishing.com

CPSIA information can be obtained
at www.ICGtesting.com
Printed in the USA
LVOW11*0410110417
530382LV00004B/15/P